The
Scared
Stiff

The
Scared
Stiff

JUDSON JACK CARMICHAEL

An Otto Penzler Book

CARROLL & GRAF PUBLISHERS
NEW YORK

The Scared Stiff

Carroll & Graf Publishers
An Imprint of Avalon Publishing Group Inc.
161 William St., 16th Floor
New York, NY 10038

ISBN: 0-7867-0954-5

Printed in the United States of America

I would like to thank Jeannette for the dessert. It was delicious.

The
Scared
Stiff

1

I don't know, maybe it's because we wanted so much, Lola and me, that we wound up with so little. So far, I mean. The moneymaking schemes, the trends we latched onto, the brass rings we kept reaching for, none of them ever worked out.

The problem is, the world keeps changing. It just keeps changing all the time, too fast for a simple little couple like us to keep up, much less to succeed. Today it's VCR, tomorrow it's DVD. Today it's day-trading, tomorrow it's Chapter 11. Today it's dot com, tomorrow it's dot bomb, and we managed to get burned, one way or another, on every one of those. But through it all, through it all, Lola and I just kept hustling. What else was there for us to do?

When I first met Lola, fourteen years ago, I knew; I absolutely *knew*, and so did she. Alone, what were we? Not much: me, a middle-class nobody from Long Island with a community college degree in Communications (even *I* didn't know what that meant exactly); Lola, a penniless South American beauty with a charity scholarship to some minor Florida college because she was the brightest child of her generation down there in Guerrera. Alone, each of us was just another anonymous commoner, shuffling along with the crowd.

But *together*? Together we were special; we were fantastic from the very beginning. We were glamour and we knew it; we could sense it, feel it. We could see ourselves dancing in the moonlight, the couple everybody looks at and wants to be, swirling to the music that played just for us.

All we ever wanted was to live the life we'd imagined: fascinating, enchanted, forever above the herd, deserving simply because we *were*, we existed, together.

But it wasn't enough. It was never quite enough. We had scrapes and close calls and financial disasters over the years, tough times when our most exciting ideas just somehow never panned out. We lived on whatever credit we could find. When I told landlords, "I've been thrown out of better places than this," it was usually the truth. For most of our married life, we had to pretend to be a visiting houseguest if we ever answered a doorbell or a phone, and usually we preferred not to answer at all. Nor read much of our mail.

Still, we kept one jump ahead of the bill collectors for a good long time, fourteen years of perilous off-balance joy. The rackety life itself became our glamour, a desperate romantic struggle to remain true to our image of ourselves, like spies, more charming than those base creatures who could think about nothing but money.

Finally, though, there came the moment when it all caught up with us. The debts were too heavy, the most recent debtors too ruthless, the situation too dangerous, the peril finally too real. We might get our legs broken; we might even be killed.

So it was with a real sense of last resort that I at last turned to Lola and said, "There's nothing for it. We have to borrow on our life insurance."

"Oh, Barry," she said, sudden tears glistening in her eyes. "Is there no other way?"

It may seem strange that people who care as little about sordid reality as Lola and I do would even bother with life insurance, but that had also been a part of our commitment to each other from the beginning. We knew we were bound to one another, we were . . . something more than true, something more than faithful . . . *constant*. In an inconstant world, we would be, for one another, the only constant.

But what if one of us were to die, young or even not so young? The other might want to follow, but shouldn't. So the first thing we did, home from the wedding trip to Guerrera, was take out the life insurance policies, three hundred thousand on each of us, naming each other as beneficiary. That way, if one died, the last gift to the other was a starter kit for the new life.

I never thought we'd touch those policies. But now our straits were truly dire. "I hate the thought, Lola," I said. "You know I do."

"I know you do, Barry, of course you do." She put her arms around me, kissed me, and said, "Tell me what you want to do."

"I'll call the insurance agent," I said, "and ask him how much equity we've got. In fourteen years, it ought to add up to *something*."

She sighed. "You know best," she said.

So I made the call. "Steve, I was wondering. Our life insurance policies. How much equity do we have in them?"

He said, "Equity?" as though it were some word in a foreign language.

But that *is* the word they use in the insurance business, isn't it? The cash-in value of the policy, slowly growing over the years? I said, "Value, Steve, what's the value in there now, if we wanted to borrow against those policies?"

"Barry," he said, "you don't have that kind of insurance."

"What? I'm talking about our *life* insurance policies."

"I know you are," he said. "Those are term policies."

Right then, I knew. I didn't yet know *what* I knew, but I knew. Somehow, there was no salvation for us in those insurance policies. I said, "What do you mean, term policies. Don't we have life insurance policies?"

"Yes, of course," he said. "But you said you weren't interested in building equity."

"How can you have life insurance and not—? Steve, what kind of policy *is* this?"

"I thought you understood," he said. "Back when you took out those policies, you and Lola, you both said all you cared about was maximum survivor's benefits at minimum premium cost, and I said term insurance, and you both said yes. The term you chose is five years, remember?"

I did remember something about terms and five years and automatically renewable at adjusted premiums and all that, but who listens to such things? I said, "Steve. What you're saying. What does it *mean?*"

"It means," he said, "you carry insurance that will pay your survivor if you die, and double if you die in an accident, but that's *all* the policy does."

"You mean . . . ?"

"Barry," he said, "you never bought a policy that would accrue equity. That would have cost considerably more, and you didn't want it. You wanted the biggest bang for the buck. Remember saying that?"

I did. "Yes," I said.

"I'm sorry if you didn't follow—"

"No no no, not your fault," I said.

2

"It's unfair," Lola said that night, the two of us sitting up in bed, not ready for sleep. "We've put that money in all these years, and it should be there to help us when times get bad."

"Not with that kind of policy," I said. "It *is* fair, the deal they've made, if we listen to them. They'll only help us if we're dead."

"If *one* of us is dead," she said.

"Well, yes," I agreed, and very late that night, she woke me by elbowing me in the ribs, crying, "Barry! Barry!"

I opened groggy eyes and blinked at her, and her whole face was luminous in the dark.

"Barry!" she said, in a loud whisper, like a stage aside. "One of us is gonna die!"

Well, that woke me up, all right. Sitting up, gaping at her, I said, "What?"

"For the insurance!" she whispered, bubbling with excitement.

"One of us *makes believe* to be dead, so we get the insurance money!"

I was having trouble keeping up. "How can we make believe we're dead? Fake a death? Lola, they'll catch us right away."

"Not in Guerrera," she said.

I stared at her. Guerrera. Her homeland, her little country down in South America. "Lola," I whispered; now I was whispering too.

"I've been lying here awake," she told me, "just thinking about it. We know people there, we have family there."

"They keep terrible records down there," I said. "The police force isn't the most advanced in the world."

"The death can be there," Lola said. "The funeral, too."

As excited as Lola by now, I said, "We can get a death certificate in Guerrera for a pack of cigarettes!"

"A little more than that," she said, "but not much."

I contemplated this wonderful idea. "It could work," I said.

She pointed at me. "It has to be you," she said.

I said, "It has to be me? Why?"

"If I go down there," she told me, "and have a convenient accident, a local girl who moved to the States and her husband insured her for a zillion *siapas*, everybody will smell a rat. We don't want to raise suspicion."

"Okay, you're right," I said. "It has to be me."

"But not now," she said. "It's too soon since you talked to Steve about life insurance."

"You're right. We'll wait till January," I said. "We can hold off for four months. We'll wait till we'd normally go down there anyway, for our post-Christmas visit."

"Perfect," she said. "Then the gringo has his accident, and his grieving widow can talk both to the locals and to anybody who comes down from the States."

"That puts it all on you, Lola," I said. "That could get pretty tricky."

"I'd love it," she assured me. "Come on, Barry, you know me."

I did. I grinned at her. "Okay," I said. "Looks like I'm gonna die."

"I'm sure you'll do it very well," she said.

"Thank you. Only, what then? I don't want to spend the rest of my life in Guerrera."

"Barry," she said, "I thought about that too. All I've been doing is lying here thinking. I don't know everything, we'll have to figure some of this out together, but I know how to get you back to the States when it's all over."

"Good. Tell me."

"I had two brothers that died young," she reminded me. "There's birth certificates on file up in San Cristóbal but nothing else. With a birth certificate, you can make up a whole new identity."

"You mean, become one of your brothers."

"Grow a mustache," she said. "Work on your tan. You could look Guerreran with no trouble at all. Wait a minute, my brothers' names. . . ." She thought, trying to remember, then remembered. "Who would you rather be, Felicio or Jesus?"

"Jesus!" I said.

She looked at me in some surprise. "Really? I didn't think you'd—"

"No no no no no, I don't want to be Jesus; that's not what I meant. I want to be the other one."

"Felicio."

"Felicio. That's not bad."

"It means happy," she said.

"Oh, good," I said. "I've become one of the seven dwarfs."

"Felicio Tobón de Lozano," she said, rolling the name around in her mouth.

I said, "So I'd come back to the States as him—"

"And live with your sister."

"I'd like that," I said.

3

The first time Lola and I flew from New York down to Guerrera, it was to meet her parents, Alvaro and Lucía, and her brother Arturo. The second time, three months later, was when we got married in the little white stone church in Sabanon, the up-country town where Lola grew up.

Since then, we visit Guerrera regularly once a year, in January, bringing belated Christmas gifts, escaping the northern winter for two weeks, usually maxing a credit card or two. The transition from Long Island's icy damp to Guerrera's humid heat is always blurred by several hours of air-conditioning in planes and airports, but it's still a kick to step out onto the portable stairs and suddenly feel that warm moist hand of the tropics press against my face.

General Luis Pozos International Airport at San Cristóbal, capital of Guerrera, was built with American money, to keep the Commies out, and you have to admit it worked. Communism has not taken over in this part of the world; it's still feudalism around here, same as ever. But the American money meant American design, great flat open paved areas baking blindingly in the sun, surrounded by squat square buildings with flat roofs. The local people would have left trees wherever possible, and open walls and wide eaves, so shadows and breezes could moderate the air without killing it. But it wasn't their money, was it? So there you are.

The local officials, young, in their pressed uniforms and close neat haircuts, tend to be very serious, very dignified. As usual, I handed over my passport without a word and tried to look innocent. Or at least not guilty.

Lola has dual citizenship but has never renewed her old maroon passport. She travels as an American, though she always does say something to the immigration official in guttural Guerreran Spanish to let him know she's really a local, and he always smiles and thaws and welcomes her home.

Unfortunately, though I've learned a rough-and-ready Spanish over the last fourteen years, I never did become fluent, which I lately regret. It would really come in handy. Because we were doing it, we were going to do it.

That's the way it's always worked with Lola and me. One of us gets an idea, we discuss it, the enthusiasm builds, we say, "We'll *do* it!"—and we do it and never look back. (Usually don't look forward, either, which frequently becomes a problem, but let's not dwell on that.)

When officialdom finished with us, we went out the other side of the building, and there was Arturo, leaning on the twenty-year-old pale green Chevy Impala that's his pride and joy. It rocks and rolls on Guerrera's smallpox-scarred roads like a fishing boat in a high sea, and Arturo loves it, left hand out the window to press palm down on the roof, right hand clutching hard to the steering wheel.

Arturo's a big guy, big-boned, thirty-eight years old, three years older than Lola and me. He works in the tobacco fields sometimes, uses his Impala as a taxi sometimes, does fairly good carpentry and adequate plumbing and terrifying electrical work sometimes, but mostly he just hangs around. He has a wife and some children in

San Cristóbal, and technically he lives with them, but where you'll find him is at his parents' house.

Now he threw us a big grin and an *"¡Hola!"* and relieved Lola of her big leather shoulder bag and canvas overnighter. I went on carrying my own two bags, and we went around to the back of the Impala for Arturo to unwind some wire and open the trunk. In the bags went, the wire was refastened, and we all slid onto the wide front bench seat, Lola in the middle.

Arturo started the engine, and Lola said, "So, Artie, how are you?"

"How *could* I be?" He grinned and winked past her at me, then spun the wheel and drove us away from the anticommunist airport building. "Same as ever, I'm great," he said.

We drove through the chain-link fence, its gate kept open by day and closed by night; no red-eye flights in or out of Guerrera.

Lola said, "How about the other thing? Are we all set?" We'd been scheming with him the last four months, by e-mail.

"Oh, sure."

We were on the highway now, the Impala gathering speed. The capital, San Cristóbal, stood just a few miles north of the airport, but Arturo had turned the other way, toward Sabanon, eighty-five miles to the south.

The flat baking airport disappeared behind us. Dark-green hilly jungle out ahead. A few trucks laden with coffee sacks or beer cases or workers or sugarcane, and us. The wind felt good and smelled alive.

Arturo leaned forward to look past Lola at me, and grin his wide grin, and call, *"¡Hola, Felicio!"*

Felicio. Felicio Tobón de Lozano, that's me. Get used to the name. With my own big smile, I called, *"¡Hola, Arturo! ¡Hola, hermano!"*

Brother. That's a Spanish word I know.

4

Sabanon is prettier from a distance than up close. It's on the Guiainacavi River, a small meandering stream, tributary of a tributary of a tributary of the Orinoco, up in Venezuela. Sabanon is built inside one of its elbows, so that the slow-moving brown water glints past it in the sunlight on three sides.

The main approach to town is from the fourth side, the north, the road down from San Cristóbal, which here is crumbling two-lane asphalt. The first bit of the city you see, and beautiful it is, is the gleaming white steeple of the church of San Vicente, where Lola and I were married. That slender white spire striking up out of the deep greens of the jungle makes it look as though there must be a giant knight on horseback down in there, at the very least. But what's down in there, as you soon see, is Sabanon, a crumbling cluster of low buildings in the brown embrace of the river.

The town is made of wood, most of it decades from its last paint job, though here and there some owner has recently gone mad with purple or carmine or ocher, creating a little extravaganza you can't look at directly until after sunset. The town has a population of four thousand, and there are maybe seven satellite dishes perched on roofs, one of them belonging to my in-laws, which we gave them three years ago when I thought I was, or would soon be, rich.

There's only the one paved road, coming into town, running straight through it to the river, where it becomes a thick-planked wooden dock flanked by a fish market and gasoline storage tanks. The other streets in town are packed dirt, parallel to or perpendicular to La Carretera, "the highway," which is what the locals call the main drag. None of the other streets are named.

The Tobón house, painted fuchsia at my expense when Lola and I got married and at last beginning to fade, thank God, was two blocks to the right of La Carretera and one block from the river-bank. Two stories high, built on stilts, its exterior walls vertical wood planks, its ground floor is partly enclosed to hold the freezer and hot-water heater and some guns and fishing poles and Madonna, the brood sow. The open part of the downstairs contains boats and stray concrete blocks and pieces of automobile and the vertical lines of plumbing. The family lives upstairs, in a number of airy connected rooms.

The trip from the airport took just under two hours, so when we drove into town, around four-thirty, the shadows were deep black and stretched out long from right to left ahead of us, making the sunny parts of town even brighter and more intense. Then we turned off onto the Tobóns' street and our only fellow traffic was dogs, mostly parked in the middle of the road. Arturo honked and yelled and laughed and steered around the dogs, who knew him and therefore ignored him, and parked beside the fuchsia house. In the sudden silence I could hear Madonna grunting her complaints the other side of the fuchsia wall beside me.

"*Mi casa . . .*" Arturo said, and grinned at me, and raised an eyebrow, and waited.

". . . *es su casa,*" I said, and pointed at him.

"And don't you forget it! Come on, let's have a beer."

We collected our luggage and went around to the outside stair-
case, to see Mamá and Papá crowded together in the doorway at the
top, two short wide people grinning broadly and yelling at us in
Spanish. Up we went, and dropped our luggage so we could be
hugged and kissed, and then picked up the luggage again to take it
to "our" room, a small corner storage room that was converted,
sort of, to a bedroom whenever we'd visit. There we changed into
shorts and tops and went back out to be handed our first beers.

We sat in the living room, a big airy space that got some morning sun but was cool and shady the rest of the day, soft breezes
moving through the glassless windows in two walls. Arturo had
gone to another room, but now he came back, carrying a white
legal-size envelope. "Here you go, Felicio," he said.

With a flutter of excitement, I opened the envelope. The one
piece of paper inside was thick and folded in thirds. I unfolded it,
and looked at the birth certificate of Felicio Tobón de Lozano,
born to Lucía Tobón de Lozano on July 12, 1970, in Mother of
Mercy Hospital, Sabanon, Guerrera. Father, Alvaro Tobón Gutier-
rez. Birth weight, six pounds, one ounce.

We're going to do it, I thought. This makes it real.

Arturo laughed and whacked my shoulder. "Monday," he said,
"we'll go up to San Cristóbal, get your driver's license."

"Make me legal," I said.

Arturo thought that was very funny.

5

San Cristóbal, like Sabanon, is a river town, but then again they're all river towns in this part of the Americas. Until the bulldozer was born, the rivers were the only roads through the jungle. San Cristóbal is built on the Inarida, another Orinoco tributary, larger and slower and greener than the Guiainacavi. It's a border river, with the neighboring nation of Colombia across the way.

Our first goal Monday morning was the government administration building on the Avenida de los Americas downtown, a broad two-story gray concrete box with a veranda stretched along the street side. The building is, of course, air-conditioned, and right now I needed air-conditioning. I needed to dry my upper lip.

Arturo and I made our way down the long central hall to the men's room. There I dabbed my upper lip with paper towels until it was dry enough so Arturo could apply the spirit gum. Then, eyeing myself closely in the mirror above the sink, I attached the mustache.

It was bushy and dark brown, my mustache. I had bought it in a theatrical supply store in New York. Starting tomorrow, I would grow a mustache of my own. I couldn't have started it before now, but I needed photo ID right away.

"Looks great," Arturo said, peering over my shoulder at the mirror.

It changed me, it really did. My hair is dark brown like the mustache, and my eyes are dark, my nose snub, my jaw firm. Normally I look like almost any kind of American ethnic from Greek to Puerto Rican—I'm mostly black Irish, actually—but with this mustache I looked absolutely Guerreran.

Pity I couldn't sound Guerreran. Well, we'd deal with it.

The Motor Vehicle Department was farther down the hall, a doorway on the left. We went in and found that the room stretched away down to our right, beyond a chest-high counter. Two lines of people stood patiently waiting their turns in front of the two clerks behind the counter.

To our left, a chest-high shelf contained forms and pens, the pens chained to the shelf. Arturo and I went there, me bringing my new birth certificate out of my pocket, and Arturo chose a form and filled it in. When he was done, I signed it, with the new signature I'd been practicing the last two days: *Felicio Tobón de Lozano*. Then we joined one of the lines.

This first line took twenty-five minutes, during which I was sharply aware that I still had not quite broken any law. I could still back out of this, grab Lola, hop a plane, go back to Long Island, find some other way to solve our problems. (There was no other way.) But once I got to the counter, it would be too late.

Suddenly I was sure my mustache was slipping. I nudged Arturo, and when he looked at me I wiggled my mouth at him, to ask, *Is it okay?* He frowned massively, not getting my meaning. I touched two fingertips to the mustache, which felt very strange and bristly there, as though I had a woodchuck attached to my face, and he still gave me blank looks, so finally I leaned close to him and waggled my eyebrows as meaningfully as I possibly could and muttered, "Okay? S'okay?"

"Oh, sure," he said.

The couple on line ahead of us turned sadly away from the counter, and I could tell from their expressions they'd just had the experience universal in Motor Vehicle Departments the world over: they'd been sent home for more forms.

We stepped forward, and I gave the clerk my cheeriest smile along with my form, but then I felt the mustache strain against the flesh as I smiled, so I dialed down to mere comradeship. Meanwhile, beside me, Arturo had gone into the spiel.

It isn't going to work, I thought. Somewhere in this building are policemen, heavily armed policemen, and all of a sudden they're going to rush into this room and grab Arturo and me and drag us away to some basement somewhere and beat us with rubber truncheons they got from the CIA until we tell them everything, which will take about nine seconds. How could we possibly have thought we could get away with this?

While I was struggling to smile, and to keep my panic down inside, Arturo told our story to the clerk behind the counter. What he said was: I had laryngitis. I'd been working in Mexico for years and knew how to drive but didn't have my Mexican driver's license anymore, and was going to become my brother Arturo's partner in his taxicab business, but had to have a license first, and couldn't wait for the laryngitis to clear up before coming in to apply, because I have this big family to take care of, which Arturo (winking at the clerk) has no intention of supporting. And here's my form, filled out and signed. And here's Arturo's driver's license and his cabby license.

The clerk looked at my form. He looked at me; I coughed. He turned the form over, made a red X on one line, and slid it toward me, along with a pen. "Sign here," he said, too fast. I understood some of what people said, and most of what I read, but generally people talked too fast for me.

I signed: *Felicio Tobón de Lozano*. I did it fluidly, easily, as though I'd been doing it all my life. I returned form and pen to the clerk, and he compared the two signatures as though that would tell him something.

Without waiting to be asked, I brought out the birth certificate and opened it on the counter. The clerk looked at me, looked at the birth certificate, lowered his head over it for a minute, and then said, *"Gracias."*

I moved my lips, nodding, and put the birth certificate away.

Next was the eye chart. I saw the clerk gesture toward it, as he spoke to the both of us, and I knew exactly what he was saying: "If you can't talk, how can you tell me what letters you see?"

Easy; we'd worked that out. Arturo told him, more or less, "You tell him what line to read, and he'll write the letters down."

"Oh, okay."

The clerk found a scrap of paper and slid it over to me, with the same pen as last time. He said something too fast for me to catch, and I looked at Arturo's left hand. He was to my left, leaning forward, forearm on the counter, left hand dangling down, now showing four fingers, the thumb tucked in out of sight. So: fourth line of the eye chart.

I looked at it. I wrote A F D E P G, turned the paper around, and pushed it and the pen back to the clerk, who looked at the letters, turned to look at the eye chart, nodded, and made a notation on the form.

There were a few questions, which Arturo mostly dealt with. Twice he turned to let me know I should answer, the first time nodding just slightly (I nodded), the second time not nodding (I shook my head).

Now all that remained was the road test, and for that, we were told, the wait would be between two and three hours. We could reserve a place without waiting on line, so we went and had lunch and then returned to the same building, where Arturo led me to a different room, a waiting room lined with uncomfortable green plastic chairs screwed to the floor.

And here, the worst of it was, I couldn't read. Arturo had bought a newspaper on our way back from lunch, but that was no help to me. So I just waited it out, and eventually Arturo stood up, which meant my new name had been called. I hadn't recognized it.

Apparently, in Guerrera, the job of road test inspector is given to policemen when they're too old to be policemen anymore. This fellow was ancient and leathery inside his brown uniform and looked mostly like an old saddle. He was also short-tempered, maybe because his shiny teeth were so ill-fitting or maybe because it had been too long since he'd had a rubdown with saddle soap. He seemed to believe that one symptom of laryngitis is deafness; once Arturo explained my problem, this guy yelled every instruction directly into my right ear, with a great clacking of those teeth, which up close sounded like castanets.

We rode in the Impala, in which I'd already done some driving to acclimate myself. The inspector sat beside me, Arturo in back, leaning forward in a companionable way, forearms crossed on top of the front seat. His right hand rested on my left shoulder, to give me the signals we'd worked out. A tug to the left meant turn left, to the right meant right. A push down meant stop, a pull back meant park. Four fingers tapping on my shoulder meant go faster, a smooth sideways caress meant go slower.

It worked very well, except that my right ear would never be the same. It was a short road test, eight blocks or so, and there we were back at the admin building, where I angle-parked with such smooth savoir faire that even the inspector was impressed. Most Guerrerans park by ear.

Armed with the inspector's form, back we went to Motor Vehicles, where we were led through the opening in the main counter and back to the fellow with the camera, where once again Arturo explained my disability. The guy shrugged, not caring; as Arturo told me afterward, what he said was, "So what? This isn't a sound camera."

Impatiently he gestured for me to stand with my toes on the white line on the floor. I did, and faced the camera. Arturo stood behind the cameraman, who gave me instructions, and Arturo did whatever he said: Step forward, lift his head, brush back the hair on the right side of his head. I echoed Arturo's movements, and *flash!* the picture was taken.

Now it was another half hour on the same line in front of the same counter, but when we finally got to the same clerk there was nothing to it at all. We handed over our documents, he handed back a temporary driver's license consisting of thick blue paper folded in half to make a little book, and we left.

Outside, Arturo said, "We had our choice. Either they'll mail it to us, or we come back in two hours and pick it up."

Two hours would be four-thirty; not long from their closing time. I said, "What did we decide?"

"*Hermano*," he said, "if you mail something in this country, that means you don't care if you ever see it again. I said we'd come back in two hours."

Two hours and five minutes later, I walked out of the Motor Vehicle Department for the last time, with my brand-new laminated driver's license in my pocket. "Shall I drive?" I said.

Arturo stared at me. "*My* car? You kidding me?"

I was, actually. I got into the passenger seat, and as we drove out of town I took out the driver's license and looked at it. That face. That signature. That seal of official approval.

It was so easy. And already I looked like somebody else. Already I *was* somebody else.

I liked that fake mustache, in the picture, and I was very reluctant to remove it; I'd already grown used to having a little furry pet under my nose.

Until about halfway to Sabanon, that is, when heat and sweat and wind finally did their job, and all at once the mustache fell like a woolly caterpillar into my lap. It was about to blow out of the car when I grabbed it and put it in my shirt pocket.

I could hardly wait to grow my own.

6

On Tuesday, the day after I got my new driver's license, I reverted to tourist mode; Lola and I got into the back of Arturo's Impala, he became the cabby, and off we all went to San Cristóbal again. Yesterday I'd worn my scruffiest old black chinos, a white open-collared short-sleeved shirt that had seen better days, and heavy black sandals without socks, because yesterday I was Felicio. Today I wore a bright red San Francisco 49ers cap, a lavender Ralph Lauren polo shirt, brand-new khaki shorts with a tan leather belt, high white socks, and black-and-white sneakers the size of apartment buildings. I'd started growing my mustache but had disguised the fact by not shaving at all, which is what tourists do the first two days of vacation, before it starts to itch.

Lola, beside me, was an edible vision in a white sundress, white sandals, white turban, large gold hoop earrings, deep red lipstick, and very dark large sunglasses. When she laughs and shows those sparkling teeth, strong men have been known to faint.

For much of the trip, Lola regaled Arturo with the local gossip she'd picked up yesterday. She was just the visitor, but he was male, so she would learn more dirt in a day than he would gather in a year. For my benefit, they did all their dishing in English, but I knew none of the people involved, so it hardly mattered. The basic idea seemed to be that people cannot keep their hands off each other.

There was one woman in the stories, named Luz, apparently one of the cousins, who appeared in so many of the adventures, causing so much mischief in so many directions, that I finally asked just how many Luzes there were in the family, which made both Arturo and Lola roar with laughter.

"Just *one!*" Arturo assured me.

"Just one too *many!*" Lola cried.

In San Cristóbal, on Avenida del Liberación, a too-narrow parallel street just one block east of the main Avenida de los Americas, we had our choice of four American car rental agencies, one Brazilian agency, and two locals. They all offered the same basic VW Beetle (or bigger cars if you wanted, which cost more and don't fit anywhere), and the prices varied depending on how much the companies spent on advertising back home. The local agencies, which barely had advertising budgets big enough to include an appearance in the San Cristóbal Yellow Pages, were the cheapest, and of them Arturo thought Pre-Columbian Rent-A-Car was the most reliable, so that's where we went. Arturo dropped us off in front of the office, I made a show of paying him—it was a show, but he never gave me the money back, so I'm glad at least I underpaid—and the two of us opened the sparkling glass door and went inside.

Air-conditioning, since the customers are tourists. The office was a tiny cubbyhole in a street of narrow storefronts. In this front room, there was barely space for the old wooden desk, the nice but chubby girl behind it, and the two wooden chairs in front of it. A bulletin board on the side wall contained charts, keys, folders, and all sorts of things that I'm sure were meaningful to the girl, if to no one else. The rear wall contained filing cabinets, calendars, a clock, rather forlorn color photos of Guerreran tourist attractions, and a closed wooden door.

The clerk gave us one look, smiled, and greeted us in English. We responded in kind, told her what we wanted, and sat down. And now my old ID was possibly being used for the very last time: my driver's license—the American one—my passport, my VISA card. I filled out some forms, signed *Barry Lee* with my usual flourish, and the girl asked if Mrs. Lee would also be a driver.

"No," I said. "My wife doesn't like to drive away from home."

"I get nervous," Lola said, with her sunniest smile, and it seemed to me obvious that nothing on earth could make this woman nervous.

When I slid back over to the girl the form I'd filled out, she turned to the closed door behind her and yelled, "Jorge!" and almost immediately the door was opened by a dark sweating man in a dirty undershirt and dirty work pants. He also had a droopier, scragglier version of my mustache.

The girl rattled off some directions at this fellow with the brisk bark of a drill sergeant. He listened without any visible reaction, and when she was finished he shut the door again.

She turned back to us, smiling sweetly, and said, "He'll bring the car to the front."

"Thank you."

But we weren't quite finished; she still had the VISA card authorization to go through. But enough juice remained in that account so there wasn't any problem. She got her approval number over the phone and wrote it on the slip. Then I signed the slip, she stapled a bunch of papers together, put the resulting stack of documents into a folder, pressed the heel of her hand down onto the folder to establish the crease so it might stay shut, handed the folder to me, and said, "Enjoy your stay in Guerrera."

"I'm sure we will," I said.

"Your first time?"

"Oh, no," I told her. "We've been here before."

"Well, enjoy it anyway," she said, which I thought cryptic, and the front door opened behind us, to show the same undershirted man, just as sweaty and dirty as before.

This time, he was the one who barked out the remarks, while she listened poker-faced. She nodded when he was finished and said to us, "The car is here. The gasoline tank is full. If you bring it back full, there's no additional charge; otherwise we charge three dollars and fifty-one cents U.S. per gallon."

Which was, in this particular case, not going to be an issue. But that was hardly a point I'd mention, was it? So I thanked her and gripped my rental contract folder, and Lola and I got smiling to our feet.

The undershirted man held the front door open for us, then held the passenger door of the Beetle open for Lola. The little mounded vehicle was white and gleaming, like her outfit. It looked like an igloo that had skidded south.

I got behind the wheel in the slightly cramped space and put my hand on the ignition. Before I started the engine I looked at Lola, who was looking at me. We were both very solemn. "Well," I said, "looks like we're gonna do it."

"Looks like," she said.

7

The next day, Wednesday, I was back in the Impala with Arturo, this time headed for Rancio, way up north, and once again I was in my Guerreran clothing.

The reason for this trip? There would soon come a time when I shouldn't be in Sabanon but would still need somewhere to stay in Guerrera. Up in Rancio, it seemed, there was Cousin Carlos, extremely trustworthy. "You remember him from the wedding," Arturo assured me.

"No, I don't."

"He was there."

"Arturo, *everybody* was there."

"He's Tia Mercedes's son, a big guy, great big belly on him, long mustache that droops down next to his mouth."

"That's half the cousins who were there," I said.

So finally he gave up. "You'll remember him when you see him."

"Fine."

Well, I didn't, but it hardly mattered. He remembered *me* from the wedding. "You put on some weight," was the first thing he said to me.

"I think you're about the same," I said, gazing at all that stomach in a formerly white T-shirt.

What Cousin Carlos mostly looked like was a pillow that was trying to stand upright. From a thick balding head with a face even more stubbly than mine (plus that droopy mustache and ocher teeth), he proceeded downward and outward through meaty sloping shoulders to a virtual ski slope of a body. Tree-stump legs supported this mass of flab, so he looked both powerful and extremely out of shape. If you ran, he probably couldn't catch you, but if he caught you, watch out.

Cousin Carlos was in the auto parts business. He had a long low tin-roofed building that was one-sixth shop and five-sixths garage doors. Two of the garage doors were open when we arrived, with trucks and truck parts scattered inside and out and half a dozen grease monkeys—and never had that phrase seemed more appropriate—roaming over the mess as though trying to remember what the trucks had looked like when they were all in one piece.

Rancio, being the smallest and poorest part of a three-nation border with Colombia and Venezuela, mostly supports itself by smuggling, and I had no doubt that Cousin Carlos's auto parts business was more or less a front, but it did look like an active and prosperous one.

Once Arturo had introduced us and we'd admired each other's form, Cousin Carlos squinted at the huge sun high in the sky and said, "Let's go eat."

"Good," I said.

He turned to yell what sounded like dire threats at his crew, who blinked at him and scratched their behinds with their screwdrivers. Then he walked off down the dusty street, and Arturo and I followed.

The chief characteristic of most Guerreran towns, it seems to me, is dogs, but the chief characteristic of Rancio is motorcycles. Also mopeds and motorbikes. Everywhere in Rancio you can hear them, a block away, on the other side of the house, zipping past, or just idling in front of a bodega. And the ones that aren't in motion are usually upside down in the roadway, being worked on by the owner and half his family.

Cousin Carlos walked us through about five blocks of this, during which I began to believe I'd never be able to hear again. But then he stopped at a whitewashed board wall, ten feet high, with razor wire along the top, a full block wide. He had a key for the whitewashed door in the middle of this wall, which he unlocked; he stepped inside and looked back for us to follow. So we did.

Quite a contrast. Here we had a low plain white stucco house of the style you see in the better Florida developments, with a red-brick patio between it and the wall, flanked on both sides by tall lush tropical plantings: many bright flowers, many huge leaves. The inside of the wall was painted a light brown, and abstract metal sculptures had been fastened to it here and there.

"Very nice," I said, and I meant it.

"Better around back," he said, and led the way to the left, where a path went around the house, flanked by more wall.

The back was an even bigger surprise, because here was a green lawn, and there was the river. It wasn't a swimming river, so where the wall ended in the shallows on each side, razor wire had been strung, in several coiled lines, just beneath the surface of the water. This was a viewing river. Seated here, you could view it without the slightest worry that anything out there would come ashore to view you back.

In addition to well-tended green lawn, the rear of the house also featured a small and sparkly swimming pool, all light blue interior and pink stone surround, and another patio, this one shaded by a large blue-and-white canvas awning. A white plastic table and six white plastic chairs stood on the patio.

Cousin Carlos waved toward the patio. "Sit," he said, and went on into the house.

Arturo and I sat. "This is a hell of a great place," I said. "Is this where I'll stay?"

"Oh, sure," he said, and grinned and pointed a finger at me. "*Mi casa . . .*"

". . . *Es* his *casa*," I finished, jabbing a thumb toward the house.

"Very good, *hermano*," he said, and he smiled, approving of me.

I said, "Do I talk money with him?"

"No no no, I did that," he said. "Mostly, he isn't doing it for the money anyway, he's doing it for family. I told him, you're working a little scam; when it's done you're gonna get a whole shitload of money, and he gets forty million."

"*Siapas*," I said.

"Well, yeah, sure. Two hundred bucks, right? That's around forty million."

"It's easy to be a millionaire in Guerrera," I said, and Arturo laughed.

An older woman came out of the house then, clearly a servant, heavyset and waddling, dressed in a white apron over an ankle-length black dress. In thick gnarled hands she carried plates and snowy napkins and silverware. She set the table for three, then said, to both of us, "*¿Cerveza?*"

"*Sí,*" we both said, and she nodded and went away.

Arturo grinned at me. "You learned *that* word pretty good."

I knew what he meant, but I said, "*Sí?*"

"*Cerveza,*" he said. "Gimme another *cerveza*."

"Here it comes now."

Heineken; very nice. Cousin Carlos didn't pay for all this stuff from his auto parts business.

Arturo and I sat in companionable silence for a few minutes, drinking our Heineken from the bottle, watching the lazy river, and then Cousin Carlos came out in better pants and a guayabera shirt that on him looked like a balloon just starting to lose its air. He was carrying his own Heineken bottle. Plopping heavily down into another chair at the table, he said, "I ain't goin' back there today. Fuck 'em. I hate the fuckin' place, Arturo, but when I don't go there I get bored. And those assholes I got workin' there . . ." He shook his head.

Sounding mildly interested, Arturo said, "Yeah? Who's that? I didn't see anybody working there."

"Yeah yeah," Cousin Carlos said, and to me he added, "You like guacamole?"

"I love guacamole."

"Good, 'cause that's what we're havin'."

Arturo said, "Where's María?" To me he explained, "Carlos's wife."

"Up in Caracas," Cousin Carlos said. "She'll come back the weekend. She's got her dealer up there."

"I'm sorry I'm gonna miss her," Arturo said. "Maybe next time."

"Maybe so."

Dealer, I thought. Drug dealer? Arms dealer? Who are these people? Is Arturo certain I can trust them? Am I certain I can trust Arturo? Maybe Lola and I should have one more discussion about this.

The servant woman came out again, with one big bowl nested among three little bowls. She put the little bowls around on our plates and ladled guacamole for us from the big bowl, then left the big bowl in the middle of the table and waddled away again.

We didn't stand on ceremony here. Cousin Carlos leaned his head over the table, tilted the bowl up with one hand, grabbed his tablespoon with the other hand, and started shoveling. Arturo did a modified version of the same thing—that is, a bit more civilized—and I did a modified version of what Arturo was doing.

The servant woman came back with a plate of tortillas; we ate them. She came back with more beer; we drank it. She came back with a big platter of fried chicken legs; we ate them. Meanwhile, she was taking away the empties, and now she brought more beer; we all sat back and belched and considered the river. Life seemed good. I wasn't even very much worried about the missing María's dealer.

After a few minutes, Cousin Carlos roused himself a little, like a cloud changing shape, and I saw that he was thinking about his responsibilities as a host. He frowned at me and said, "You want coffee?"

I looked at him. "For what?"

He considered that. "Clean your teeth," he decided.

I pondered that concept: coffee as a tooth-cleaning agent. It almost seemed to make sense. "Nah," I said. "But thanks anyway."

"*De nada,*" he said, which was perfectly true.

We spent some more time contemplating the day. I was reaching the stage where the low flat green movement of the river was becoming a metaphor for life itself—I was becoming stunned into philosophy, in other words—when Cousin Carlos, looking at the river, said, "You comin' here soon?"

"Oh, yeah," I said, and roused myself. I sat up more straight in my chair, became businesslike. "By the weekend," I said. "At least I hope so. It depends on a lot of things."

"*De nada,*" Cousin Carlos said.

Arturo said, "I'll phone you when."

"*De nada,*" Cousin Carlos said, and the servant woman came out, looking faintly worried or aggravated or upset. She stood next to Cousin Carlos's chair, bent forward as though she were in church, and muttered some things to him.

Cousin Carlos at first looked startled, then irritated, then fatalistic. He shrugged and grumbled something, and the servant woman bowed even more deeply and went away, rubbing her hands in a fretful manner, as though she'd been told to go get the doctor.

Cousin Carlos looked over at me. "You get to practice," he said, and touched his finger to his lips.

Oh, good: a dress rehearsal, completely unexpected, and me half zonked from beer and sun and heat. But what the hell, I was going to have to do this eventually, so why not start now?

The plan was, I intended to stay at this house of Cousin Carlos for any length of time from one week to three, depending how things progressed in the outer world and how my mustache was coming along. During that time, I would have to pretend to be Guerreran, because I couldn't exactly be hidden, in a small town like this, even behind Cousin Carlos's fine privacy wall, and I certainly couldn't present myself as the mysterious American. Which meant I had to be a Guerreran who, somehow, didn't speak fluent Guerreran Spanish.

Okay. The story was that I was Ernesto Lopez (chosen because I could both pronounce it and remember it), an old friend of Cousin Carlos from his days in Ecuador, managing the Coca-Cola plant, and that now I was a deaf mute as an aftereffect of syphilis. The syphilis was cured now and I was getting back on my feet and would only be staying with my old friend—*compadre*—Carlos until I got a job and my own place.

The syphilis part wasn't my idea, it was Arturo's. He said it gave the story believability, that anybody in Guerrera would understand a person might have some lingering problems after syphilis. I think the real reason for that detail was that Arturo is a smart aleck, but what was I going to do? Go along. I went along.

So now the story would be told for the first time, and we would all see how it flew. I felt suddenly very nervous, full of stage fright, and I didn't want to turn around to look at the house when this visitor should come out, but there came a moment when Cousin Carlos and Arturo both stood up and turned around, so I did too.

My first thought was: I don't want this woman to think I have syphilis. She was a beauty, probably in her mid-twenties, black-haired, chisel-cheeked, with a generous red mouth and large dark fiery eyes. Her body was hard and tightly curved, as though it had been constructed to contain electricity. She looked like Lola crossed with a panther, and I thought, *Oh, my*!

She came out of the house prancing, as though going onstage, which maybe is what she was doing. She fell all over Cousin Carlos with hugs and kisses, which he accepted with small nods and small smiles, patting her in safe spots. Then she suddenly discovered the presence of Arturo and fell all over *him* with hugs and kisses, and Arturo wrapped her in a bear hug, lifted her feet off the ground, and bit her neck until she squealed. Then he released her, grinning and whacking her on the behind, and she turned, disheveled, giddy, delighted, having the time of her life, to discover *me*.

She almost fell all over me too with hugs and kisses—I could see the automatic response gathering in her eyes and her mouth and her shoulder muscles—and then she realized she had no idea who I was.

And why should she? Even assuming she were somehow another relative, another cousin, who had been at our wedding, that was fourteen years ago. She would have been in her early teens, at most, and she was unlikely to remember much about the gringo groom from way back then. And even if she did have some memory of that former me, this present me, unshaven and shabbily dressed, would not serve as much of a reminder.

So she didn't know who I was, but this woman was direct: she asked me. I could more or less make out the words, in her rattle-quick Guerreran, as she looked directly at me, and I was so disorganized and surprised that I almost spoke. I don't know what I thought I was going to say, but I could feel the words welling up, and just in time I clamped my lips shut and gave Carlos a wide-eyed look, as though to say, Who is this, and what does she want?

Cousin Carlos took her near arm and started to explain. Arturo wrapped an arm over her shoulder, folded his hand against her side next to her breast, and did his own share of the explanation. Surprise crossed her very mobile face, and then pity for the poor deaf mute—I smiled bravely—and then—oh, yes, I could tell when Arturo, that bastard, got to the syphilis. You could see her knees press together.

After that, I was more or less left out of the conversation, which was what we'd wanted, wasn't it? We all sat at the table, and more beer was brought out, including one for our new guest. We sat in an arc behind the table, so we could all see the river, with the woman at one end and me at the other, Arturo next to me. The three chatted, enjoying one another, she going on with a great deal of animation, and I sat and watched her. From time to time she'd catch my eye and toss a quick smile in my direction, like one flower petal out of a basket, and then she'd concentrate again on the other two.

We drank that beer, and then all at once Cousin Carlos heaved himself to his feet and made a pronouncement that seemed to me to be saying, one way or another, "The party's over."

The woman pouted prettily but then also got to her feet, and so did Arturo and I. Arturo gave her another bear hug and bite and gestured to me that we were leaving.

For the hell of it, I stuck out my hand to her. She hesitated, just the fraction of a second, then showed her own brave smile as she took my hand in her strong narrow fingers and gave it one strong shake. I smiled my gratitude, and as I turned to shake hands with Cousin Carlos (who had no trouble with the concept), I noticed the woman was now holding her right hand out from her side, and her smile was more fixed than before.

I smiled and nodded farewell to Cousin Carlos, who merely nodded at me, not being a man to waste his smiles. He and Arturo said a word or two, and then Arturo and I departed, taking again the path around the side of the house. As we left the lawn area, I looked back, and it seemed to me the woman was just turning toward the swimming pool. I knew what she was going to do: rinse that hand in chlorinated water.

I followed Arturo around the house and through the door in the wall and out to the grubby street again, full of the sounds of motorcycles. We walked along toward Cousin Carlos's shop and the Impala, and I said, "I just wish it didn't have to be syphilis."

Arturo laughed. "She got to you, *hermano*. I knew she would!"

"What do you mean?" I felt a little bad-tempered in this noise and heat, what with being full of beer and not liking to be a syphilitic. "Who was she, anyway?"

"We talked about her in the car the other day," Arturo said. "Lola and me. Remember Lola?"

"Oh, don't be stupid, Arturo," I said. "Who is she?"

"Luz," he said. "Luz Garrigues."

"Oh," I said.

I remembered now. Luz. If it weren't for this Luz, the Tobón family wouldn't have any gossip worth mentioning.

We walked another dry noisy half a block, and I said, "You mean, she and Cousin Carlos . . . ?"

"No, no," he said. "She's his niece. Carlos, he's her uncle, he wouldn't do a thing like that."

"Oh," I said.

We walked some more, and I became aware that Arturo was watching me, with that overly boyish grin of his. I said, "What now?"

"Don't go get yourself in trouble, *hermano*," he said. "You know what I mean."

I looked at him. "What, me? You don't have to worry about me."

8

Friday was the day: Two days after my meeting with Cousin Carlos, almost a week after our arrival in Guerrera, and the beginning of the weekend. What better time for it? And what better place than Vista Alegar, the closest thing Guerrera has to a tourist attraction?

At 837 feet, Vista Alegar is the highest spot in Guerrera, up in the mountains along the southern border with Brazil. As the crow flies, it's probably sixty miles from Sabanon down to the border, but roads are few in Guerrera and meandering, mostly following the rivers and circling around mountains, so it can take nearly three hours to make the trip.

The last several miles, one drives due south but steeply uphill, beside a narrow rocky tumbling northbound river called the Conoro. As the road climbs, the descending river becomes more and more agitated, till there are actual rapids, visible from the road, and swirling deep pools that the more adventurous tourists swim in, and even brief noisy white waterfalls. Vines dangle down over all, and there's huge-fronded and huge-leaved jungle growth and incredibly gaudy birds flickering here and there, occasionally making sounds like a Marine Corps drill instructor.

For the last few miles to the border and the town of Vista Alegar, the road veers away from the river, and soon there are dirt roads angling off leftward toward tourist spots constructed along the steep banks. Most of these turnoffs are marked by rough-and-ready signs painted on or carved into wooden planks. The one we wanted had two such signs: GLOBAL WARMING CAMP and THE SCARLET TOUCAN, that being the restaurant we were headed for.

We turned in there and jounced over the roots and stones and brick-hard ruts of the narrow tan road through the jungle, the Beetle bounding around like a Christmas ornament in a hurricane and the both of us holding on for dear life, me to the steering wheel, Lola to whatever she could find. Twilight came more rapidly in the jungle, and I had to stop at one point to find the headlights.

Soon those lights picked out another car ahead of us, going the same way, even more slowly; a bright red Honda Accord with a rental company sticker on its bumper. "Not our undertaker," I said, "but he drives like an undertaker."

"He's an undertaker in northern Michigan," Lola decided. "Here he's just a guy afraid of potholes."

The Scarlet Toucan's parking lot is gravel, a broad, more or less flat area to the left of the restaurant, with a flimsy rail fence marking the edge of the dropoff to the river below. The lot is lit at night by kerosene-burning torches spaced around the perimeter, but that glow is nothing compared to the electric floodlights under the restaurant itself, which is cantilevered out over the cliff. All that light makes the river and its rocks and the surrounding jungle brighter and harsher and seemingly closer than by day.

While the cautious driver of the Accord angled off to find a spot as close to the restaurant entrance as possible, among the ten or twelve cars already parked there, I steered the other way, to the nearest free spot along the fence. I parked with the Beetle's nose not quite touching the rail, and when I got out I could look down at the sharply lit picture of the rapids. I could hear them, too, rushing and shushing down there.

Not speaking, holding each other's arms, we walked toward the restaurant. I could feel Lola's tension trembling in her arm, and I suppose she could feel mine as well.

The Scarlet Toucan, like most interesting restaurants in really obscure out-of-the-way places around the world, was owned, or at least operated, by a New Yorker who'd decided to get away from town for a few years. This particular Rick, whose name was Mike, was a wiry sharp-featured guy of indeterminate age and a deep tan and black hair flat on a stony skull. He's aggressively friendly without content, but that's okay; the food's good.

The restaurant seems rickety and probably is, but it's stood this long and might stand awhile longer, so why worry? There isn't much by way of building codes out here in the jungle, so what you have to rely on mostly is Mike's self-interest. If the restaurant someday were to fall into the rocky river below—way below—we might or might not be here that day, but Mike certainly would. So it's his confidence in the joint's stability we're relying on, and let's hope he's right.

The restaurant is bamboo-walled, with a conical thatch roof, like a coolie's hat. The interior is dark, mostly, except at the far end, facing the view. The mahogany tables and chairs are clunky but comfortable local workmanship. The decor makes me think of the South Seas, but I guess it's just supposed to be generic expatriate.

While waiting for Mike to come deal with us, I glanced at the other diners here, a mix of tourists and well-off locals, and tried not to guess which one would be my undertaker. I had deliberately avoided meeting the man, leaving all that part to Arturo. He would be here, that's all, having a nice meal at my expense, ready to do his thing when the time came.

Now Mike did come over, to shake our hands and introduce himself—we'd met him before, of course—and gush over us and say, "You folks having a great time?"

"Great," I agreed. I was a little drunk, just enough to be noticeable. "Even the wife is loosening up," I said, "and that's saying a lot."

Lola glowered at me but kept silent. Mike turned swiftly to his registration book. "Lemme see, lemme see: Lee. You requested a table by the view."

"I'm about ready for a view," I said.

Not looking at us, he reached for two menus and a wine list. "Come this way."

Lola and I both decided to follow him first, so we bumped into each other. She glared at me, while Mike tried not to notice, and I did an elaborate satiric bow, saying, "After *you*, your Majesty."

"A gentleman," she commented caustically, and we followed Mike out to the view, which is to say, out to the far edge of the plank platform the Scarlet Toucan is built on. Out there, where the floor stops, there's a rough wooden railing at waist height, but that's all. Nothing else: no glass, no screens, nothing. When you sit at a table along this edge, you look down past your thigh at white water and black boulders way down there.

"Enjoy your meal," Mike told us before he left, but his heart didn't seem to be in it. And we sat there, me particularly resplendent in all that light in a royal-blue shirt, worn especially for the occasion.

Our waitress arrived a minute later. A nice slender convent-bred local girl with a sweet smile, she was difficult to be rude to, but I did my best. When she stopped beside our table, before she could ask a single question or even wish us a good evening, I fixed a slightly drunken stare on her and demanded, "Do you know what Tanqueray gin is?"

"Oh, yes, sir, would you—"

"I mean *Tanqueray*," I interrupted. "I don't mean booga-booga or some other local crap, I mean *Tanqueray*. You know what that is."

"Yes, sir," she assured me, her smile only slightly dimmed. "It is in a green bottle. Our barten—"

To Lola, with elaborate astonishment, I exclaimed, "A green

bottle! How do you like that? It's in a green bottle! Civilization has come to wherever the fuck we are."

"Oh, shut up, Barry," Lola said, clearly having had it up to here with me. "Since I suppose you're going to insist on having a drink, why don't you just go ahead and order it?"

"Oh, I have your permission," I said. "Oh, how wonderful. How *gracious*."

Lola, tight-lipped, stared down at the river and the rocks.

To the waitress I said, "A Tanqueray Gibson. Can your bartender handle that?"

"Oh, yes, sir, he—"

To Lola I said, "And you, my darling? What would *you* like most of all on this lovely evening?"

She glowered at me, and everything she wasn't saying hung in the air over all heads in the immediate vicinity. Beneath their shimmer, after a little pause, she turned to the waitress, smiling politely in an effort to return civility to the table, and said, "Just water for me, thank you."

"Yes, ma'am."

The waitress would have turned away, but I said, "You didn't write it down."

The look she gave me was cool. "I don't need to, sir."

"Oh, of course! Stupid me, I do beg your pardon." I flopped first my left hand, then my right, onto the table, palms up, as I looked at each in turn and said, "One Tanqueray Gibson, one glass of water. Even *I* could remember that."

The waitress, without her smile, made her escape, and I grinned savagely at Lola.

"Water. If you want water so much"—thumb gesture at the river down below—"why not just jump?"

She leaned closer across the table. "Do try to keep it down, Barry," she muttered, in a tense undertone that nevertheless, I'm certain, carried very well. "People are looking at you."

"If people are looking at me instead of their food," I said, not at all keeping it down, "they'll stab themselves in the cheek with their forks. And deserve it, too."

Well, it went on like that. I wasn't funny, I was merely boorish. Clearly, I was either someone who couldn't hold his liquor or I was someone who'd had more liquor than anyone could hold.

It was hard at night to get rid of liquids at that table. There was no potted plant handy, to corrupt with alcohol. If you just poured your unwanted drink over the side to join the river, it would glisten and gleam in the floodlight glare all the way to the rushing water below.

So what we did, we both drank our water right away, and I poured the first two Gibsons into those glasses after I'd fished out and eaten the onions. The third (and last) Gibson arrived just after the white wine had been delivered in a nice traditional ice bucket containing water and ice, so from then on the gin went to help cool the wine, and so did some of the wine.

Meantime, I was picking at my food, getting drunker, slowly becoming louder without ever reaching the point where Mike might have to come over to have a word with me, and sniping without letup at Lola, who occasionally snarled back but usually just sat there in grim forbearance, frowned at her plate, and mechanically ate her food.

Food. I really should eat something. I put down a couple of mouthfuls, which gave our neighborhood a moment of blissful rest, and which I ended by abruptly hurling my fork down onto my plate with a hell of a clatter, as I jumped to my feet, threw my napkin at the jungle—it floated downward through the air like a flawed parachute, in all that light—and yelled, "I can't take it anymore! Do what the fuck you want! *Stay* here in this godforsaken place, if that's what you want!"

Stunned silence all around, except of course for the river, which went on with its own busy shushing sounds just as though some person weren't making a scene right overhead. And now, as no one in the entire room ate, and no one spoke, and no one looked directly at me, I spun about, corrected myself in time so that I didn't march into space, spun about in the other direction, and marched out of the joint.

"You *pig!*"—said in clear tones of utter outraged contempt by Lola—was the only sound that followed me.

Mike, near the door, looked as though he wasn't sure whether he was supposed to hit me or I was supposed to hit him, but whichever it was he was going to hate it. As I swept by him—no fisticuffs—I snarled, "*She* can pay for dinner. About *time* she paid for something!" And out I went.

The Impala now was parked to the left of the Beetle, and as I ran from the Scarlet Toucan's front door across the parking lot, Arturo got out from behind its wheel and came around to the car's right side. The Impala's interior light had never worked, at least not during the car's years in Guerrera, so when he opened both right doors no lights went on. Nevertheless, I could see me slumped in the passenger seat. I recognized me, of course, from my royal-blue shirt.

9

In a small poor South American country with few records, where people still emerge from the jungle not knowing how old they are or how to write their names, unknown bodies are not rare. People live their lives, and then they die. If they're still in the jungle, their families bury them right there. If they've come to the city, solitary, doing casual labor, living on the margins of society, when they die there's nobody to claim them or bury them except the government. My undertaker, tensing over his dinner in the Scarlet Toucan at the moment, in addition to his regular family trade also had a contract with the government to deal with the unknown and the indigent. And that's how we'd gotten our body at a reasonable price.

Very reasonable. In addition to the meal at my expense that my undertaker was I hoped enjoying this evening with the companion of his choice, he could expect to be paid at American rates for his services to the late Barry Lee, not at Guerreran rates. Arturo had provided him with a second set of clothing identical to what I'd worn this evening, he had provided the clothed body, and I had provided dinner.

"Quick!" Arturo whispered.

"One second, one second."

The only thing I carried that mattered was my wallet. I went to one knee beside the Impala and pushed my substitute leftward so I could slide the wallet into his hip pocket. He was cold but not stiff; in fact, he was unpleasantly soft, not at all what I'd expected.

The Beetle's interior light switched on when I opened the driver's door, but no one else was in the parking lot and it wouldn't be lit for long. I grabbed the royal blue shoulders and Arturo grabbed the chino knees, and we lugged him out of the Impala and behind the wheel of the Beetle. I put one of his hands on the steering wheel, and in the brightness of the interior light I saw his hand was soft and pudgy, with a clear mark on the third finger where a ring had been removed. And wasn't that a recent manicure?

What was this? This was no indigent, no unknown peon. I tried to see his face, but he was slumped too far forward, I could only see that his cheeks and neck were not scrawny and his hair was neatly barbered.

Something was wrong here, but there wasn't time to do anything about it. I'd have to ask Arturo later. Who are we getting rid of here?

"Come on, *hermano*."

"Yes, yes," I said, "I'm coming!"

I stood up out of the car and shut its door and the light went off. He was a peon again; he was me again; he was no longer a mystery. I reached in past him to start the engine, which immediately coughed into life. I shifted into DRIVE and got my arm out of there, and the Beetle moved forward to poke the rail fence, insistent but not strong enough to break through.

Now, while I stood there, Arturo ran to the Impala. He got in, started it without switching on the headlights, and backed up to get behind the Beetle. As I stepped backward out of the way, he suddenly accelerated as fast as he could at the rear of the Beetle, hitting it with a *crunch* that popped the smaller car forward, through the fence and off the edge.

Out it arched, into all that light above the river, a white descending balloon. No. A white descending refrigerator.

Arturo slammed on the brakes, and the Impala stopped just before the drop. He backed around in a tight circle, and I turned away from the dramatic instant of my death. As I ran for the Impala and jumped into the backseat, I heard the screams start inside the restaurant.

I could pick out Lola's scream. It was the loudest one of all.

10

When next I saw her, Lola described for me the scene after my departure from the Scarlet Toucan. Into the at-last-calm atmosphere of the restaurant, the shiny white Beetle made a sudden dramatic appearance in the middle of the air, hung there like a surrealist painting, then crashed with a great geyser of foam and spray and auto parts.

The patrons, of course, were horrified and began to scream and point and leap to their feet. Naturally, Lola had recognized the car, and she made it clear that she knew at once what must have happened, and after her first horrified shriek she blamed herself, loudly and inconsolably: "It's all my fault! I never appreciated him! I drove him to it!"

The first thing that happened was that two guys in dirty aprons from the kitchen scrambled down the boulders and among the support pillars under the restaurant, carrying flashlights. They came out into the floodlit area, standing on the brink of the rush-

ing river, while the observers above crowded dangerously close to
the edge of the platform to watch. The staff guys couldn't get very
close to the car, but they stood on wet boulders and shone their
flashlights into it and saw the royal-blue mound slumped in the
front seat. Then they looked up at the people on the restaurant rim
and shook their heads. One of them made a horizontal motion in
the air with one hand, palm down, while the other drew a finger
across his throat. The driver is dead; no hope.

Fortunately, there just happened to be, among the diners in the
Scarlet Toucan that evening, one Señor Ortiz, a well-known and
widely respected mortician from the city of Marona. Grasping the
situation at once, Señor Ortiz promptly volunteered his services,
which Mike was happy to accept.

Señor Ortiz ordered Mike to take down the names and addresses
of all the patrons in the restaurant, as witnesses to the tragic accident, while he himself got on the phone. First he called his staff in
Marona and told them to rush to the Scarlet Toucan with the
ambulance used for dead bodies. Only then did he phone the
police, but he didn't call the small local constabulary in Vista Alegar, just up the road, but police headquarters instead, in San
Cristóbal, 170 miles away.

Meanwhile, other patrons gathered around poor Lola to calm
her, give her solace, and reassure her (without quite saying so) that
once she was over the shock she'd realize she was better off without that bum. And Mike and his waitresses moved among the
patrons, taking down names and addresses and distributing free
drinks of the patrons' choice.

People didn't want to leave, but they didn't want to eat anymore
either. After Mike's free round, they began to buy their own
drinks, and the occasion turned into a kind of Halloween party, a
premature wake, while everybody waited for the police, or Señor
Ortiz's ambulance and crew, whichever got there first.

It was, in fact, the police who arrived first, but not the ones from
San Cristóbal. He was one young cop from Vista Alegar, who
seemed mostly embarrassed to be the center of all this attention.
Headquarters at San Cristóbal had phoned him, and it was his job

to maintain order until more experienced police arrived from the capital. He was given the entire story several times over, was offered (and accepted) a rum drink by Mike, offered in his turn his condolences to Lola, and then decided to sit at her table until reinforcements came. A rich beautiful widow, and a native-born Guerreran at that; he might be young, that cop, but he wasn't foolish.

An hour and a half after Barry Lee's final flight, Señor Ortiz's ambulance arrived. The three-man crew carried their canvas stretcher and white sheet down under the restaurant and out into the light. They'd also brought along a strong rope, one end of which they tied to a restaurant support pillar, the other to the nearest rear window frame of the Beetle, so they'd have something to hold onto when going out and back. Then they carried the stretcher out to the car, and from above everyone saw that flash of royal blue as the body was moved from Beetle to stretcher.

And then it was over, or at least the interesting part was over. The body was brought up over the boulders and stuffed into the ambulance, the ambulance drove away, and Señor Ortiz came back in from overseeing the operation to receive the thanks of the proprietor, the admiration of the crowd, a kiss from his adoring Señora Ortiz, and one last complimentary planter's punch for the road.

Now the patrons began to drift homeward, all pausing for a final word of condolence to the widow, so that it actually was very like a wake, except that the viewing was over. Lola had to stay, of course, to wait for the real cops to arrive from San Cristóbal. The bashful young cop had to stay, and the Ortizes, and Mike, but he did send the staff home and from then on tended bar himself.

Twenty-five minutes after my supposed departure in the ambulance, and two hours and ten minutes after my presumed departure from this life, the police from San Cristóbal at last arrived, in two vehicles: a van containing eight uniformed policemen, and a Land Rover bearing a uniformed driver and two inspectors in plain clothes. Well, relatively plain; one, named Rafez, was in an off-white linen suit, pale yellow dress shirt, and tan sandals, while the other, named Loto, wore a pink guayabera shirt, pressed designer blue jeans, and black cowboy boots with silver decorations. Rafez in the suit was the suave one, while Loto in the boots was the blunt pragmatic one.

At first, when they were introduced to Lola and she said a heart-broken word or two in Guerreran Spanish, these inspectors made the mistake of thinking that her dead husband must be local too, and not the rich northerner they'd been led to believe was the victim here. A dead Guerreran was not worth an exhausting midnight drive across most of Guerrera, as any fool was supposed to know. Until the situation was explained, they were quite frosty, but then, having been assured that Barry Lee, the departed, was indeed a North American, even a New Yorker, they relaxed; their dignity had not been impaired, after all.

It was Loto, in the boots, who questioned Mike and the Ortizes and the bashful young cop, while Rafez, in his linen suit, joined Lola at her table to murmur delicate questions about her marriage and the events of the night. Lola answered tearfully but bravely, confessing there had been trouble in the marriage recently, brought on by financial reverses they had suffered, and that this vacation had been their last desperate attempt to recapture their earlier passion. "Ah," Rafez murmured, smiling soulfully at her, "when passion has gone . . ."

"But we wanted to try. We wanted to hope. And *now* . . ."

Inspector Rafez reached across the table to grasp her hand in sympathy. "At such moments," he said, "we can only bow to the will of Fate."

"I'm sure you're right," she agreed, and released her hand so she could sip chardonnay, the only drink she was permitting herself during this dangerous time.

Down below, the soldiers had clamped the Beetle with grappling hooks and metal cables. The cables ran up to a pulley on the front of their van, so the van's engine could be used to winch the Beetle out of its watery resting place and grindingly up the boulder-strewn slope until, no longer quite recognizable as an automobile, it reached the parking lot.

Had this been a crime scene, that would have been a terrible way to treat the primary piece of evidence, but it wasn't a crime scene, was it? It was an accident scene.

And now everyone was finished. Mike was turning his back to yawn, even the Ortizes were coming down from their self-satisfied high, and the bashful local cop had resigned himself to the fact that Inspector Rafez had the inside track with the beautiful rich widow. Rank, as everyone knows, has its privileges.

Lola was driven home by the inspectors. Loto sat in front with the driver and Rafez sat in back with Lola. She'd expected she might have to fend him off, but he behaved himself as he and Loto and Lola chatted about Guerrera, the changes since she'd moved away (not many), and people they might know in common (a few).

After a while, Loto began to doze. The silences lengthened. "I've been thinking about moving to the States myself," Rafez said.

"Oh, yes?"

"Sure. New York City, I was thinking. I read about New York City a lot, and there's a lot of Spanish people there."

"That's right."

"The police there," Rafez said, "they could use some cops talk Spanish, I bet that's true."

"I'm sure they've got some," Lola said.

"Oh, yes, sure, they'd have to do that already. But look at this, Señora . . . Señora Lee. May I speak to you as Lola?"

"Yes, I'd like that."

"Thank you. And I am Rafael. Rafael Rafez."

"How do you do," she said politely.

"Well, Lola, here's what I think," he said. "I think they got cops there that speak Spanish and maybe know the people from the south, know them a little, but you look at me. Already I'm a cop, and already I'm here in South America; I got dealings with all kinds of Spanish people in this country. Not just Guerrerans, all kinds. Look at all the borders around us."

"That's true."

"I think, if I got to New York," Rafez told her, "I'd get a job with the cops in New York, they're glad to have me, a guy knows the people like I know the people, and already a *cop*. Already took *two courses* in police technique, up in Miami. U.S. government courses, you know about them?"

"No, I don't," Lola said.

"Very good, very professional. I got diplomas, I'll show you sometime."

"That would be nice," Lola said, and they arrived in San Cristóbal, and the van behind them peeled off, and Loto woke up to say to the driver, "Take me home."

So they had a little middle-of-the-night tour of the empty streets of San Cristóbal, with the widely spaced pinkish streetlights and all the facades shuttered and shut up for the night. They stopped at a newish concrete apartment building and Loto yawned, got out of the Land Rover, and then stuck his head back in to say, "Condolences, Señora."

"Thank you."

Once they'd left the lights of San Cristóbal behind, on the road to Sabanon, Rafez did make his move. Apparently he was a little heavy-handed, the bastard, and Lola had to defend herself with increasing vigor. She'd hoped the presence of the driver would be some sort of deterrent, but the driver never saw a thing, never even looked in the rearview mirror.

She tried to remain gentle about it, the heartbroken and dazed widow lady, but Rafez just got more and more aggressive, and it wasn't until she gave him the nosebleed that he accepted the idea that no meant no.

Tenderhearted Lola; the nosebleed worked, but she still felt badly about it. "He'll never get the blood out of that linen suit," she said.

Good.

11

"Arturo," I said, bouncing around in the backseat like a single piece of popcorn, "stop a second." I was in back as we drove too fast out the potholed dirt road from the Scarlet Toucan after we'd drop-kicked the Beetle into the river, because I was supposed to be changing clothes, out of Barry and into Felicio, but the road flung me around so much I couldn't do a thing. "Stop, will you?"

"I don't know, man," he said. "We gotta clear outa here."

"Just stop while I get these pants on, Arturo."

So he did stop, though reluctantly, and I at last finished getting dressed, switched to the front seat, and slammed the door, before Arturo sent us leaping forward again. Braced, I said, "One question."

"It was beautiful, man," he said. He grinned, and his teeth gleamed in the reflected headlight glow; the dashboard lights didn't work on the Impala either.

I repeated myself. "One question, Arturo. Who *was* that guy?"

He risked a quick glance at me. "What guy?"

"The guy we put in the Beetle."

"How do I know?" he asked me. "He was just somebody Ortiz had around. He said we was lucky, he had a guy the right size and sex and age and everything."

"Arturo," I said, "that was no peon, that was no nameless indigent. That guy had a *manicure*."

"He did?" Arturo made the turn onto the main road, heading north, and we could both relax a little. "A manicure," Arturo repeated, and grinned and shook his head.

"What's going on, Arturo?"

"Looks like," Arturo said, "somebody else got a scam working."

"Just so it doesn't make trouble for *me*."

"How can it? The body come from Ortiz, the body's goin' back to Ortiz."

"Well, that's true."

He gave me another grin. "And whaddaya thinka that Beetle, out there in the air?"

I grinned back at him. "It was great."

He nodded, watching the dark road. "It was beautiful, *hermano*. I shoulda brought a video camera."

I laughed, feeling the tension ease down another notch. "Arturo, we couldn't stand there making a *movie*."

"Be a hell of a movie," he said.

It was almost two-thirty in the morning when we finally pulled to a stop in front of the anonymous wall surrounding Cousin Carlos's place. Carlos had given a key to Arturo, who gave it to me, and it worked first time, as simple as if I'd been coming here this way for years.

I waved to Arturo, who yawned and waved back, and I went on inside as he drove off. I'd asked him earlier if he didn't want to stay here tonight, rather than do more hours of driving, but he said that was okay, he wasn't going all the way home to Sabanon but would stay over in San Cristóbal. Maybe that meant his alleged wife and putative children were about to get a rare and precious Arturo sighting.

In any event, I was now on my own. I let the door in the wall snick shut behind me, which put me in darkness alleviated only slightly by star shine, just enough to make out the general shape of the building. Arturo had told me what I should do next. The same key would unlock the front door of the house. I should go in there, and I'd see a nightlight down the hallway to my right, which would be in the kitchen. I should continue on past the kitchen to the door at the end of the hall, which would be open. That was my room.

Yes. The key worked on the house door, as promised. I stepped inside into greater darkness, with what might have been a living room in front of me. I could vaguely see hints of the windows that would overlook the pool and the lawn and the river. A hall extended to my right, as advertised; the spill of light from a doorway on the left down there must be the kitchen. And the black rectangle beyond it would be the doorway to my new room.

I moved slowly and silently down the carpeted hall, not wanting to wake anyone. More of those free-form metal sculptures were on the walls here, like the ones I'd noticed on the inside of the perimeter wall. They were interesting abstract things, at the same time both primitive and sophisticated. They didn't seem to go with Cousin Carlos at all. But you never know about people.

I reached the kitchen and looked in, and Luz was there, looking at me. She was seated facing me at a large heavy mahogany table, a paperback photo novel open in front of her, along with a beer bottle and a plate containing half a thick sandwich. She gave me a very loose smile, with mischief twinkling in those large dark eyes, and said, "How you doin', Ernesto?"

I knew enough now to pretend I hadn't heard her, but that I would realize she'd spoken because I'd seen her lips move. So I smiled and nodded and waved my hand at her, and continued on along the hall, thinking, Damn it, what's *she* doing here?

Can it be she wants to check me out anyway, that the thought of syphilis—cured, after all—is becoming less of a deterrent? I don't need this, I really don't. I don't need Luz hanging around, and I don't need Lola *hearing* that Luz is hanging around.

I was closing the door of my pitch-black room when what she'd said floated through my brain again: "How you doin', Ernesto?"

In English.

12

I woke up late; ten-forty by the Rolex, which I still had. I'd thought long and hard about whether to accessorize Mr. X with my watch and wedding ring, in addition to my wallet, and finally decided there was too much likelihood they'd be lost in the crash. So the heck with it; they *were* lost in the crash. I'd keep them both with me, but hidden, until I could get back to the States as Felicio, when they would be given to me, as part of her dead husband's remaining effects, by my grateful sister, Lola.

This was the very tricky part now, when I was floating among identities. I couldn't very well claim to be Lola's brother in front of her family, most of whom weren't in on the scam, so that's why I was having to be Ernesto Lopez, the pitiful but no longer scabrous deaf mute, until the time was right to leave the country. I was hoping it would only be a week or two.

The idea was, Barry Lee would be buried on Monday, after a very touching funeral mass in the same church in which he'd been married only fourteen years ago, and on Tuesday Lola would fly to New York, carrying with her the death certificate and the funeral card and videotape of the funeral and a copy of the order for the gravestone and Señor Ortiz's undertaker bill and the deed for the grave plot, and turn all that over to our insurance agent. Then she'd go out and buy a lot of black.

How I'd love to fly north with her, but of course I couldn't. Or, that is, her brother Felicio couldn't, since he didn't at this point have a passport. Soon he would apply for one—with, as usual, the invaluable assistance of his brother Arturo—but we didn't think it would be safe for Felicio to make any official move until after the insurance company, having decided there was no problem, had paid off. Then, once Lola had that check in hand, Felicio would leave the land of his birth for the very first time just as quickly as he could, to fly north to comfort his widowed sister in her hour of travail.

The death certificate was the key to all this, and one of the reasons we'd decided to work this scam in Guerrera instead of at home is that, in Guerrera, the coronor doesn't actually have to see the body to give you a death certificate, just so he has a signed statement from a mortician. The reason is that there's only one coroner for the whole country, but there are morticians everywhere there's a graveyard. So Señor Ortiz would drive his statement to San Cristóbal on Monday, come back with the certificate, and Lola would catch her plane north on Tuesday.

That was the plan, and for the next part of it my job was to do nothing. Not that I had to stay in this tiny room all my life. Seen by the light of day, it really was very small and plain; the word *monastic* comes to mind, and not only because of the huge mahogany crucifix hanging above the bed. The bars on both windows also helped.

The furniture, apart from this fairly comfortable single bed, consisted of a very crude clunky small dresser, which looked as though it had been made by a Shaker on speed, and a bulky uncomfortable mahogany armless chair built by the same person during rehab.

Well, it was a small room, and it was very late, and yet I was reluctant to get up and start my day, and the reason for that was Luz. She'd spoken to me in English last night. She didn't buy Arturo's story, masterful though it had been. She believed something else, but what?

She believed I could hear, and she believed I spoke English.

So Luz was a problem, though I didn't know yet *what* problem she was. But it was a problem that would have to be dealt with.

Finally, though, it wasn't the need to deal with Luz that got me out of bed and into the white terry-cloth robe draped over the chair. It was my bladder. I needed a bathroom.

When I opened the door, the hall was empty and the house silent. I stepped out and saw an open door on my right, before the kitchen, and when I looked in I saw it was a bathroom. It was very modern, with a stall shower and a stack of thick white towels on an attractively graceful small white-painted wooden table completely unlike the usual cumbersome mahogany creations with which so much of Guerrera is littered.

The medicine chest was stocked with unwrapped toothbrushes and combs and disposable razors and all the usual accessories. I could shave!

So this was the guest area of the house, and this was the guest bathroom, and it was not at all what I would have expected from Cousin Carlos, but I was grateful. And that shower looked very tempting.

And refreshing. When I went back into the guest room fifteen minutes later, I felt much more positive about life. I was clean and rested. My face was tingling with aftershave rather than itching with stubble, and in the bathroom mirror I had seen a man with a definite mustache: not nearly as luxurious as his driver's license photo yet, but showing promise.

Now that I felt physically better, I felt better about everything else, including Luz. She was family, after all. She might be a provocateur, but there was no reason for her to make real trouble.

Next to the dresser in my guest room, on the floor, stood the ratty little cardboard suitcase Arturo had brought up to Rancio earlier, containing Ernesto/Felicio's few shabby possessions. I emptied it now into the dresser, putting some of the clothing on my fresh new body along the way, and then I went out at last to see what the day had to offer.

This morning, in the kitchen, it did not offer Luz but rather the woman servant who'd fed us all lunch outside last time I was here. She was slicing plantains when I walked in, but she turned around at once, smiled at me, dried her hands on her apron, and gestured for me to sit at the table. (I obviously couldn't be the deaf mute with this woman, not and live here, so Carlos had told her *she* should be the deaf mute outside this house, in re me.)

I nodded my thanks, took the same chair as Luz had used, and the woman started bringing me things: a tall glass of fresh orange juice, a huge colorful mug of strong black coffee, and, when I made pouring gestures, a tan earthenware jug of warm milk to pour in with it.

And more: Three eggs, sunny side up. More coffee. Then half a melon the color of gold accompanied by half a lime the color of cash.

I could get to like it here.

13

After breakfast, feeling better, I went from the kitchen to the patio, planning to sit quietly in the shade and watch the lazy river while I slowly digested. There were a few white chaise longues over by the pool, under the extensive blue-and-white awning; I started in that direction and then stopped when I realized I wasn't alone.

She realized it at the same instant and turned to look at me. She was seated on one of the chaises, legs up, in profile to me, but she immediately stood, a tall striking woman who was all bronze and black; bronze skin, black one-piece bathing suit, large black sunglasses, thick black hair pulled back through a glittering bronze figured circlet. She spoke to me in firm aristocratic Spanish, telling me that whoever I was, this was not my proper place.

I gaped at her, partly doing my Ernesto number and partly just gaping at her. I don't know if she was beautiful, but she was certainly dramatic, with a firm jawline and strong nose and full-lipped mouth and the tall lean body of a swimmer to go with that bathing suit. She was one of those women about whom it is impossible to guess the age; surely over thirty, most likely under fifty, but who could know?

I had no idea who she could possibly be, but I thought I should get out of her way so, maintaining my blank expression, I began to nod my head and back toward the house door I'd just come out.

But then she abruptly shook her head, and her expression changed. Her whole body language changed, from sternly authoritarian to casually dismissive. Bending one knee slightly as she turned a fraction away from me, she said, in English, "Oh, you're the one the cousin married."

Who *was* she? Could Cousin Carlos possibly have a mistress who looked like this? (She certainly seemed as though she ought to be *somebody's* mistress, but the somebody should be a high-ranking government official, at the very least.) Was she another cousin, from a loftier realm of the family than I'd so far met? Or possibly an important local woman, waiting for Carlos, here to hit him up for a charitable contribution to something or other?

In a bathing suit? And why the switch to English? And what did she mean when she said I was the one the cousin married? Did she mean Lola? Does she *know* what's going on?

She frowned at me, and no doubt I was still wearing the stupid expression, honestly earned, because she shook her head and said, "Oh, come sit down out of the sun." Then, turning away to spread herself out again on the chaise, she said, "The mustache is a good idea."

I moved forward until I was in the shade under the awning, but I didn't feel comfortable enough to sit. I said, "I take it I'm not Ernesto Lopez at the moment."

"Is that the name?" Seated there, one long bronze leg stretched out on the white waterproof cushion of the chaise, the other knee lifted, she looked up at me appraisingly through the sunglasses. "Why not?" she decided. "Ernesto Lopez. And the clothing is good, that's what confused me. How are you, Ernesto? I'm María."

María. I should have remembered having heard the name, but I was feeling a little flustered, not knowing if I had to worry that my secret was out, my security compromised, my cover blown. So I merely stepped forward closer to her, stuck out my hand, and said, "How do you do?"

She took the hand, and hers was firm, maybe a bit too much so. Looking up at me, amused, she said, "You have no idea who I am, do you?"

And then I did. *María.* María was Carlos's wife, up in Caracas to see her dealer and now home. "Oh, for God's sake," I said, as she gave me my hand back. "I'm sorry, I've been a little . . . distracted."

She laughed, a musical sound, if throaty, and said, "*Do* sit down, Ernesto, you're giving me a crick in the neck."

"Sorry." I was saying sorry a lot; I *must* be rattled. I pulled the foot of a nearby chaise closer to her, so we'd see one another at an angle, and sat. "This is a beautiful place," I said.

"Thank you," she said. "We brought most of the furniture from Ecuador. You know Carlos used to manage the bottling plant there."

"Is that where you're from?" She had almost as little accent as Lola.

"No," she said. "Argentina."

"Way south," I said, thinking, *We've gone directly into cocktail party chat.*

But then she said, "How did your death scene go?" and I found myself laughing. I said, "It looked great when I left. I haven't heard from anybody since. Tell you the truth, I just got up."

"Do you need something? I could have Esilda make some breakfast—"

"No more," I said, pressing both hands to my stomach. "Esilda—she's the woman in the kitchen?—she just fed me very well."

"Good," María said. "She'll take care of you."

"I can see that. My real name, you know—"

"Oh, don't be silly," she said. "I know your real name. I was at your wedding."

"You were? I'm sorry, I don't—"

"Grooms aren't supposed to remember the other people at their wedding," she assured me. "You were very handsome, and Lola was very beautiful, and you both looked as though you couldn't wait to get away from everybody and fuck yourselves silly."

Being around Lola's family and friends, I've noticed that people never treat dirty words in their second language as seriously as those words in their primary tongue. The taboo words you grew up with keep their strength, whether you use them as a grown-up or not, but other languages' taboo words are never more than merely funny. Still, it is always startling—and it was now—to have an elegant woman say *fuck* early in a first conversation.

Trying to stay in the spirit of our chat, I said, "As I remember, we succeeded."

She smiled. "Congratulations."

"Still," I said, "I think it was wrong of me not to remember you."

"That's very gallant of you, Ernesto," she said. "Thank you."

"Ernesto." I tasted the name, since I was hearing it addressed to me for the first time by a new person, and I didn't much like it, not for me. "Ah, well," I said, "I'm a deaf mute, so I don't actually have to get used to answering to that name. And it's only for a little while, anyway."

"Carlos says you might be here a month."

"Oh, less than that, I think," I said, then hastily added, "Not that this isn't a great place. It's just that—to be without Lola. You know."

"Of course." She smiled in sympathy. "But I'll be pleased for you to stay," she told me. "It can get a little boring in Rancio."

"You preferred Ecuador?"

"Not particularly," she said. "It's all the same to me. Every place can get boring sometimes. But after that ridiculous business about the embezzling, of course, Carlos couldn't stay in Ecuador any longer, and he does like to be near his family, so here we are."

Embezzling. She'd said that casually, as though, being a member of the family, I would know all about it. I didn't know all about it, but I couldn't think of a way to ask, so I'd find out from Lola when I saw her again. In the meantime, I had another question, even more urgent. Trying to sound as casual as she had, I said, "The last time I was here, I missed you, I'm sorry to say. Carlos said you were in Caracas to see your dealer."

"To have scenes with my dealer, in fact," she told me. "To threaten I would go elsewhere. I may have to eventually."

This didn't help much. I said, "Has he been your dealer long?"

"Twelve years," she said. "And really, he throws wonderful parties, you can meet the most astonishing people, but after a while you want more than that. You want a real *hit*."

Increasingly befuddled, I said, "You go to him for parties?"

She looked confused, then amused, and said, "Ernesto, don't you know what we're talking about?"

"Well, no," I said.

She went off into arias of laughter, rocking on the chaise, looking very alluring but also very self-contained. "Oh, Ernesto," she said, when she could speak again, "that's wonderful. What kind of dealer did you think? Did you think it was my *drugs* dealer?"

"No, that didn't seem to fit," I admitted. "Nothing seems to fit. If it's a riddle, I give up. Tell me the answer."

"Sweetheart," she said, which I knew was horribly condescending, but there was no way out of it, "he's my *art* dealer."

"Your art dealer." She was buying art?

She shook her head at me, still broadly smiling. "The sculptures on the walls? You've noticed them?"

Oh, so that's what she's buying. "Yes," I said, "they're very striking, very interesting, I remember think—"

"They're *mine!* I make them! Later on, I'll show you my studio; it's at that end of the house down there."

"You're an artist!" I said. I was feeling stupid and abashed, and she was right to condescend to me.

But then she softened, saying, "I thought Carlos would have told you. Or Arturo. Yes, I am an artist, and my dealer sells me

very well in Europe and in South America, but not at all in the
United States. He has no contacts there, and I'm feeling a frenzy,
because legitimacy comes from magazine articles, and the important magazines are in the United States, and they know *nothing*
about me."

"Ah," I said.

"I *need* to get into Soho," she declared. "Not LA; that just ghet-
toizes me as another Hispanic. I need to get into Soho, and
Friedrich isn't getting me there, and I *will* go to someone else
unless he can come up with something."

"Friedrich," I said, "is your art dealer in Caracas."

"Yes." Then she smiled at me again and said, "I'm sorry I
laughed, I was wrong. You couldn't know, and you're very sweet."

Which was more condescension, I realized, but that was all
right. Speaking sincerely, I said, "I'll have to go back and look at
those pieces again, now that I know something about the mind
that produced them."

"You're going to understand me," she said, openly mocking.

"I doubt that," I said.

Which pleased her. "Good," she said. "Will you forgive me for
laughing?"

"Of course," I said. "Will you forgive my ignorance?"

"We forgive each other," she decided, "and now we are friends.
Would you like to swim? Esilda will get you a suit."

"Later," I said. "It's too soon after breakfast for me."

"Well, I need to swim now," María told me, and she got
smoothly to her feet, strode to the edge of the pool, and dove in.

I sat there and watched her swim laps, with strong unhurried
strokes. I was thinking that Lola was about to go away for weeks,
for who knew how many weeks. I was thinking that this woman
could be something of a torment, and that Luz could be something of a temptation, and I certainly hoped the time spent waiting for the insurance company didn't drag out very long.

Tuesday she would leave, flying home to New York, while I
stayed here. Between now and then, we had to get together, some-

how, somewhere. That was definite. I sat in the chaise, under the white-and-blue awning, in the warm air, and watched María swim her steady laps, and schemed how to get together one more time with Lola.

14

Carlos appeared around five-thirty in the afternoon. By then I'd swum, in the bathing suit Esilda had brought me, boxer-style, very colorful, with matadors waving capes fore and aft. I'd also dealt with lunch, and dozed a bit in one of the chaises, and was feeling very comfortable and at home, pleased to be around María.

In midafternoon, she'd showed me her studio, a bare concrete room at the opposite end of the house from my guest room and about twice its size. It looked mostly like an auto repair shop, with its acetylene torches and stacks of pipe and all the tools scattered around, including an array of hacksaws on the wall over the workbench. I looked at it all and said, "You should be covered with scars."

She laughed. "For the first few months, I was, but that was years ago."

I looked at what was apparently a work-in-progress, a two-foot-high twist of metal clamped in a vise at the end of the workbench. It was a kind of spiral that bent in on itself, as though in pain. I don't know why it seemed so strong, but it was hard not to go on looking at it. I said, "I now realize you don't do your work justice, hanging it in a row on the wall out there. One at a time, it's more powerful."

"That isn't display," she said, dismissing the work on the wall with a careless wave of the hand, "that's storage. I send photos to Friedrich, and then sometimes he asks me to ship this one or that one."

"He can tell from pictures?"

"Now he can. And the dealers in Europe."

I looked at the bending spiral again. "I've never understood abstraction," I said. "I don't mean to look at, I mean to make. How do you know when it's right?"

"The emotion," she said, and shrugged. She wasn't really interested in talking about her art, just I guess in doing it. "Come back out in the sunlight," she said.

So I did, and was still there in my matador trunks when Carlos came home.

I hadn't really been thinking about Carlos all day, not in the aura of this strong woman, but now I looked at them together and I just didn't get it. I know it's a common thing for couples to look completely mismatched, so that only they themselves know why they're a team, but María and Carlos took that notion to extremes. Here was this dramatic sophisticated woman, this artist, and over here in this corner we have a slob in a torn white T-shirt whose belly is so fat it lies on his belt buckle. He came out to the patio, nodded at us seated there on adjoining chaises, and said, "You met."

"Ernesto is very amusing," María told him. "He thought I was in Caracas to see my drug dealer."

Carlos hid his amusement very well. "Huh," he said.

"Come for a swim, darling," she said.

"I got to shower," he said, and nodded at me. "Tell Esilda we want drinks."

"Beer?" I asked, as I stood up from the chaise.

"She knows what we want. You tell her what you want."

"Okay."

María swam again, arms rhythmically moving, legs slowly scissoring, black-sheathed body thrusting smoothly through the clear water. Carlos went into the house, and I walked over to the kitchen entrance and inside, to find Esilda seated weeping in front of a small TV set that stood in the corner of the counter. It was a Spanish-language soap opera, fiercer and more passionate than American ones. The three people raging around what looked like a Holiday Inn motel room with the drapes drawn shut seemed somehow to have hurt one another deeply. They were discussing it.

Esilda wiped her eyes and looked at me. I was sorry to tear her away from her fun, but I was on a mission, so I told her Carlos and María wanted drinks, then pointed at myself: *"Cerveza."*

She nodded, got to her feet, and abandoned the trio in the motel room without a backward glance. Over at the counter, she poured white wine into a graceful long-stemmed glass, then combined half light rum and half Coca-Cola in a heavier cut-glass tumbler. Seeing me still standing there, she made a shooing gesture that I should get out of her kitchen, so I did.

Outside, María was still swimming laps. I considered joining her but felt too lazy, so I sat instead. Every once in a while, a grungy motorboat would go slowly by, out there on the river, and one did now, so I watched it until it was out of sight.

Then I looked for a while at Colombia, which was the land on the other side of the river. Some of the riverside over there had been cleared for grazing, and scrawny cattle moved around picturesquely against a background of mountainous jungle. Where the land hadn't been cleared, the jungle petered out as it approached the river, becoming a kind of messy savanna. Bird calls electrified the air from time to time, but which side of the river the birds were on I couldn't tell.

Esilda came out with a silver tray. Because it was the cocktail hour, I suppose, she had poured my beer into a frosty glass stein with a handle. She turned the tray so I could take it, and I said,

"*Gracias.*" She smiled, put the tray on the round white table near the chaises, and went back into the kitchen.

María, seeing the drinks arrive, got out of the pool, wrapped herself in a golden towel that made her look like a creature who would have been worshiped in this part of the world a few thousand years ago—and who's to say they would have been wrong?—and came over to pick up the wineglass. I'd known the wine was hers. She raised the glass to me: "*Salud.*"

"Prosit," I said, and she laughed, and we sipped from our glasses, and Carlos joined us.

Well, he'd shaved, and his flattened hair suggested he'd showered, but he was now wearing only red bikini swimming trunks, so I can't say he'd made an overall improvement. In fact, at first I thought he wasn't wearing anything at all, because his belly hid the trunks in front, and it was only when he turned away that you could see that crimson globe behind.

Arriving, he said nothing to me at all but went over to kiss María lightly on the lips—I hadn't expected that—then picked up his drink and held it toward her and growled, "*Salud.*"

"Cheers," she said, smiling fondly at him, and they clinked their glasses together.

He downed about half his drink, put the glass down, nodded at me, and went over to hurl himself into the pool with a huge splash. He did walrus and whale imitations for a while in there, while María lay back on the chaise beside me and seemed to go to sleep. I spent the time sipping my beer and wondering if Carlos would be able to get word to Arturo that I needed to spend some time with Lola before Tuesday. I'll ask him when he comes out of the pool, I decided.

But when he came out, wrapping himself in another of the golden towels and now looking like the Sun King, picking up his drink on the way by and then sitting on the edge of the chaise on my other side, he had things he wanted to say to me, so he went first. "Tomorrow we gotta go to church," he said. "It's expected. Ten o'clock. You'll meet people. You know how to do that."

"Sure."

"You want to go to the funeral?"

For just a second, I couldn't think what funeral he was talking about. Then I remembered: mine, of course. I said, "How could I? I don't dare go back to Sabanon."

"I got a chauffeur suit," he said. "You wear it, with the hat, you stay in the car. You don't go in the church, but you see it all from outside. And the procession, and in the graveyard."

A chauffeur in the funeral procession. I would get to go to my own funeral. "You're on," I said.

15

Sunday morning. Was I already used to this new doppelgänger existence? It seemed only natural to put on Ernesto's best (not that good) clothes and meet Carlos and María in the living room to go to mass together. Both were dressed well, she in a pearl-gray high-neck long-sleeve blouse, long black skirt, and dangling earrings in crimson and gold, he in a black suit, as well-tailored as a suit could be on that body, with a pale blue shirt and a black string tie. He was actually presentable.

María and I exchanged good mornings, and then Carlos said, "You won't talk when we go out, so we talk now."

"Okay."

"While you're here, you can help me sometimes, a little bit."

"Sure," I said. "I'd like to be useful."

"Good." He nodded once, sealing the bargain, then said, "There's gonna be a guy at mass this morning. I think he's there. If he's there, I'll touch your elbow."

I thought, What's all this? "Okay," I said.

"If he's there," Carlos said, "after mass, you and me, we take a walk with him."

"Okay."

"So you're just along to be another guy, like there's no problem."

"*Is* there a problem?"

"No, no, I just gotta talk with him," Carlos said. "He screwed up a little, that's all, messed up a deal I had over in Colombia, so we gotta talk about it."

"Okay," I said. "Whatever you say."

"Good," he said, and took María's arm, and she smiled at me and we left the house.

The church was about four blocks away, and as we walked Carlos and María shared greetings with several other people. A few times Carlos introduced me, and I stood there smiling like a dummy. Twice, men extended their hands, which I shook, still smiling to beat the band.

The church itself, when we got to it, was small and neat and very white. Wide stone steps led up to the entrance, and as we started up them Carlos touched my elbow. I looked at him, and he nodded and waved his hand to a snotty-looking guy who stood with two other guys over to one side, watching the people arrive. The snotty-looking guy gave a kind of self-satisfied smirk as he waved a languid hand in Carlos's direction. He was tall and very thin, with a black pencil mustache and slicked-back hair, like a silent-movie Romeo. He wore pointy white shoes and white pants with a sharp crease and an off-white shirt with brown piping. Draped over his shoulders was a gray linen jacket, as though he thought he was an Italian movie director.

Inside, the church was whitewashed stucco walls, crude bright renditions of the Stations of the Cross, rough tile floor, and heavy pews of rich-patina'd wood. The place was about half full, and Carlos led us to a pew near the back. We sat, and a minute later the snotty guy went by, saying amusing things to his two friends. They found a place near the front.

The mass was interesting, and then less so, and then it was over and we shuffled out to the bright sunlight, where María said, "I'll see you at the house," with a fond smile at Carlos. She walked on, nodding hello to the people as she went, and Carlos and I stood to the side of the entrance, and at last here came the snotty guy and his two friends.

He saw Carlos, and his smile faltered, then came back stronger than ever, with something challenging in it. Carlos gestured, and the guy came over, trailed by his friends, and the conversation began, as usual a little too fast for me to get it all. Carlos didn't bother to introduce me but told the guy, Let's take a walk, and the guy said, No, thanks, some other time. So Carlos put a little growl in the voice and said *this time*, and the guy made a face—*how tiresome*—and shrugged an acceptance inside his draped linen jacket.

We started to walk, and the two friends came with us, until Carlos stopped and said I'm talking to you, not these jerks. Another *how tiresome* look but the guy nodded, so then the three of us walked, and the other two stayed put.

We walked, and Carlos talked. The guy was in the middle, and Carlos talked low and hard, so I didn't get it all, only that the guy was impatient at first, making it clear he didn't see why he had to be bothered with this crap. But Carlos went on, the growl coming and going in his voice, and the guy began to accede a bit. He gave some explanations of his own, which Carlos didn't buy.

From the church we walked first down the dirt street beside it, then right along another dirt street lined with small rickety houses. When we made the turn I looked back, and the other two were trailing, not quite a block back, looking uncertain.

More talk, more walk. The guy was no longer supercilious but now understood Carlos's position completely. He was prepared to do what he could to make things right, but Carlos must realize his hands were tied; there was only so much he could do.

Another block, another turn, and the river was ahead of us, with shacks full of dogs and kids on the left, tin warehouses on the right. Then Carlos stopped. He said something brief and guttural. The guy became offended, gathered himself up to be haughty, and Carlos slapped him across the face.

We were both astonished, the guy and I. He stared at Carlos, then in that instant he switched from aristocratic panther to snarling mongrel, bent forward, hand slicing back toward his hip pocket.

Holy Christ! What should I do?

Nothing. Before the guy could bring anything out of that pocket, Carlos punched him *hard* in the stomach, putting all of his considerable weight behind it. The guy said, "*Hhhh*-uh!" and bent way over.

Carlos stepped back, took aim, and kicked him on the knee. Not with the toe of his shoe but the side, a sharp angled kick, snapping against the kneecap. I heard a *crack*. The guy shrieked and hit the dirt.

The other two! I looked back, and they were standing there, tense, openmouthed. They didn't come forward, and I understood I was the reason for that.

In some of the houses along here, little kids stared out at us. Nobody else reacted at all. Bright sunlight, a shrieking man on the ground, and nobody notices.

Carlos walked in slow circles around him, here and there giving him another hard kick, methodical and relentless. The guy jumped and shrieked at every kick, but Carlos remained calm, the technician at work.

It went on for a while, until I was beginning to think I should suggest that enough was maybe enough, but then all at once it stopped. Carlos stepped back from the quivering mess on the ground, said one short hard sentence, and turned away, gesturing to me to come on.

We walked back the way we'd come. The guy's two comrades rushed past us, goggle-eyed.

Carlos said one thing, as we walked: "Now I got an appetite."

16

Monday. I was to be buried today.

I put on my chauffeur's suit—charcoal-gray pants and jacket and hat, all of which more or less fit—and joined Carlos and María in the living room. He was in his Sunday suit again while she was striking in a short black dress with a gold chain around the waist and very dark stockings and black stiletto heels.

They looked me over in my chauffeur rig and María said, "Perfect. With that mustache, you even look as though you don't like your employers."

"But I do," I said. "And I'm not just saying that in hopes of a raise."

María laughed, and Carlos growled, "Time to go."

We left the house, and Carlos led the way across the dusty street to a windowless two-story wooden shack, one of a row of similar structures along this side of the street. He undid a padlock, and opened two wide wooden-slat doors, to left and right. In the dimness inside hulked a very recent Buick Riviera, black and gleaming, with black leather upholstery. The Batmobile could not have looked more incongruous in that shed.

Carlos extended a set of car keys toward me, saying, "You know this kind of car?"

I took the keys. "I've driven most cars," I assured him. I had noticed the license plate on the front of the Buick, in the Guerreran colors of gold numbers on a red background, though these weren't numbers: C   M. Simple and clear-cut.

I stepped inside the garage to get behind the wheel, adjust the seat backward, start the engine, and drive out into the sunlight. With the windows closed, and the AC on, I could barely hear the many motors of Rancio singing their song.

When I'd cleared the building, Carlos opened the rear door behind me to let in María and a blast of heat and noise; then he shut the door while she settled herself comfortably and smiled at me in the rearview mirror. Still outside, Carlos shut and locked the doors of his garage and came around to the other side to let in himself and another blast of noise and heat.

Once they were settled together back there, I looked in the rearview mirror again and said, "You'll have to give me directions, at least until we get out of town."

"Turn right," he said, and I did, and from then on, through Rancio, I followed his directions to steer this nice car through the scruffy town, avoiding many collisions with motorcycles. Out of town, there was only the one road.

It's 130 miles from Rancio to Sabanon through San Cristóbal. The funeral would be at one, so we'd left shortly before ten, to give ourselves plenty of time to deal with all the slow traffic one invariably meets on Guerreran roads. During the first hour, María made up her face, though I hadn't realized she needed to. She'd brought along two little bags of cosmetics, and every time I glanced in the mirror she was hard at work on herself back there.

After a while, she put the bags away, and then she and Carlos got into quiet conversation together, just chatting, the way Lola and I would. At one point, I even saw Carlos laugh, showing his teeth. An astounding sight.

I enjoyed the car and the day, even though the traffic was as lame and halt as expected. But mostly, I had to admit I was getting a kick out of thinking, *I am going to my own funeral!*

In the backseat, Carlos dozed for a while with his mouth open. María took a memo pad from her black leather shoulder bag and made lists. And I made pretty good time.

We arrived in Sabanon at twenty to one, and the Plaza Iglesia was full of vehicles and people. It looked as though all the many cousins who'd come to our wedding were also showing up for my funeral, and I was touched by that.

Both of Lola's parents come from large families, well scattered around Guerrera and the neighboring nations and also well scattered through the economic classes. Some of her cousins were schoolteachers and administrators, and some were day laborers and milpa farmers, poor as squirrels. Carlos was a cousin with money and influence, but there were other cousins, illiterate and unpropertied, who barely existed in the modern world. We don't get that kind of diversity in the States because our society is more settled, so the ranges of class within a family are usually not very broad.

Señor Ortiz's people, in black suits and gold armbands, were maintaining order, holding back the unwashed, ushering the cars through. I stopped in front of the church, an Ortiz employee opened the right rear door, a blast of heat and crowd noise came in, and Carlos and María stepped out onto the cobblestones. As they went on to the church, the Ortiz man opened the right front door, letting in more heat and noise, and leaned partway into the car to shout something at me and point off to my left.

What did he mean? Cars were being parked straight ahead, along that side of the plaza. But when I looked to my left, where he'd pointed, I saw three important-looking cars with chauffeurs standing next to them, parked over near Club Rick, the local hot spot for dancing. Lola and I love to dance and we go there once or twice every trip, though not this time. So I nodded, and he backed out of the car again and slammed the door.

Three other chauffeur-driven cars: a black Cadillac, a dark green BMW, and a white Jaguar sedan, all new and gleaming. I hadn't known I'd get such a grand send-off.

The three chauffeurs stood around in the sunshine, hats tilted to the backs of their heads, sunglasses on, adorned in mustaches like mine, leaning against the side of the Caddy and jawing together. They looked at me curiously when I didn't join them. There were maps in the door pocket beside me; I pulled one out at random and studied it, hoping none of them would come over to offer to help.

Shit, one was moving this way. I looked at him, smiled, made a big negative hand wave, and went back to the map. He took offense, as I'd hoped he would, and went back to his pals, shrugging. I could imagine what they were saying about me: "Thinks he's better than us."

Those other damn drivers just couldn't forget about me. Every time I took a surreptitious glance in their direction, one or another of them was looking my way. So I just kept on studying the map, which was of Colombia and therefore nothing I understood.

Finally, one time when I looked up, the chauffeurs were moving away. Yes, and the plaza was clearing, as the mourners had finished entering the church and the sightseers had started to drift off. The chauffeurs, I saw, were taking this opportunity to spend a little time in Club Rick.

I wished I could join them, in fact, but obviously could not; being unable to speak Guerreran Spanish could be awkward. But I could open the windows and shut off the engine, so I did. And I also put away this map to places I wasn't going.

But the wait was boring. I looked around and found the Buick's owner's manual, which was in Spanish and English, and I read that for a while until I realized I didn't actually want to know this stuff, so I put that away too and just sat there, watching nothing happen in the plaza.

Then two things happened at once. Across the way, the hearse and the flower car and the limo for immediate family were all pulling up in front of the church. And ahead of me, the chauffeurs were coming out of Rick's, putting on their caps and wiping their mouths with their sleeves. The funeral was over.

I started the engine and shut the windows. The AC came on, the chauffeurs all gave me dirty looks as they got into their cars ahead of me, and across the way my casket came out into the sunlight, gleaming like old money, borne on the shoulders of eight cousins. Arturo was at the front right. I believe he was weeping.

17

What a beautiful widow Lola made, there on the broad stone steps in front of the gleaming-white church, as slinky and sexy in her long black dress as the vamp in a movie from the twenties. I could see the outline of her pelvic bones from across the plaza. Mamá and Papá supported her on both sides, and she moved with sinuous exhaustion, a golden hanky to her cheek.

The casket was in the hearse, and the cousins all stood to one side, watching Lola's pelvis. The flower car was bedecked. Señor Ortiz's men shepherded Lola and Mamá and Papá and Uncle Nestor and Aunt Mercedes to the limo. Others of Señor Ortiz's men waved to us chauffeurs, and we drove around in a loop to the church, lining up behind the limo. The rest of the mourners had started to ooze from the church by now and to hurry away in the sunlight to their cars, in plebeian rows at the end of the plaza.

I recognized Luz, in a short purple dress, purple shoes, purple hat, and purple handbag, on the arm of a man old enough to be anything she wanted. I suppose purple was as close to black as she could get. I hadn't seen her since that first night at Carlos and María's, when she'd spoken to me in English, nor had I asked either Carlos or María about her. Let sleeping Luzes lie, that's what I thought.

I didn't know any of the people who were ushered into the three cars ahead of me, though I supposed they had to be related to Lola in one way or another. They all mostly made me think of drug cartels: large swarthy gold-strewn men and overripe platinum-blond women. Carlos and María, when they approached the Buick, looked utterly middle-class after those people. They got into the backseat, as before, Señor Ortiz's man shut the door, and I followed the white Jag. The cars of the hoi polloi fell in line behind me.

The cemetery, Campo Santo Lúgubre, was eight miles north of town, off the main road, in a hillier drier area where it was easier to dig and things didn't rot quite so rapidly as down by the town and the river. Our long cortege drove toward it at a stately funereal pace not because we were a funeral procession but because we were following a timber truck loaded far beyond capacity with huge mahogany logs, teetering far above the slat sides of the truck body. The driver was lucky the vehicle would move at all under that weight, and when he got to some of the hills farther north, it seemed to me, he would come to a dead stop.

Speaking of dead stops, here's the cemetery, with a wrought-iron archway entrance featuring the name of the place spelled out in spidery letters. Carlos and María had been chatting cheerfully together on the way out from town, gossiping about the other mourners, but now they fell silent as we passed under this grim arch.

It wasn't a cheerful place. Most of the graves were sunken; many of the stones leaned this way and that in exhaustion; most of it was weedy and scraggly. The occasional well-tended grave, with fresh flowers and gleaming stone and carefully weeded neat rectangle of lawn, was somehow even more depressing than the rest, because it said that someone who's been left behind by a loved one

comes out here all the time, with nothing better to do than turn a
grave into a garden.

It was an old graveyard, Sabanon being a very old town, settled
before 1700. The gravel roadway meandered past graves ancient
and modern, and our slow conga line followed the hearse deeper
and deeper in. Dark green jungle surrounded us, and just when I
had begun to think we would never get wherever we were going and
would become a loop, a circle following itself, out ahead I saw
something bright yellow and metallic, and I knew we were almost
there.

Yes. A backhoe, standing beside the new open hole in the
ground. Once, gravediggers would stand at that spot, leaning on
their shovels as in Shakespeare's day, but today it's the backhoe,
with one fat guy in a dirty white T-shirt, a red bandanna around
his neck, leaning against the side of his machine.

Everybody stopped. Señor Ortiz's men were quickly out,
encouraging the cars behind us to come up along the grass to our
left, so everybody could get nearer the grave, which was just off
the road to the right. I sat there watching it all, until María leaned
forward to tap my shoulder and murmur, "Sorry, Ernesto, but the
chauffeur opens the door."

"Oh! Of course, sorry."

The other chauffeurs were already out and doing their duty, and
now I popped out of the Buick and opened the rear door on my
side, so María could step out first, followed by Carlos. Cars were
passing right next to us, being hustled along by Señor Ortiz's busy
and efficient men.

María and Carlos walked around me and headed along the road
toward the new grave, where the priest now stood, holding his
black book, with purple cinctures (for funerals) over his white sur-
plice over his black cassock. He had to be hot.

The other chauffeurs, after unloading their cargoes, had gotten
back behind their wheels, so I did the same. They kept their
engines running, though it seemed to me a fast getaway was not in
the cards here, so I did too.

I hate to have to admit this, but even your own funeral can get boring after a while. I was seeing it from a distance, but it looked exactly like a funeral. A bunch of people in dark clothes stood in a horseshoe shape, facing a hole in the ground. The priest spoke, though with the windows closed I couldn't hear what he was saying. And, of course, there was no one from my family present.

We'd agreed on that ahead of time, that one of the many reasons for a fast burial was so she could assure my parents by telephone it would be impossible to get here in time; we didn't want our scam to louse things up for them more than absolutely necessary. They'd find out the truth once it was all over. But that meant I was rather unrepresented at my own funeral.

And here came Arturo, walking briskly, an unlit cigarette in his mouth, matches prominent in his hand, obviously looking for a place where it wouldn't be irreverent to smoke. After he'd passed the Jag in front of me, everybody else now behind him, he signaled me to open my window, so I did. As he walked by, he tossed something onto my lap, and I buttoned the window closed again.

It was a small white envelope, containing two objects: a slender rectangular card of the sort hotels use as keys, and a note scrawled on a torn-off piece of lined paper, which read *Inter-Nación 2217 7 P.M.*

Inter-Nación was the hotel by the airport, outside San Cristóbal; *7 P.M.* must mean tonight, since Lola would be flying to New York tomorrow.

I looked in the rearview mirror, and there was Arturo, strolling amid the parked cars, trailing cigarette smoke. Ahead, the crowd had started shifting from foot to foot. I caught a glimpse of my casket being lowered, bearing somebody else's scam to his final resting place. The man with the red bandanna climbed up into the seat of his backhoe.

A few minutes later, as the mourners straggled back to their cars, at least one chauffeur, as he leaped out to open the rear door for his passengers, was grinning from ear to ear.

18

There was no one there. It's true I was three minutes early, but there was still no one there. Room 2217 of the Hotel Inter-Nación was dim and cool and completely empty.

I'd told María and Carlos about the message from Arturo and asked if I could borrow a vehicle to keep the appointment. I hoped, of course, the vehicle would be the Buick.

Carlos, sounding almost avuncular, told me there was no problem, he'd loan me a vehicle, but it turned out the vehicle he had in mind was anything but a nice air-conditioned Buick. It was a scooter, an Italian Vespa, a motorized kitchen chair with a shield stuck on the front. The word *vespa* in Italian means *wasp*, and that's exactly what the thing sounded like, nasty and nasal and snarling.

So, having driven Carlos and María home to Rancio, I'd changed from chauffeur back to peon, accepted the Vespa with many expressions of gratitude, and rode my mobile kitchen chair among the trucks back down to San Cristóbal, through town, and out to the Inter-Nación.

Room 2217 sounds as though it should be on the twenty-second floor, but in fact the Inter-Nación is only three stories high, a squat building across the road from the airport. They'd stuck an extra *2* in front of the room numbers to make the place sound more impressive. So I went diagonally across the lobby without attracting attention from the staff, ignored the elevator, and climbed the stairs to the second floor. The card key produced a small green light above the doorknob, the door opened, and I entered an empty room.

She hadn't been here. The closet was empty, the bed untouched. I went to look out the window, but this room didn't face the road and the airport, it faced the jungle. As I stood gazing out at the greens, I heard clicking sounds from the door and turned with a smile of welcome. But then I heard voices. She was with somebody else.

It had to be the bellboy. She'd have all her luggage with her for tomorrow morning's flight. And the bellboy shouldn't see a man in the widow's room, especially a man who just might be identifiable later on as her dead husband. As the door to the hall opened, I made a dash for the bathroom, sliding in just as the two Spanish-speaking voices entered. Yes, Lola and a young male. She was directing the placement of the luggage, and he was explaining the wonders of the room.

And his voice was coming this way. Quickly I stepped into the tub, behind the half-drawn shower curtain. If he were to come all the way to the tub to demonstrate the faucets, I didn't know what I'd do.

But then the lights came on in the bathroom and I saw the mirror. The wall facing the door was all mirror, and in it I could see the doorway, where the bellboy stood, a short young guy in a red uniform jacket, hand on the light switch. Beyond him, back in the main room, was Lola.

If I could see them, they could see me. Except that the bellboy was calling Lola's attention to other things and wasn't looking toward the mirror. Lola was; I saw her eyes widen with surprise, then amusement. She said something, drawing the bellboy away, and as he left the doorway she came forward to switch off the light.

It took her another couple of minutes to get rid of him. At last I heard the outer door snick shut, and as soon as it did I stepped out of the tub and into the other room, where Lola in her traveling clothes sat on the bed among her suitcases, laughing. Looking at me, she said, "Speedy Gonzales, I presume."

God, she was beautiful. I never want to be away from her, not for a second. "Oh, no," I said, walking toward her. "Not speedy. This is going to be very, very slow."

Early in the morning, before I snuck out of the Inter-Nación to climb back aboard my Vespa, we had a conversation that we'd had before and was the basis of our life together.

"I'll be here," I said.

And she said, "Of course you will, you're the net."

"And you're the net," I said.

"You know I am."

We smiled at each other. I said, "We're out there alone, nobody to be sure of in the whole world except you and me. I'm your net and you're my net. The only net we've got."

"The only net we need, Barry," she said.

19

Time dragged after my funeral and Lola's departure. All at once, I had nothing to do. I trailed after Carlos to his truck place a few times, but I sure didn't fit in there, and Carlos wasn't what you'd call encouraging. At the house was María, self-sufficient, at work in her studio or reading or swimming, obviously feeling no need to find ways to keep her house guest amused. I could watch television or swim, but mostly what I did was wait.

And, of course, watch María. And finally to wonder, What was her view of me? We were alone together in the house most of the time. She seemed amused by me, and friendly, but I couldn't tell whether or not that amusement was linked to any level of sexual interest. Was there an offer in her half-mocking smile? I was certainly not going to take her up on any offer, if it indeed was there, but was it?

Of course I wouldn't respond. If I didn't have Lola to restrain me, and I did, the memory of Carlos delivering that Sunday morn-

ing beating would keep me in check all by itself. Still, without a
word being said, without even a glance that was no more than
ambiguous, I found myself feeling somehow less of a man for not
having taken María up on . . . on what?

Watching her swim, sometimes, the powerful legs scissoring, the
form-fitting black bathing suit, the long sleek body, the concentration in those eyes, I found myself drifting into unexpected shoals
of thought. Was this somehow time out? If I were no longer Barry
Lee, but not yet Felicio Tobón de Lozano, did neither Barry's vows
nor Felicio's filial duty come into play? Keeping one eye out for
Carlos, could Ernesto Lopez take a little taste of the sweetness this
household offered?

I began to avoid the pool, if María was in it. I was beginning to
avoid my own lecherous brain.

Saturday, the eighth day of my afterlife, the three of us were having lunch out by the pool when María said to me, "Arturo phoned;
he's coming up today. I think he's heard from Lola."

"Oh, good!" I said, and felt myself smile all over. Just to hear
Lola's name helped. And it kept those other impulses at bay as
well.

Finished with me, María turned to Carlos. "I'm going to Miami
on Monday."

Carlos glowered. "Who with?"

María seemed amused by the question. "By myself, sweetheart," she said.

Carlos is a jealous guy? That surprised me and might have worried me. I'm here alone with his wife every day and he never seems
to think about it, but maybe I've been wrong about that. A good
thing he couldn't read my mind. I watched him more carefully as
he said, "Friedrich gonna meet you there?"

"He can't this time," Maria said, easy and unaffected, as though
Carlos weren't showing jealousy at all. "He's sending me to a
woman with a gallery in Palm Beach. I think Palm Beach is too . . .
bourgeois for me, but Friedrich says this woman has excellent contacts in New York."

Carlos said, "When you comin' back?"

"Wednesday. Unless I go see Friedrich on the way back. I'll phone you, darling." Smiling, she said, "You won't be lonely, you'll have Ernesto here."

He grunted at that and went back to his lunch.

She said, "My plane's at eleven-twenty. Can you take me?"

"The chauffeur'll take you," Carlos said.

"Oh, good," María said, and smiled at me.

The chauffeur? Listen, I'm not *really* the chauffeur. But before I could figure out what if anything to say, Arturo bounded out from the house, a Heineken in his hand. "*¡Hola!*" he cried, and everybody greeted everybody, even Carlos lightening up a little. Arturo dragged a chair over to join us and grinned at me. "How you doin', *hermano?*"

"Oh, going along," I said. "Helping out where I can."

Arturo turned his happy smile on Carlos. "That right? Felicio being useful?"

"Ernesto," María said.

"He's a good driver," Carlos said.

I said, "I've got my own chauffeur suit."

"A whole new career," Arturo said, happy for me.

I said, "You heard from Lola."

"Oh, sure," he said.

María said, "Carlos and I are finished. You sit here and get your messages."

"Thanks, María," I said.

They went away, and I said, "What did she say, Arturo?"

"Well, she couldn't say much, you know. On the telephone and all."

"She could say *something*."

"Yeah, but you know," he said, "she had to talk like you was really dead, so what I had to do was—uh, waddaya say?"

"Translate," I suggested.

"No. Get at the *meaning*. You know?"

We both thought about it. "Interpret," I suggested.

"That's it," he said, and slapped his knee. "I had to interpret what she says, so when she says, 'I love Barry so much, and I wish he was still around so we could be together and I could tell him how much I love him,' I interpret that, you see, that it means I should say, 'She loves you and misses you and wishes you could be together.' "

"Me, too," I said.

"I told her that," Arturo assured me. "I told her, 'Wherever he is, Lola, I'm sure Barry feels the exact same way.' "

"Thank you, Arturo. Did she say anything about the insurance?"

"She give all the stuff to the insurance man, and it don't look like a problem. It looks like a week or two, and then they send the check."

"That's great. It's time for me to get my passport."

"Sure. When?"

"I gotta drive María to the plane Monday," I said, "so I'll be right there in San Cristóbal, dressed up in my chauffeur suit, with the tie and all. How about then?"

"Easy," he said.

I grinned at him. "Every day in every way, Arturo," I said, "I'm getting less and less dead."

20

Monday, after lunch, I put on my chauffeur suit and drove María to the airport. She sat in back, explaining it looked better that way, and the fact that she felt the need to offer the explanation took the sting out of it.

But it also confirmed the realization I'd come to after the cool way she'd dealt with Carlos's show of jealousy at lunch. There was no invitation for me in that woman. She was self-contained to a remarkable degree. She'd brought Carlos into her life, for whatever reason, but she mostly inhabited her world by herself. I needn't feel I was letting an opportunity slide; there was nothing there.

So as we drove I spent more attention on the beautiful day outside than on the beautiful woman behind me, and when I thought about beautiful women at all, it was mostly Lola. How close we were to being together again.

We were a quarter hour out of Rancio, amid the usual traffic, when María said, "You're very quiet today, Ernesto."

I looked at her in the rearview mirror, and her ironic smile was aimed at the back of my head. "Well," I said, "I am a deaf mute."

"Even for a deaf mute," she said, "you're being very quiet. I believe you miss Lola."

"A whole lot," I said.

She nodded. "You know, when you first came to stay, I wondered if you were going to be difficult. You understand what I'm saying."

"Yes," I said.

"My response was all prepared," she told me, and met my eyes in the mirror, and smiled again. "I was going to be flattered but distant."

"And just a little contemptuous," I said.

The smile became a laugh. "Just a very little," she agreed. "It would have been amusing for both of us. Poor Ernesto, you're a faithful husband."

"I am," I said.

"There are very few faithful husbands in this part of the world," she said. "It is not a trait that is particularly valued."

"I think that's true everywhere," I said. "But Lola and me . . . it isn't that I'm being faithful to her. It's that I don't have any other way to live. To go do something else would be like breaking a bone."

"Yes, of course," she said, and switched to look at the back of my head again, speculatively. "It seems like a contradiction, but it isn't," she decided. "You aren't the faithful type, actually, you're a rogue."

"Thank you—I think," I said.

"Oh, I know you like being a rogue," she assured me. "What the English call a chancer. You're unfaithful to the entire world, so why are you faithful to your wife?"

"Maybe that's why," I said, and met her eyes in the mirror.

"Maybe I need one little island in a sea of untrustworthy water. And so does Lola."

"You're each other's island."

"We *are* the island," I said, "and I need to be with her again."

"Poor Barry," she said, which was the first time she'd used my former name, and without the usual mockery.

I didn't think I could stand sympathy. Smiling back at her, I said, "Poor Felicio, in fact."

That made her laugh and restored our relationship. "You aren't a man," she said, "you're an anthology!"

I was about to say something, I don't know what, but when I looked in the mirror I saw, beyond her, a red light flashing. "A cop is stopping us," I said.

"What?" Annoyed, not at all worried, she twisted around to glare out the back window. She said something in Spanish that I doubted was a prayer, then faced front and with great irritation said, "We might as well stop."

"I thought so too," I said, pulling over to the weedy verge and touching the brakes. "But what do I do, María? He's going to ask me questions."

"Leave your window closed," she told me, "and I'll open mine. When he comes to the car, I'll order you not to speak, to let me handle it. So he'll hear me say it."

I was now stopped, and the police car was going past to pull onto the shoulder in front of me and switch off its red dome light. It was a big American car, black and white, POLICIA on doors and trunk. A brown-uniformed driver was at the wheel, and two plain-clothes men in back.

I said, "Can we get away with that?"

"Of course," she said, and I realized that in her mind a person with her capacity for imperiousness, in a country like this, should be able to get away with anything. I hoped she was right.

Both rear doors of the police car opened, and the two men got out. Both wore white guayabera shirts and black sunglasses and modified black cowboy hats with gold stars pinned on the front.

One wore dark jeans and boots, the other tan cotton slacks and soft tan shoes. Both had black holsters on their belts, on the right side, flaps shut.

The one in jeans leaned against the trunk of his police car, unsnapped his holster flap, then folded his arms and looked at me, without expression. The other one came forward, and I heard María's window lower and felt the sudden moist hot air stroke the left side of my neck. She snapped at me in Spanish to let her handle this, sounding very aggravated, and I sat to attention, staring back at the one staring at me. The other one stopped next to me and tapped my window with a knuckle, and I pretended not to hear him. My hands were on the steering wheel, correctly, at ten and two o'clock.

María demanded to know what this fellow wanted, so he gave up on me and moved farther back along the car. He called her María, with a little too much familiarity, and hoped Carlos was well, and she told him not to worry about Carlos, and he said but he did worry about Carlos.

It was quite a battle they had, without ever stating the topic, all words and attitude. He used the power of his position, and she used the power of her imperial status. He spoke insinuatingly, as though to say, I could be rough, but I'm choosing not to, and she spoke with condescending grace, as though to say, I could dismiss you like the peon you are, but I'm choosing to give you a moment of my valuable time.

Then he straightened, as though tired of it or having made his point. "You want to be careful on this road," he said. "And tell Carlos I might come visit him."

"You won't," she said, but he'd already turned away. As he strolled back to his car, making a laughing comment to his deadpan partner, María slid her window closed and said, "¡*Lechón!*"

In the rearview mirror, her face was very angry. She caught my eye and made a brushing-along gesture. "Drive on!"

Now I really was the chauffeur, and she really was her highness. "Yes, ma'am," I said, but at the moment she was impervious to irony. I put the Buick in gear, and we drove out around them as they got back into their car. In the rearview mirror, I saw them U-turn and recede.

We drove in silence for a few minutes, and then she said, "I'm sorry, Ernesto, that pig had me out of sorts."

"I got the idea you didn't like him. Is it okay to ask what it was all about?"

"It was nothing to do with me," she said. "Carlos had a disagreement with a man a week ago—"

"Sunday before last?"

"Yes. You know about it?"

"I was there."

"Oh. Well, that man is a friend of this pig, Rafez, and he—"

"Rafez? Rafael Rafez?"

Her expression in the mirror was astonished. "You know him? How on earth do you know him?"

"He groped Lola, the night I died," I said. "She had to give him a bloody nose before he'd lay off."

Delighted, she said, "Really? Lola gave him a bloody nose?"

"All over his white linen suit, the bastard."

"But that's wonderful," she said. "Brava for Lola. Oh, now I feel one hundred percent better. Thank you, Ernesto."

"*De nada*," I said.

21

Laryngitis again, and in two hours I had my passport. I loved it. It was a dull red, with harder covers than my old American passport, and the picture inside looked just like Felicio Tobón de Lozano, with his round swarthy face, bushy mustache, messy dark hair, and a black necktie this peasant was obviously not at all used to wearing. With this passport, I could travel the world.

With this passport, I could get back with Lola. That was the point. This passport was my passport to Lola.

Arturo promised he'd phone Lola to tell her their brother Felicio had a passport now, find out what news there might be, and then come let me know.

But it wasn't Arturo who snuck into the house two days later, Wednesday afternoon, while I was reading last week's *Newsweek* out by the pool. It wasn't Arturo who went *hiss! hiss!* at me until I finally heard it and turned around to stare at the living room doorway. It was Luz.

Damn. I'd almost forgotten about Luz. The only time I'd seen her, since the night I'd come here and she'd spoken to me in English, was at the funeral, all in purple. But now here she was, hunched in the doorway, her face a Kabuki mask of stress and agitation, her breasts threatening to jump out of her gold scoop-neck blouse as she clutched the air with scarlet-nailed hands, gesturing to me to come over, hurry, come over quick.

Well, I'd have to deal with it, that's all. Not looking forward to this, I got to my feet and went over to the living room, as she receded into the dimness ahead of me. I went in, prepared to explain whatever was necessary to explain—the sanctity of marriage?—and she said, with a broken sob in her voice, "Oh, Barry, I'm sorry. I'm sorry. It's all my fault."

"Ernesto," I told her. "Or maybe Felicio. Anything but Barry."

"It's all my fault," she repeated, and clutched at my arm to draw me toward a sofa. "I'm sorry. I just didn't know they were so stupid."

"You didn't know who was so stupid?" I asked, as we sat together on the sofa. Her black skirt ended where her legs began, and her knees were angled toward me.

"My cousins," she said, which covered half of Guerrera.

I said, "Which cousins?"

"From Tapitepe," she said, naming the southeasternmost town in the country, at the border with Venezuela and Brazil. "Manfredo and Luis and the other Luis with the bad arm and José and Pedro and *poco* Pedro, little Pedro."

"Ah," I said.

"You met them," she assured me, "at your wedding."

"I met all the cousins at the wedding," I said. "I don't necessarily remember them. What's the problem, Luz?"

"I tol' them," she said. "Not *them*, exactly, I tol' a few others—in the family, you know—and now they know too, and it's all my fault. But I didn' know, Barry, I didn' know they—"

"Felicio," I said.

"I didn' know how they'd be," she said. "I swear it. I didn' know."

"How they'd be about what? You mean, you told them about *me?*"

"They know about it," she said. "How you not really dead. Because you gonna get millions of dollars from the insurance and the whole family's gonna be rich."

"Well, no," I said. "Not millions, and the whole family—"

"So they think that's good," she said. "Very good. But I tell them, We can't say anything outside the family, because if the insurance finds out, then the family don' get nothing."

"Luz," I said, "the family was never going—"

"So they say," she went on, "if the family gets all this money if Barry Lee is dead, how come he's alive?"

I looked at her. "Say that again?"

"Why have the risk?" she asked me. "That's what they say. Why have the risk? If the insurance find out Barry Lee ain't dead, nobody gets nothing."

"Luz," I said, "they were *never* going to get anything."

"Millions," she said.

"Not millions," I told her. "Listen to me, Luz. Not millions. It isn't millions. Carlos is getting a couple hundred, and Arturo is getting some, and Mamá and Papá are getting some, and that's all. The rest of the family isn't getting anything."

"Millions," she said, blinking at me.

"No," I said.

She looked at me, and I didn't say anything else, and gradually I could see it sink in, until finally she said, "You not gonna share with the family?"

"Not a penny," I said. "Not a *siapa.*"

"But they helpin' you!" she exclaimed, and sat up straighter on the sofa, aiming her breasts at me.

I said, "No, they're not. Carlos is helping, and Arturo is helping. What are the rest of those people doing?"

"They come to the funeral!"

I sat back and stared at her. "They came to the funeral, so I'm supposed to give them millions of dollars?"

"Everybody knows it," she said. "The whole family knows it."

"From you."

"I tol' a couple people, Barry, I'm sorry—"

"Felicio."

"—I was wrong, but I tol' a couple people, and *they* tol' every-body else. Just in the family, Barry, I swear."

"Felicio."

"But this is what happen," she said. "So Manfredo and Luis and the other Luis with the bad arm and José and Pedro and *poco* Pedro, they come to me and say, Where is he? and I say, At Carlos's house, and they say, Luz, you can get a man to do things, get him to come out of Carlos's house—see, they don't want trouble with Carlos, they're much afraid of Carlos—and I say, Why? and they say, If we gonna get millions if he's dead how come he's alive? and I say, You can't mean you gonna kill him, and they say, Why not? He's dead already; we went to the funeral."

"Luz," I said, "that's completely wrong. Nobody's going to get millions, and *they* aren't going to get anything."

"Not if the insurance find out you alive."

"Not at all."

"If it just Lola," she pointed out, "they can tell her, You gotta give us the money. Some for everybody."

I sat back and thought about that. I'm truly dead, and these lowlifes from the least-civilized branch of the family lean on Lola. Or if Lola isn't around they lean on Mamá and Papá. And they'll never believe there isn't millions. Money from America. That's what everybody wants, and this is how they'll get it.

So now what? Here's Luz, fidgeting, saying she's sorry, falling out of her dress—already I know for sure she isn't wearing under-wear—and telling me I've got in-laws that plan to kill me for the insurance money.

I'm killing me for the insurance money! There's no room in this scheme for freeloaders. I said, "So you're here because you're sup-posed to talk me into going outside, so they can kill me."

"No, no, not now," she said. "Barry, I come to—"

"Felicio, Luz, *please*."

"Whoever," she said. "*Who ever*. I come to *warn* you. What they plan they gonna do, tomorrow a couple of them, they go talk with Carlos at his place, make sure he stay there, and that's when I come get you take me out for a beer. *Then* they do it. Tomorrow."

"Tomorrow."

"They need to get trucks and guns and things," she explained. "Shovels."

"Shovels."

"So they not ready today, but they gonna be ready tomorrow. So I come *now*, to warn you."

"So I shouldn't go out," I said. "That's easy."

"Not that easy, Barry. Whoever! Not that easy. If you don' come out, they gonna come in."

"I thought they were afraid of Carlos."

"But they want the money. So if you don' come out, they come in by the river."

"There's razor wire out there," I told her. "They can't get in."

"They know about the stuff in the water," she said. "They gonna steal a boat, run it onto the ground, right over that cuttin' stuff. Come in that way, it look like robbers. Kill you, kill Esilda, steal some stuff, Carlos never gonna know it was them."

"Carlos will know," I told her.

She shook her head. A nipple flashed and retired. "They *think* Carlos not gonna know. They think they smart, Ba—you."

"Felicio."

"Felicio."

"Thank you," I said. "They aren't smart, Luz, they're stupid."

"Very stupid," she agreed. "But they don' know that. They think they smart."

"Shit," I commented.

What was I going to do? If I stayed here, they'd come after me. But where else could I go? The only other people I knew in all Guerrera were Arturo and Mamá and Papá, and if I went to them the cousins would find me right away. I don't sound like a Guer-reran, I don't have any money, I don't know anybody, where can I go? What can I do?

Is Luz telling the truth? I thought about that, and I believed she was. She wasn't an actress, Luz, she was very up front; she let it all hang out in more ways than one. She was truly agitated and truly remorseful, and she was certainly enough of a bigmouth to have told everybody in Guerrera that Barry Lee wasn't really dead, Barry Lee was making believe he was dead so he could get millions from the insurance company and share it with the entire Tobón family, that good old Barry Lee. What a great guy Barry Lee is. Let's kill him.

I said, "What if I tell Carlos? Couldn't he stop—"

But she was already shaking her head. "Carlos ain' gonna stop them," she said.

"Why not? He's too smart to believe in all that money."

"Millions," she said.

"Luz, it isn't millions," I insisted, "and Carlos knows that. If I tell him what's going on, he could talk to—"

"He ain' gonna do it," she said.

"Why not?"

"On accounta María."

I looked at her. She gave me a very significant nod. Her legs moved. I looked firmly into her eyes. I said, "I'm not doing anything with María."

"That don' matter," she said.

"You mean, he *thinks* I'm doing something?"

"He don' know," she said. "He don' wanna know. He don' ever wanna know what María do or don' do or nothing. He woulda thrown you out already, but she want you here. So if somebody come take you away and kill you, that not Carlos's fault. Not if he don' know about it. But you outa the house, and that's okay by him."

"María," I said. "María could—"

"Gone on a trip," she pointed out. "Anyway, the cousins don' listen to María."

"Arturo," I said.

"If Artie talk to the cousins," she said, "they gonna think he want all the millions for himself."

"Oh, shit," I said. "What the hell am I gonna do?"

"I'll hide you," she told me, and moved all of her parts and bounced this way and that. "It's all my fault, Ba—Felicio."

"Luz—"

"I gotta help you, Felicio," she said, "because it's all my fault, I opened my big mouth. I do that all the time."

"Right," I said. "Who told you about me anyway? Did Arturo tell you?"

She looked indignant, shoulders back, chest out. "What do you think?" she demanded. "I'm stupid, just 'cause I like to fuck?"

"No, no, I—"

"I figured it out," she said. "Artie say all this silly stuff, you can' talk and hear 'cause you got the curse and all that, I know what's goin' on."

"Okay," I said.

"But *now* what we gotta do," she told me, "we gotta hide you. You come to my place in Napalma, we—"

"No, Luz, thank you, but no, I can't . . ."

I can't go live with Luz, with her bouncing around, falling out of her clothes all the time, telling me she likes to fuck. I'm true to Lola, like I discussed it with María, but that doesn't mean I have to torture myself.

She leaned toward me, just to emphasize the problem. "What else you gonna do?" she asked me. "I'm tellin' you the truth, Felicio. See? I'm even callin' you Felicio."

"Thank you."

"You stay here," she said, "you gonna die. For real. Where else you gonna go?"

I looked away from her, as an aid to thought. Where else *would* I go? Maybe it was true, I was going to have to hide out with Luz until I could figure out something else. Maybe get a message to Arturo, have him come pick me up, hide me somewhere safe. Safer.

I said, "You want me to go with you now?"

"Not now," she said. "They all around, those guys, they see you in the car, they gonna come get you. Wait till tonight. After Carlos go to bed tonight, you come out. You know where he keep that big car?"

"Sure, across the street."

"Next to it, on that side," she said, and waved a breast as she pointed, "is just dirt. I'm there in my car, orange Honda Civic."

"What time?"

"Whenever," she said. An accommodating girl. "I come around ten, you come out after Carlos goes to bed. You don' wanna have to tell him where you goin'."

"You're right about that," I said.

She jumped to her feet, shrugged her breasts back into the blouse, and as I also stood she grabbed my hand in both of hers and said, "I'm really sorry. Felicio. I don' want nobody gets hurt."

"I feel that way too," I assured her, and disengaged my hand.

She started away, then turned back and shook her head and other parts and said, "You know, Felicio, every time I think, *Well, now I know how stupid men can be*, I'm wrong. They always stupider."

"You're right," I said.

"See you tonight," she said, and bounced out of there, and I went the other way to jump headfirst into the pool, causing the water to steam.

Jesus H. Christ on a crutch.

22

There was a car over there, in the darkness beside that building, its headlight glass picking up a glint from the street-light down at the corner. In Rancio, as in most Guerreran towns, there are public lights only at intersections, so the mid-blocks tend to be very dark.

Still, I felt exposed out here. The street side of the wall around Carlos's property was whitewashed, and even in the darkness it seemed to me I must make a clear silhouette against it. But I forced myself to move slowly, to shut the outer door carefully, silently. In my other hand I held the cardboard suitcase, my only weapon of defense. Which meant, if I was attacked, I was dead.

The door was closed. I released the knob. I did not run across the street, but I strode fast.

Yes, that was a Honda Civic in the darkness, and by day it was probably orange. At the moment, it was merely metallic and dark, with a person at the wheel. I opened the passenger door, and the interior light leaped on, and it was Luz, wearing blue jeans cut off at the hip and a very tight white T-shirt that said LECHE in large red letters across the front.

"Hello," I whispered, and shoved the suitcase onto the minimal seat in back.

"Get in, get in." She sounded like a violin tuned too high.

I got in and shut the door, bringing darkness back, and immediately she started the engine, with a great grinding noise they could probably hear all the way to Brasilia. Then she put it in gear, and the car lurched forward and stalled. She said a word that contained one jagged syllable.

I said, "Luz, take it easy, nobody can see us."

"I heard *that* one before," she said, and started the car again, with the same racket, and this time managed to move it forward.

I wanted to settle her down some before she ran us into a tree. Trying to sound nothing but calm and serene, I said, "I really appreciate this, Luz. Thank you."

"Lemme get us outa town," she said, spinning the wheel and accelerating down the dark street. "*Then* we be okay."

I twisted around to look back at the neighborhood we were leaving and saw no one, nothing. The time was a little after eleven on a Wednesday night, and Rancio was asleep.

Luz made a fast turn at the next corner, and only then did she switch on the headlights, which meant the dashboard lights came on as well. I looked at her, shoulder to shoulder in this small car, as she concentrated fiercely on the street ahead. My own concentration was a bit more scattered. *Leche* means milk in Spanish; spelled with a slight difference, it means something else in English.

Napalma, where Luz lived, was another town along the Inarida River, like Rancio and San Cristóbal. It was beyond San Cristóbal, another seventy-five miles of meandering road alongside the meandering river, and a few miles after San Cristóbal it gives up being asphalt to become dirt. Napalma is the end of the road. Not a happy thought.

Luz's tension continued until we were well out of Rancio, and even then she would clench up at every sight of headlights, either behind us or in front. Fortunately, there was very little traffic. It was clear that nobody was following us, nobody knew what Luz was up to, but she was extremely nervous anyway. I thought she probably knew her own cousins well enough that all this fear was justified, so I didn't try to argue her out of it.

There was little conversation until we got past San Cristóbal. I tried to keep my eyes on the road. Luz did keep her eyes on the road, and we did the thirty miles from Rancio to San Cristóbal in twenty-eight minutes, according to her little dashboard clock, which on that road was pretty spectacular.

She had to slow going through San Cristóbal, but she didn't like it. "Crouch down," she told me. "Like you're asleep."

"There's no room to crouch down."

"Then put your head in my lap."

"I'll just keep my hand over my face like this," I said.

That didn't really satisfy her, but she accepted it. San Cristóbal, being the capital, was still awake at eleven-thirty of a midweek night, with bars and restaurants open, cars moving, pedestrians here and there, groups talking in little parks along the way. Luz was convinced every one of those people was in league with her cousins, and by the time we got out of town I was beginning to feel almost as paranoid as she was.

But now we had the road to ourselves. Nobody was going to Napalma tonight, and whatever farmers or suburbanites lived along here were asleep, with no lights on. By crouching a little, but not putting my head in Luz's lap, I could see in the outside mirror on my side the lights of San Cristóbal dwindling behind us, then erased, and there was nothing back there but black.

Luz had seen it too. The sigh she gave was so long and heartfelt she must have been holding her breath since Saturday. "Ho-kay," she said. "We gonna be all right now."

"Good," I said.

"Time for some rum," she decided.

"Rum? Where are we going to get rum?"

"I *got* rum," she told me. "On the floor behind you. Can you get it? Should I?"

She turned, moving her arm, and LECHE loomed. "No, that's okay," I said. "I can do it."

I waited till she had both hands back on the steering wheel and then reached into the narrow space between us, down to the floor behind my seat, and there it was, a bottle wedged under the seat to keep it from rolling. I eased it out and brought it up front with us.

"Here you are."

A quick look, and she said, "Open it, okay?"

"Sure."

It was a clear glass quart bottle of a very cheap South American dark rum, about half full. I unscrewed the cap and handed it to her.

"Steer," she said, so I put my left hand on the wheel as she put her head back and went *glug-glug-glug.* "Aw, that's good," she said, and grinned at me. Wiping the bottle mouth with her palm, she said, "Have some."

I took the bottle and she took the wheel. My first reaction was, No, I don't want cheap rum, I don't want to share the bottle with you, I want to keep my wits about me. That was followed a nanosecond later by an opposite reaction, much stronger. "Thanks," I said, and tilted my own head back.

Very sweet. Molasses. A waterfall of sweetness, but attached to a dynamo. Powerful, like an engine of sweetness, like a love song from a heavy metal band.

"Wow," I said.

"Good stuff," she said.

"You want more?"

"Not yet," she said. "Keep it in your lap, and if I want it I'll reach for it."

"Right," I said.

You smell Napalma before you see it. It isn't a bad smell exactly; in fact, it's yet another kind of sweetness, like a little spray of sugar caught high in your nose; and it comes from the factory. The

town is situated inside a deep curve in the Inarida, where a natural
rock shelf makes for an unusually deep harbor, and the factory is
built there, partly out over the water.

It's a fish processing plant, taking all kinds of fish from the river
and turning them into great sacks of fertilizer. The sacks are
loaded on barges that float down the Inarida to San Cristóbal, and
from there they're flown all over the world to feed gardens the people of Napalma could barely imagine. Luz worked at the factory,
not on the factory floor but as a clerk in the billing department.

It's a twenty-four-hour factory, one of the few late-night opera-
tions in the entire country. We drove past it, the main town being
just beyond, and the primary factory structure was three stories of
rattletrap sheets of corrugated tin, many bare lightbulbs, a parking lot full of little beat-up cars, and a few people visible in shorts
and T-shirts and yellow hard hats.

Just beyond the factory were four bars, mostly open-air beer
gardens, all open and doing business. Then the lights faded, and
we were actually in Napalma, another little river town with rickety
wood houses on stilts. Some of the houses on stilts were built out
over the river, and one of these was where Luz lived. There was a
row of similar houses, the front third on land, the rest on pilings
over the water. All the houses were dark. A streetlight gleamed far
away and stars shone on the river, but still the neighborhood was
very dark.

Luz stopped the car in front of her place. The interior light
popped on again as she opened her door, and then I opened mine,
and got myself and the rum bottle and my suitcase all out onto the
weedy ground. I said, "Should I leave the bottle in the car?"

"How much is in it?"

We bent down at the opposite open doors, I held the bottle in
the light in there, and we both looked at it. There was less than two
inches of amber liquid left.

"Bring it in, we'll finish it," she said.

Was that a good idea? Probably not, but I was past worrying
about good ideas. I shut my door, picked up my suitcase, and followed her into the house.

It was shoe-box shaped, with a front room that was part living room and part kitchen. Luz turned on a table lamp perched on the TV set, with a bright pink shade on it that made the room dim but rosy, as though it were a pleasant comfortable place just a little too near Hell.

A doorway with a scarlet curtain over it led farther back, to the part of the house over the river. Luz went through this curtain, me following, and turned on a lamp on her dresser, with a bright golden shade that made this room look as though it had been deep-fried.

This was Luz's bedroom, with her clothing and her shoes and her scent and her personality strewn all over it. It was dominated by a low double bed with extremely wrinkled orange sheets and distorted pillows. Many many photos from magazines were on the wall above the bed, ranging through all levels of piety and celebrity, from the Madonna to Madonna.

Luz grinned at me in a loosely ironic way, gestured at the bed, and said, "I know you don' wanna sleep there."

"Thank you," I said. Nothing else I could have said, it seemed to me, would have been safe.

At the back of this room were another pair of doorways covered by scarlet curtains. Luz went to the one on the left, saying, "I got no electricity back here, but there's a kerosene lamp."

"Okay."

She pushed aside the curtain and went in. I pushed aside the curtain and stood in the doorway, since there wasn't room for both of us in there. A window without glass let in the sight and sound of the river, plus its aroma, mixed with the odor of the factory. Luz bent and lit a wooden match and from that lit a small kerosene lantern with a clear glass chimney. It smoked at first, until she lowered the flame.

The room was very small. A futon on the floor was neatly covered with one sheet and one blanket. In the corner beside it stood a wooden crate, its open interior facing the futon. This would be my bedside table, with the kerosene lantern and a beer bottle containing a bright red hibiscus standing on top of it.

I said, "That flower's great. Thank you, Luz."

"Make it like home," she said. "Come on, I show you the rest."

I backed into the main bedroom and she followed and then turned to the other curtained doorway, saying, "This is—oh, I don't know." She shook her head. "*Lavatorio*."

"Lavatory," I suggested.

"Where you piss and like that."

"Yes," I said. "I get it."

She pushed aside the curtain, and it was a closet. That's all. A closet. No light in there. But then, with whatever golden glow managed to creep in there from the bedroom, I saw the round hole in the floor. And the river was below.

All at once, I remembered my entire lifetime's experience of North American plumbing, North American bathrooms. All those great huge tubs, Jacuzzis, bidets, powerful flushing equipment, masterful drains, gleaming porcelain and tile, thick towels, mirrors rimmed with gleaming lightbulbs.

Okay. I'm going through these things now, and I can do it because I'm going to get back. I'm going to have that other life again, and this time I'm going to keep it. Because it's mine, I'm supposed to have it, and I want it. Six hundred thousand dollars. Just keep saying that, I told myself. Six hundred thousand dollars.

Luz looked at me, quizzical, wanting to be sure I grasped the concept. "Ho-kay?"

"Okay," I said. "I get the picture."

"You wanna go?"

"Not at the moment."

"Well, I do," she said. "You get us a couple glasses. In the shelf beside the refrigerator."

"Right," I said, and she let the curtain drop with herself inside. I turned away, and as I crossed the bedroom I heard the strong stream hit the river.

I had left the rum bottle on the square table at the kitchen side of the front room. Now I found two jelly glasses on the shelf, put them on the table, and was just carefully pouring an exact amount of rum into each glass when Luz came in, smiling broadly, saying,

"Boy, I needed that. That's a long time. You sure you don' want to?"

"Later," I said. "Here's your rum."

She took the glass and clinked with mine. "To your long life," she said.

"Afterlife," I said. "And to yours."

We drank, and she said, "I gotta get up early, be in the office six-thirty, so I gotta set my radio alarm, but you don' need to get up. And, just in case, you know, you shouldn' go out and around."

"I won't."

"There's food here, what you need. And beer in the refrigerator. After work tomorrow, I gotta go to Rancio to lure you out, then I gotta find you not home, Esilda say you gone, I tell the cousins, I get back here maybe around seven."

"Okay."

"Could be we go out dancin' then," she said, and grinned at me. "I bet you like to dance."

Danger? What the hell, this situation was dangerous all the time. "I love to dance," I said.

"I knew you would," she said. "Lola wouldn' take up with nobody didn' like to dance."

"That's right."

"And other things," she said, and laughed, and then yawned, holding the back of her hand to her mouth.

I said, "Time for—uh, time for sleep."

"You bet."

She raised the glass to me again, and we both finished the rum. She switched off the light and crossed to open the curtain, and illumination from the bedroom made it possible for me to find my way.

She stood beside her bed, yawning. I said, "Good night, Luz. And thanks again."

"You gonna have a good time here," she told me.

"Not too good, I hope," I said, and she laughed and unzipped her cut-offs, and I went into my new room.

23

Luz got back from work later than she'd said the next day, almost seven-thirty, and when she came in she seemed rattled and angry and a little scared. She also looked very different, because she wore her office clothes. It was interesting to see she could contain all that animal exuberance when she wanted to: not hide it, that wouldn't be possible, but not flaunt it either.

Her white blouse was cut full and buttoned to the neck, where a small gold crucifix hung from a wispy gold chain. Her skirt was black and not too tight, and ended just below the knee. Her shoes were black and low-heeled and maidenly.

She hurried in, dressed like that, with this upset and distracted look, carrying a brown paper bag, and thrust the bag at me. "Open that. I gotta change."

"Okay."

I was feeling a little dopey. I'd spent most of the day with her photo novels, a kind of comic book that uses posed photos of actors instead of drawings. Luz had a whole stack of them on the floor beside her bed. They were in Spanish, of course, but the stories were not hard to follow. They were mostly love stories of the most sentimental sort, like Esilda's soap operas, but they were also quite sexy, and several of the women looked a lot like Luz. The only difference was, these were actresses faking it. I couldn't imagine a situation in which Luz would fake it.

Now she marched away through the scarlet curtain into the bedroom, taking her upset and alarm with her, and I looked into the paper bag. It contained two bottles of rum. I opened one, put the other on the shelf, and was pouring when she came tripping back in.

Now, *this* was Luz. A tight red skirt the size of a sweatband, glaring orange blouse with nipples that pointed at me as though to say *I know you*, great golden hoop earrings with parrots in cages in the middle of the hoops, and thonged clogs that rattled. "Gimme that glass," she said, and emptied it in one.

I drank more moderately, then held the bottle up. "Yes?"

For answer, she held the glass toward me. I filled it, and this time she took only a healthy swig before she said, "I don't like it."

"What don't you like?"

"I tol' 'em, he isn't there, that Barry Lee he's gone, the maid told me he gone away, she don' know where he gone to; they get mad at *me*."

"Who gets mad at you?"

"All them from Tapitepe. Manfredo and Luis and the other Luis with the bad arm and José and Pedro and *poco* Pedro."

"They got mad at you? They think you warned me?"

"No, no," she said. "Come on, we sit down."

The sofa was very old. It had sagged to about an inch from the ground and then been covered with serapes. Luz dropped into it as though going backward into a swimming pool, while I levered myself slowly downward, holding the sofa arm.

When I finally reached bottom, she said, "They think I'm stupid, I say something got you scared. Not today, they know you not there today, 'cause Carlos say that to Luis with the bad arm and

poco Pedro when they talk to him to make sure he's at his shop,
you know. What they figure, these guys, I'm the one, I'm the stupid, I said something *before* that got you scared. So now they
gonna cut me and all this shit."

"They're gonna cut you?" This was terrible.

But she dismissed it with an angry wave of the hand. "No, they
just talkin', 'cause they mad, 'cause you got away, now they gotta
look for you."

"Where?"

"They gonna go talk to Artie." She gave me an angry smile.
"Maybe he's gonna punch their heads in, whaddaya think?"

"I'd like that," I said.

"So would I," she said, and bounced all her parts around on the
sofa, and said, "You hungry? You wanna go eat?"

"Luz, you know," I said, "I got almost no money. I've been living on Carlos."

"So now you're living on me," she said, and whomped herself
on the chest. Her grin was now less angry, looser, more Luz. And
rum. "You'll pay me back some other time," she said. "I got a good
job."

"Okay," I said. "But I *will* pay you back."

"I know," she said. She finished her rum, put the glass on the
floor, and said, "So now we go eat, then we go dancin', and . . ."
She leaned forward, looking around at the floor, then over at me.
"Help me outa this, Felicio," she said. Meaning the sofa.

That was the trickiest moment so far.

24

Dancing was never going to be a sensible idea, what with me having to hide out and Luz being Luz, but I'd agreed to it last night, full of tension and rum, so here we were.

The Napalma equivalent of Club Rick, at least on a Thursday night, was a mostly open-air bar along the river between Luz's house and the factory, whose name I never did find out. It was less than a ten-minute walk from the house. There was a thatch-roofed open-sided part, with the bar and a small dance floor and some tables, and a much larger open part, with Japanese lanterns strung on poles and trees, all these soft colors of light against the surrounding darkness, like a kind of pastel chiaroscuro. There were long plastic picnic tables out there near the riverbank, and a pounded-earth dance floor between the tables and the bar. The music was a live band full of guitars and trumpets and amplifiers, all wailing away.

We ate our dinner—chicken and rice and plantains and fried

tomatoes and plenty of grease and several beers—at one of those plastic picnic tables, sharing the table with a shifting population of other diners. Luz knew almost everybody, of course, but the noise level, between the blaring band and the shouting customers, was so high she couldn't even pretend to introduce me.

After dinner, we danced, along with the rest of the happy, heaving, sweaty crowd, all moving together but not together under the pink and canary and aqua and jade lights, shifting, dipping, shoulders up with pride, mostly bare feet pounding the dirt. Luz made love to the world, to the music, to the night, to the air, to me, to everybody, and laughed through it like another trumpet.

At times we'd pause for a beer, sitting sprawled on the bench of one of the picnic tables, watching the other dancers and breathing like sled dogs, letting the air dry the sweat on our faces. But one of those times, when we reeled off the floor, she pulled at my arm until my ear was close enough, and said, "Felicio, I gotta go home."

That's right. She got up very early this morning, and by now it must be very late. (My Rolex was back at her house, in the fruit box next to the futon. It hadn't seemed to go with my Felicio costume.) So I nodded, too winded to answer, and she took my hand, and we staggered on out of there.

The night was just cool enough and dry enough to restore us some when we left that place and walked toward home. Luz had kept hold of my hand, and that was okay with me. We were pals now.

We walked in silence for the first few minutes, and then she said, "You're okay, Felicio. I like you."

"Well, thanks, Luz," I said. "I like you too. And I'm very grateful to you."

"And Lola's great," she said.

That surprised me, but I had to agree. "Yes, she is."

"Before she met up with you, you know," she said, "she was stuck-up. I was jus' a little kid, but I remember. Everybody said she was too big in the head. How do you say that?"

"Like that, pretty much," I said. "I don't see her that way, though."

"*Now* I know," she told me. "Now I know, back then, she jus' lonely. She knows she's smart and she knows she's good and she knows something good is suppose to happen, but she don' see it coming. Not till she gets away from here. Not till she meets up with you. She don' belong here, she belongs in the north."

I said, "Lola and me, we were both one leg of the same pants. We weren't any good to anybody until we got together."

She laughed. "That's a funny way to talk about pants," she said.

When we got to her place, she walked through the dark living room and switched on the light in the bedroom, and then I could follow.

Ignoring me, she was already pulling that orange blouse off over her head. I kept eyes front and beelined through my own curtained doorway.

"*Buenas noches*," she called through the curtain, and yawned in the middle of it.

"Good night, Luz," I said. I touched my warm forehead to the cool curtain. "It was a terrific night. Thank you."

No answer. I think she was already asleep.

25

So once again, in the semicool of the evening, I stretched out naked on my futon. I'm too tired to sleep, I thought, especially after doing nothing all day. So I'll just lie here and . . .

"Get out! Get out!"

It was a shrill whisper, full of panic and urgency. I sat up, completely bewildered. No idea where I was, what was going on. Stupidly, I said, "What?"

"*Get out get out get out!*"

Voices, male voices, nearby. The futon, the glassless window, the darkness, Luz's panic-stricken voice, thumps of boots on the front room floor.

The cousins! I was naked, in the dark, I couldn't remember what I'd done with my pants, where's anything, what can I do?

Still seated on the futon, I grabbed the windowsill, pulled myself up, put a leg over the sill, and my terrified toes found a tiny ridge along the outside, the same height as the floor within. The floor was the platform the house was built on, and the platform extended less than an inch beyond the rear wall.

My toes clung to that slender line, as I turned my back to the window and put the other leg over. Now I had about six toes on the narrow band of wood, and one arm around the window frame, pressed to the wall.

Light came from the other side of the doorway, turning the scarlet curtain into dark blood, a scab, a wound. The cousins were in there, in the bedroom. If they opened that curtain—

The window was very near the corner of the house. Even if I could move sideways, there wasn't room enough to hide between the window and the end of the wall. And in the other direction, toward the *lavatorio*, there was nothing to hold on to at all.

I hated this, but what could I do? I grabbed the windowsill with both hands and lowered myself. One foot reached down and down, the toes of the other turned prehensile against that sliver of platform.

It was no good. Nothing but air, nothing to hold onto. I had to let the other foot slide down off that ridge while I gripped the windowsill, so I hung there with my feet straight down. Water tugged at my ankles, warmish water, from right to left.

Above me, light increased; the curtain was open. I let go of the windowsill.

Chest-deep water, tugging at me, wanting me to go leftward with it, wanting to take me along for a ride, past the fertilizer factory, past San Cristóbal, on past Rancio into Venezuela, on to introduce me to its big brother the Orinoco, who would coast me on his broad shoulders all the way to the delta and out to the North Atlantic Ocean, the Gulf of Paria, and the narrow passage by Trinidad called the Serpent's Mouth.

No, thank you, I'm already in the serpent's mouth.

I reached in front of me and touched the slimy post holding up the house. It was an unshaped log, with the bark gone, and it was as slippery as a fish. Still, I rested my palm against it, tried not to think about the soft squishiness around my toes, the mud or worse on which I stood, *in* which I stood, and tried instead to concentrate on what was happening above my head.

Dim light was at the window up there, which meant the curtain was still drawn back and I was seeing illumination from the bedroom. Somebody was looking into the back room and not seeing anybody.

What now? Would he come in the rest of the way, light the kerosene lantern, look around, find my Rolex? Find my passport, my driver's license, my clothing, my suitcase?

No. The light dimmed. It was a person he was looking for, not a Rolex. In what dim light he had to work with, he'd seen there was no person in that room, and that's all he wanted to know.

Plainly I could hear their boots, above me, scuffing around in the bedroom. Indistinctly I could hear the voices, Luz trying to be outraged but merely being scared, the male voices gruff and discontented.

Splash-sssssshhhhhhhhhh. . . . Oh, for God's sake, one of them's using the *lavatorio*!

I couldn't stand being here, in this piss-warm water, while piss splashed down twelve feet away: downstream, thank God, but still. What if somebody in the house just over here to my right decided to get rid of tonight's beer? Or tacos?

Where I stood was not completely inky black. There was starlight, and it reflected off the water, and I could make out the post in front of me and the building above me and the other houses up and down the row. And I could see a support board attached to the post in front of me at an angle just above the waterline, then up at a diagonal to the end of a floor beam halfway between here and the bank. Moving my feet with great reluctance, I got around to that support board and used it to pull myself along the side of the house.

The water got quickly shallower, so that it was only to the top of my thighs when I reached the other end of the board, and I was pressing my hand to the rough plank siding of the house instead. Ahead of me was land, and up beyond that point was the side window to the front room. Light gleamed from there, a searchlight band of it that I didn't dare walk through. Of course, it wasn't as bright as a searchlight, it was merely the rosy glow from Luz's pink-shaded living room lamp, but it would show movement.

Where were they? The sounds of voices, it seemed to me, still came from the bedroom. They weren't going to have sex with her, were they? They were all cousins. On the other hand, these guys struck me as the kind who'd go to family reunions to pick up girls.

I couldn't go past the window, but maybe I could get close enough to peek inside, if I stayed out of the band of light. I moved forward, the water now to my ankles, the mud under my feet firmer, the slope steeper. I came up to land, very steep and stony, pulled myself along the side of the house, and here was the window. I chanced a peek inside, and the room was empty.

The voices seemed different now, Luz less scared, the males less belligerent. Everybody was still talking, but it seemed to be merely a general discussion at this point, without suspicion in it. Talking about me? Where I might be, probably.

Out here, wet and naked.

The quality of the light changed in there, and I had just realized that must mean the bedroom doorway curtain had been pulled back when into my line of vision stepped a Mexican bandit. It's true he didn't wear a sombrero or a bandoleer, but he did have the slouching walk and the walrus mustache and he did carry—oh, Lord!—a machete.

I pressed myself against the wall of the house. He turned, almost facing me, and spoke, and two more of them entered the picture. So that was Luis with the bad arm: ugly son of a bitch.

Next Luz came into view, smiling nervously, wearing a great white cotton sack of a nightgown she must own for hospital stays and visits to grandma's house; I couldn't believe that was how she normally spent her nights.

Did I hear her use the word *cerveza*? If she was being a hostess now, asking them to stay, it was a perfect way to remind them they had to go; they had miles to travel, podner, and an ornery in-law to kill.

Yes. That was the way it was working; they were all trending toward the door. Six of them in all, and there's *poco* Pedro; I could probably take him if he weren't carrying that machete. Three of them held machetes; the other three apparently would prefer to rip me apart with their bare hands.

Out the door they went, still taking their time, Luz wishing them luck in their quest, assuring them there was no problem in their having showed up so unexpectedly, drop in any time, bring your machetes, come by when you can stay longer, give my love to the dogs and the chickens back at the hacienda. . . . Would they never *leave*?

Yes. There they go, *poco* Pedro last. Luz stood in the doorway for more farewells, these hushed for the sake of the neighbors. I crept forward, trying to duck under the light from the window, and saw their pickup truck, big and dirty and saggy. They came into sight one at a time, moseying toward their truck just as though it actually was a passel of ponies. They climbed aboard, three inside the cab and three in the open back. It wasn't as dramatic as a posse on a passel of ponies, but it would do.

I was so absorbed in watching them, I almost forgot to duck out of sight of the headlights. The truck faced the house, which meant it faced me. But then the starter ground and ground, and I suddenly realized what was going to happen next, and I moved back and downslope along the side of the house as far as the window. I looked in there, and Luz still stood in the open doorway, smiling, waving bye-bye, until she was suddenly flooded with glary light. Then she slammed the door and turned, and her expression had switched to great worry.

I wanted to speak, but the truck was slowly backing off, headlight beams spraying everywhere, and I didn't dare move. Luz hurried away, toward the rear of the house, no doubt looking for me, and the truck at last completed its turning retreat. It stopped, then moved forward, engine rasping, and limped away toward San Cristóbal.

Now I hurried around to the front and in. I shut the door behind me just at the instant Luz came rushing back through the doorway from the bedroom, still looking deeply worried until she saw me, then becoming joyously relieved. "Felicio! You're okay!"

"I don't know," I said. "I've been in the river. I've probably got most of the world's tropical diseases by now."

"Oh, we gotta get you washed," she said. "C'mere."

I followed her to the sink, where she pulled out a gleaming metal contraption and attached it to the faucet, saying, "Here. This's how you get clean."

Ah. It was a telephone shower, a shower head attached to a flexible metal hose. I took it, and she said, "There's the soap. Get the water hot like you want it. I'll do your back."

I said, "Luz, I'll get the whole house wet."

She pointed down and said, "You stand there."

I looked and there was a metal grid, about two feet by three, in the floor in front of the sink. "That's terrific," I said. "What'll they think of next?"

I ran warm water over my chest and arms. Some splashed on the floor, but most of it ran down me and through the grid.

Luz said, "I'll do your back."

"Okay." I gave her the shower head and started to soap my front. She ran water over my back, and all at once I saw the situation I was in: wet and naked, being washed by Luz Garrigues. Then, to make matters worse, I immediately produced physical evidence of my awareness.

"Okay, here's the water," she said, coming around front. "Gimme the soap, I'll do your back." Then she did her loose smile and said, "Well. You *are* glad to see me."

"Warm water," I said. "It's a well-known turn-on."

"Uh-huh." She took the soap, went around behind me, and soaped me *very* well indeed, while I tried to think about other things. Any other things.

Even those guys. I said, "Why did they come here, anyway? Did they think I was here?"

"They don't know what they think, those bums," she said in disgust. "A couple of them—I think Manfredo, maybe not—they said I give you a warning so you could run away. They argue, did I do it, did I not do it. Then I was dancin' with somebody tonight nobody knows. Somebody got on the phone, called Manfredo or somebody, ask about this guy. So they come down, look around, just in case you're here."

"Somebody called your cousins about *me*?"

"They wanna know who you are. Nosy people. So they call a cousin of mine: Who's this guy stayin' with Luz? So that's why they come down. I say you ain't stayin' with me, you're a truck driver work for the factory, you off on your run."

"Jesus, that was close."

"I pray to Jesus, too, lemme tell you," she said. "Those guys can get mean. Especially that *poco* Pedro, he's a mean guy even when he ain't drunk."

"Luz, tomorrow, from the factory, could you call Arturo? Tell him to come down here. Don't say why, just tell him come down, it's important."

"Sure, in the morning. Okay, you're done. Here's the water."

I kept my back to her. "Thanks, Luz, I'll just rinse the rest, you know, myself."

"I seen those before," she told me. "I'm goin' to bed, I'm tired."

"Thanks," I said. "For—you know, for everything."

"Sure. Goo'night."

What with one thing and another, it took me a long while to get back to sleep.

26

Friday. Another slow day, alone in Luz's house. I was running out of photo novels, and the river was running out of different kinds of boats to show me. The Rolex said it was only eleven-thirty, too early for lunch, but I decided to eat anyway, just for something to do. I got up from the saggy living room sofa, meaning to go to the refrigerator and spend a long time choosing my menu, when a car stopped out front.

Oh, no. The cousins again? I didn't *want* to go back in that miserable river, this time with all my clothes on. Crouched over, I ran to the front window and looked out and saw Arturo just climbing out of his Impala.

Arturo! I'd forgotten all about him. I'd asked Luz to phone him, so this morning she must have, because here he was.

I forgot lunch. I hadn't actually been hungry anyway. I went to the door and opened it and said, "Hey, Arturo, how you doing?"

"Better than you," he said, and gave me a grim smile, and shook his head as he came in. "I hear you had a rough night here."

"You bet."

He shook his head again. "Those *bufóns* from Tapitepe."

"Yeah," I agreed. "Manfredo and Luis and the other Luis with the bad arm and José and Pedro and *poco* Pedro."

"Yeah, them. They're stupid as shit," Arturo said, "but they can be dangerous."

"I got that," I assured him.

"You told Luz to call me," he said, "so she did, and I come down and had a talk with her."

"And?"

"And they could come back, *hermano*. That story, how she's dancin' with a truck driver from the factory, that don't hold up."

"It don't?"

"How come nobody around here knows this truck driver, never seen him before? Manfredo's stupid, but he ain't that stupid. He might ask around, Who's this truck driver? Then he comes back."

"Would he hurt Luz?"

"Not if you ain't here. Luz can talk her way out of it, unless they got you right here like evidence."

"I suppose so. You got any ideas?"

He said, "I'll take you back to Sabanon, to begin with. You got stuff to pack?"

"Not much." I felt a pang at the thought of leaving. Two days ago, I'd thought the house a hellhole and Luz a dangerous tramp, and now I realized I was going to miss them both. I said, "I'd like to say so long to Luz."

"I said your so-longs," he told me. "Luz says to tell you she liked having you around; you're a funny guy. And a good dancer."

"She said that, huh?"

Arturo grinned at me. "You never know, *hermano*," he said. "A few more days around here, you might begin to forget Lola. Good thing I'm takin' you away."

"Saved again," I said, and went to get my stuff.

27

The next few days at Mamá and Papá's house were, I suppose, restful, but also unsettling. The problem was, I now slept in the bed where Lola and I always sleep together when we visit, so the night memories got really intense.

I preferred the days, where I now had a new persona. My name was Felicio, and I was a friend of Arturo's from San Cristóbal, and I'd had a recent terrible tragedy that nobody would talk about—a death for which I held myself responsible was hinted—as a result of which I had taken a vow of silence. This story was not broadcast all over the place but was brought out as necessary for the consumption of neighbors and friends.

Arturo had more phone conversations with Lola, and the insurance situation continued to go along smoothly. And he'd found me some recent American magazines, to help pass the time.

Monday afternoon, I spent an hour alone in my bedroom, reading those magazines, until I got bored, so I got up and opened the door, and in the living room were Arturo and Mamá and Papá seated with a man whose back was to me, but who was somebody I was sure I didn't know. He wore a suit and tie, in all this heat and humidity, and he had a clipboard on his lap and a pen in his hand. He looked like an American real estate salesman, but he was speaking fluent Spanish. He was asking questions. About *me?*

Arturo saw me in the doorway and did a quick urgent headshake: Stay out of here. I stepped back, retreating into the bedroom, and quietly shut the door.

What was this? Something to do with my death? Or something else entirely? What should I do?

Mamá came sidling in, shutting the door behind her, putting her finger to her lips. I looked at her, full of questions, and she pointed at me and then pointed at the window.

What? This is the second floor. She wanted me to go out the window?

Yes. To demonstrate, she picked up my magazines and tossed *them* out the window. Then she came close and whispered, "The insurance!"

"Insurance investigator?" I was appalled. Everything was supposed to be going so smoothly.

She nodded, pointed urgently at the window again, and went over to stick my suitcase under the bed.

Every bedroom I'm in, sooner or later somebody wants me to go out the window. While Mamá smoothed the ruffled bed, I went over to look down at the magazines strewn on the hard ground eight feet below me.

Damn it to hell. All right, all right. One leg over the sill, then the other, lower myself more slowly than Mamá likes. I dangled a few seconds, then dropped and hit the packed earth, first with my feet, then my knees, then my elbows. My forehead landed on *Newsweek*.

I was at the back of the house. Beside me was the enclosed part of downstairs, the fuchsia-colored vertical slats behind which were the freezer, the hot-water heater, some guns and fishing poles, and Madonna, the brood sow.

And me, until the insurance investigator went away. Rising, I became aware of a whole lot of new pains in my body, including my head. When I stooped to pick up the magazines, I felt briefly dizzy. Carrying the magazines under my left arm, I went around the corner and under the house, into the open part with the concrete blocks and old truck parts and vertical plumbing pipes. The door to the enclosed section was under here, and that's where I headed.

As I went, my mind was full of questions. What had gone wrong? In her last two phone calls, Lola had thought this was almost over, that everything was going along exactly according to plan. Was this somehow just a formality, down here in Guerrera? Wouldn't that be awfully expensive, to send a man all this way? We'd been counting on it being too expensive.

Could it be that the insurance company keeps a man in South America to run a simple check on cases like this? Or maybe a bunch of insurance companies share the expense of keeping the guy, to cut down on fraud? Exactly the kind of fraud that comes out of little countries with less than first-rate record-keeping.

But that's why we'd been so thorough. How could there be any question of fraud in this case? There were all those eyewitnesses, there was the death certificate, there was the funeral, the grave, the undertaker's bill. For God's sake, there was videotape of the funeral, this whole huge family all in mourning. What more could they possibly want?

I plagued myself with all these questions while I hurried around to the door under the house that led into the enclosed area. When I opened that wood-slat door, Madonna snorted a question of her own: What's with you, buster?

"Pay no attention to me," I muttered, shutting the door. "Go on with what you were doing."

Madonna snuffled her disdain and rooted around in her straw, pretending I wasn't there. It was dim in here, but not dark. Two very dusty windows gave illumination, one at the side, over Madonna's pen, and the other facing the street. While Madonna, a thousand-pound bloated white sausage almost seven feet long, grumbled about this intrusion into a lady's boudoir while refusing to look at me or acknowledge my presence, I worked my way around all the stored (and forgotten) crap in here to the front window and looked out. Would I be able to see the inspector when he left?

Oh, good, it was perfect. From here, looking at an angle, I could just see the bottom of the stairs down from the living room. And across the street, that white Land Rover must be his vehicle.

There was someone in the Land Rover, at the wheel. He looked as though he was reading a photo novel. A chauffeur? He wore a white panama hat, not very chauffeurlike at all. Then he lifted his head to look over toward the house, and I flinched.

The cop. Lola's cop, the one she'd had to punch in the nose. Rafael Rafez.

28

He stayed upstairs for an hour, driving everybody crazy. Madonna didn't like me down below any more than I liked the insurance investigator up above, but we both had to put up with it.

At last I heard the *clomp-clomp* of descending footsteps. I'd been sitting on an old massive television set, leafing through my magazines without really absorbing—or reabsorbing—much content (or contentment), but now I stood, put the magazines atop the TV, and went over to look out the window.

Here he came, a sour-faced, pale-skinned black-haired guy of about forty, wearing black-rimmed glasses. He had a nose like a can opener. He didn't look satisfied.

Rafez got out of the Land Rover as the insurance investigator reached ground level. They walked toward one another and chatted briefly in the middle of the road. It seemed to me that Rafez asked if the investigator wanted Rafez to go upstairs and kick some ass, and the investigator told him No, or Not yet, or Maybe later. They looked along the street and spoke a bit more, and then they got into the Land Rover, Rafez at the wheel. They made a U-turn and went away.

For sure? Leaving the disgruntled Madonna behind, and my magazines as well, I crept out of the enclosed area and along its outside wall under the house until I could see down the street, just in time to watch the white Land Rover turn left onto La Carretera, headed out of town.

Oh, boy. I raced up the stairs and into the living room; everybody in there was extremely upset. Mamá paced back and forth, rubbing her hands together, and Papá was so overwrought his beer bottle kept clicking against his teeth. Arturo had a beer bottle in each hand. He gave one to me and said, "We gotta talk." He was very solemn and serious, much more than I'd ever seen him before.

I said, "Arturo, I don't get it. What's going on with that guy?"

"He's suspicious," he said. "He don't know what he's suspicious about; all he knows is, he's suspicious."

"His driver," I said, "is the cop that investigated my death, the one Lola socked."

Mamá and Papá both wailed at that news, and Arturo's brows lowered so far it was a miracle he could still see. He said, "Rafez?"

"That's the one." I drank beer like Papá, then began to pace like Mamá. "What's *wrong* here? What's the problem? Everything we did was perfect."

"Maybe *too* perfect," Arturo said. "Maybe that's what got them suspicious, they never seen such a perfect case before."

"No," I said, "it doesn't work that way. If they don't see something wrong, they don't follow through. So what the hell do they see wrong?"

"I don't know," he said. "Just so they don't see *you*. You can't stay here no more."

"Hell and damnation," I said. "Where can I go next, Arturo? I've been all over the country."

"Well, you can't be here," he told me. "They're sniffin' around, and so's Manfredo and them from Tapitepe. They'll be hearing about a deaf mute up in Rancio and a guy with a vow of silence been livin' *here*, and if the insurance guy don't show up, Manfredo and them *will*."

"So where can I go?"

"I'm rackin' my brain," he said. "The problem is, you can't go to nobody else in the family, because everybody that's lookin' for you is gonna go to the same people. I don't know what we do, because you can't go to nobody we *know*."

"That doesn't leave much," I said.

We all paced for a while, except Papá, who found walking a distraction when he was drinking beer. Then, dubiously, Arturo said, "Maybe . . ."

We all looked at him. I said, "Yes?"

Arturo looked at Mamá and said, "Ifigenia?"

Mamá, whose name is Lucía, briskly shook her head and said a lot of words very fast, some of which I caught; it was the Spanish equivalent of *Are you out of your mind?* Arturo said it was worth a try. Mamma told him it was on his head, not hers. Arturo said what the hell. Then he turned to me. "What the hell, it's worth a try."

"What is, Arturo?" I asked him.

"Everybody knows," he explained, "me and my wife Ifigenia is estranged. I go there every once in a while, we make a baby, have a fight, I come back here for a couple years. In the family, anybody that knows about what you're doin' knows Ifigenia never liked Lola, never had any use for her, and didn't want me to do nothing about this anyway. I had to 'splain to her, over and over, that even if it all went to hell, I wasn't doin' any crimes and nothin' bad could happen to me, but she still don't want nothin' to do with it and don't want *me* to have nothin' to do with it. So who would expect you to hide out at *her* house?"

"Nobody," I said.

"Exactly," he said.

"Including me," I said. "If she's that against the whole idea, she won't let me stay there. Or she'll turn me in."

"It's worth a try," he repeated. "I can't think of nothin' else, so what the hell. Lemme at least call her on the phone."

"Okay," I said. "Any port in a storm."

He looked interested. "Yeah? That's nice. You just make that up?"

"Yes," I said.

"You're pretty good," Arturo told me, and crossed over to the telephone to make his call.

Well, I could see him regretting *that* one right away. He got a few sentences into the conversation, saying, "Ifigenia," in honeyed tones two or three times, and then the squawks started out of the earpiece. Not in *her* house. How dare he make such a suggestion, doesn't he ever think about his *children?* How long is she supposed to put up with a lowlife? When is he gonna fix that stair he promised to fix last *September?*

Arturo said this, and he said that. His eyebrows lifted, and they lowered. He bobbed and weaved, moving from foot to foot, as though in an actual physical boxing match. Mamá gave me the evil eye—*see what you've done to my son?*—and Papá went off for more beer, bringing back four bottles. I was grateful for mine.

Well, Arturo finally managed to get off the phone, and when he looked at me his expression was speculative, as though he were wondering if it would relieve his feelings if he kicked the crap out of his troublesome brother-in-law. I said, "Sorry, Arturo."

"*De nada*," he said, and sighed. "I gotta do *somethin'* about you, man," he said. "It's come down to it now. Either we find someplace safe, or I gotta get rid of you myself."

I blinked. "What?"

"I wouldn't give you to Manfredo and them," he said, "they'd screw it up somehow, leave evidence; they'd get your fingerprints or somethin', the cops would. I'd rather feed you to Madonna."

"Arturo," I said, "don't joke."

The look he gave me was not comical. "Barry," he said, using the wrong name for emphasis, "don't you know what's goin' on?"

"I don't know," I said. "Maybe I don't."

"You think we're goin' through all this for *you?*"

"Well, it's mostly for Lola," I said. "I understand that."

"That's right."

"And everybody else that's involved," I went on. "None of us wants to get caught at this."

"Caught?" He looked at me as though I was very dumb. "Who's gonna get caught? Doin' what? What are you talkin' about?"

"Well, the family."

"No," he said. "Don't you worry about *us*, we're not in trouble, we didn't do nothin' to break the law. And neither did you."

I frowned at him. "I didn't?"

"No," he said. "You wanna play a joke, pretend you're dead, go ahead, nobody can stop you. Nobody can stop us, we go along with the gag. That ain't a crime."

"Busting up that car is."

"Big deal. They make you pay for a Beetle."

"Arturo, wait a minute," I said. "You're wrong about this. We *are* committing a crime."

"No, we ain't," he insisted. "Don't you know the only one that broke the law here? That if *you* get caught, *she* goes to jail? That's right, man: Lola. When she put in that insurance claim *that* was a crime, the only crime anybody committed. They wanna go after you for conspiracy? Too much trouble. They got the one did the fraud; they throw her in jail; that's it, next case."

"Arturo—"

"I like you, Felicio," he said, sounding as though he didn't like me at all, "but you ain't my sister. You ain't even my brother. I'll do anything for Lola, you know that, so that's why I'm playing along with this. But I gotta tell you, it's *her* I'm worried about, not you. I know she wouldn't be happy if you got killed, so I'll do what I can to keep you alive. But one way, you know, Manfredo and them from Tapitepe are right. If you're dead, *nobody's* in trouble. So if it comes down to you dead or Lola in jail, I'm sorry, but I'm gonna lose another brother."

29

What do they call it, the law of unintended consequences? You think you're so smart, you think you're so clever. You scheme and scam and think you've got it all doped out, and there's always some other angle you didn't take into account.

So what had I done this time? I *thought* what I was doing was scamming an insurance company, which was already scary enough, but it turns out what I actually did was put a six-hundred-thousand-dollar price on my head. And then I marooned myself in a place full of people anxious to collect, where I didn't have any resources of my own and where, it now turned out, I didn't even have any allies. Not when push, you know, came to shove.

All of a sudden, I didn't want any more beer. More beer would just muddy my head, and if we'd reached the point where Arturo contemplated feeding me to Madonna, I could not afford a muddy head.

I put down my beer. I said, "Maybe . . ."

They all looked at me. They were very interested in what I had
to say. Unfortunately, I didn't *have* anything to say. I'd been thinking, Maybe I could get the American visa now and leave Guerrera
right away, but in the first place it wouldn't be right away, and in
the second place I shouldn't call attention to myself while insurance investigators were wandering around Sabanon. So I didn't
have anything to say after all.

Arturo said, "Listen, could you be an American?"

He was sounding friendly again, as though he was on my side. I
said, "What do you mean?"

"Mamá," he said, "we still got some of the Barry Lee stuff,
don't we?"

"Oh, sure," she said.

I said, "Some of my old things are still here?"

"Lola had her own stuff to carry," he explained. "She took some
of yours, left some. One suitcase. We got it downstairs, under the
house."

I hadn't noticed it. I said, "What do you mean, be an American?"

"It's not workin', you bein' Guerreran," he said, "because you
can't talk."

"It's driving me nuts," I admitted.

"So what if you put on American clothes," he said, "and went
somewhere Americans go, and be an American for a while?"

I said, "How do I do that?"

"You don't know how to be an American?"

"Not without a passport," I told him. "Not without credit cards.
Even if I had the cash, and I don't, nobody expects cash from an
American. What do you want me to do, go to some hotel? Hi, I'm
an American, I'll pay you in *siapas*? And the hotel always asks to
see the passport. They've got some police form to fill out."

"That's right, dammit," Arturo said. "But it would be so perfect, you know? An American is something you could play."

Mamá said, "Dulce."

Arturo turned to her, frowning. He thought about it. Slowly he nodded. "Son of a gun," he said. "She might do it. Only whadda we tell her?"

I said, "Her?"

Instead of answering, he said, "You're an American, right? And you gotta hide out. Only not for the reason you really got to, for some other reason. What's the reason?"

"*I* don't know," I said. "I don't know what you're looking for."

"A reason for you to hide out," he explained, "that makes you a sympathetic guy for a friend of mine."

"You mean noncriminal," I said. "Like I'm hiding from my ex-wife."

"Maybe," he said. "Why you hidin' from your ex-wife?"

"She's trying to serve me papers," I said. "It's a financial settlement, and she's vindictive, and she wants it all. And there's a deadline. If I can keep out of sight for a month I'll be okay."

Slowly he nodded. "That might do it," he said. "Let me make a phone call."

"To Dulce," I suggested. "Who is she?"

"Let's just see if this works," he said. "You go get your suitcase; I'll make the call."

I said, "This is just a ploy to get me down there with Madonna."

He laughed. "Not a bad idea. If the phone call don't work, I'll tell you, Take the suitcase back down again; here, I'll come with you."

"Please don't joke, Arturo," I said. "I've been under a lot of stress lately."

"Lemme call," he said.

So I went downstairs and Madonna snorted. You again?

"Don't mind me," I told her. "Carry on." I looked around, and there was my green vinyl bag with all the zippers. "I won't be bothering you again, I hope," I told Madonna, and carried the bag upstairs.

Arturo was still on the phone. Mamá smiled at me: *it's working out.*

I carried the vinyl bag into the bedroom and put it on the bed next to the ratty cardboard suitcase I'd been lugging around. Boy. Already you could tell these were two different guys, and you didn't even have to look inside the luggage.

I opened the vinyl bag, and here were a lot of old friends. My Reeboks: great. I'd never been really comfortable in those peon shoes. A nice variety of touristy clothes. Underwear. My toilet kit. Fantastic. Wow, I'd missed all this gear.

"Okay," Arturo said, in the doorway.

I looked at him. "Okay? I've got a place to stay?"

"Put on some American stuff," he told me, "and let's go."

"Sure." I pulled out tan chinos, a light blue LaCoste pullover. "Where we going?"

"I tell you in the car," he said. "We gotta get outa here, man. Leave that other stuff behind."

"Right," I said.

30

"**B**ackseat, tourist."

"Oh, right."

I got into the back of the Impala, Arturo got behind the wheel, and we drove away from Mamá and Papá's house. I said, "Where are we going?"

"Up by Marona."

A long way, nearly two hundred miles, up where the Siapa River, for which the local currency is named, meets up with the Conoro River, the one my rented Beetle belly-whopped into.

There was pretty country up around Marona. The Siapa is the cleanest and freshest and fastest of all the waterways of Guerrera, tumbling north out of the mountains of Brazil. There are nice resorts and rich people around there.

Come to think of it, that was also where my undertaker, Ortiz, came from. That wasn't the idea, was it, to have me hang out at a mortuary for the next couple of weeks?

Then a worse thought occurred to me. Was this instead of Madonna? As casually as I knew how, I said, "Where by Marona are we going, Arturo?"

Instead of answering, he said, "Take a look in the seat pocket there, the hotel brochures."

The back of the front passenger seat had a wide pocket, like a kangaroo's pouch. I reached into it, and it was full of different kinds of brochures and pamphlets, hotels and tourist attractions. All because of Arturo being a sometime cabdriver, I supposed. "Got them," I said.

"Take a look at Casa Montana Mohoka."

I leafed through them and found it, and it was actually Casa Montana Mojoca, but pronounced with that airy *j*. "Got it."

"Look it over."

I did. It was an expensive full-color brochure that opened out to eight pages, and what it described was a pretty snazzy-sounding destination resort. A golf course. Tennis. Olympic pool. Full gymnasium. Meeting facilities for conferences. Private airstrip and helicopter pad. Nature trails. World-famous orchid-viewing walk. Horseback riding. Rafting the Siapa.

What a place. This was the kind of resort being built all over the world these days, in out-of-the-way locations where the costs are low and the regulations nonexistent. Corporations use them for all kinds of conferences, and then the corporate executives come back and use them for their vacations. They fly into some little country like Guerrera, go straight to the resort, spend their three days or their week, fly back out, and they've never been anywhere at all. Corporate people love that kind of place, because it comes with a guarantee of the removal of all doubt and danger. A vacation with no surprises: what a concept!

"Look," Arturo said.

We were just passing the church, going through the plaza, and out ahead of us to the right was the white Land Rover, stopped in front of Club Rick. We drove on by, and the Land Rover was empty.

"Asking questions," I said.

"You got it."

I looked out the rear window, and that white vehicle just sat there in the sun, as innocent as an ice-cream cone. Then we were through the plaza, and it was out of sight, and I faced front again.

This brochure, Casa Montana Mojoca. I said, "Is *this* where I'm gonna stay?"

"Right."

"But, Arturo," I said, "these people don't take some bum in off the street. I don't mean I'm a bum, I mean I don't have any ID, I don't have any money—"

"It's okay," he said. "It's all taken care of."

We were leaving Sabanon now, thank God. I said, "You mean, this person Dulce?"

"That's right."

"Tell me about her."

"Dulce and me," Arturo said, "we go back a long time together, early schooldays, know each other forever. Shit, she might even have been my first, I don't remember. I think I was maybe hers, too."

"Oh, yeah?"

"Haven't seen each other in years," he said. "Except, every once in a while, if I got a fare out to Mojoca—when I'm being a cab-driver, you know, not wasting my time with you—sometimes I see her out there, say hello. We get along."

"She works there?"

"She's the assistant manager," he told me. "It's a big company owns it, you know. From London, I think. So the top-guy manager, he's an American, but she's number two. Makes a shitload of money, I think."

"That's great," I said.

"I told her your story," he said, "and the first thing she ask me, Are there any kids? And I say no, this isn't whaddayacallit—"

"Child support."

"That's it, that's what she calls it. It isn't any of that, I told her, it's just this ex-wife she's a greedy bitch, so that's why you gotta stay out of California till the judge does his decision."

"California."

"Yeah, you're a big movie producer in Hollywood. That's why you just got to hole up, not use your real name, not show your passport to nobody, not even let the staff know who you really are, 'cause somebody gonna tip off the newspaper; you know, the celebrity newspapers."

"Arturo, that's wonderful!" I said.

"So the deal is," he told me, "you're goin' in under an alias, she'll fix it all in the computer, give you a room, you don't have to pay nothin' till the end, when it's safe to use the credit card. And you come to ask me for help 'cause I drove you other times you been down here, and you know my gringo brother-in-law that died, and you gotta move outa Rancio because your ex-wife traced you there."

"Boy," I said. "It all ties together, doesn't it?"

"It better tie together," he said, "or you're in shit."

Madonna. I said, "What's my name now?"

"Well, she just had a cancellation," he said, "so she put it back in the computer, because they got all the records on that guy. So your alias is, you're Keith Emory."

"Keith Emory," I said, and spelled it. "Like that?"

"I dunno, she didn't spell it out. She'll take care of you, don't worry."

"And what's my real name?" I asked. "When I'm in California, producing movies?"

"We didn't get to that," he said. "You can pick that one for yourself. You got two–three hours to come up with somethin'."

"Okay," I said.

I looked at the brochure some more. Casa Montana Mojoca. A vacation with no surprises. I could live with that.

31

As we drove through Marona, a pleasant old planta-
tion town of whitewashed stone buildings, a number of modern
banks, and the usual slums all around the perimeter, Arturo said,
"You got your name yet?"

"Yes," I said. "I'm salting myself away, so my name is Brine."

"Whatever," he said.

"And I want a first name that sounds like Barry, at last," I said.
"I've been too many other people. So I'll be Gary Brine. The big
movie producer."

"There you go," he said. "Gary Brine. That's her husband's
office."

On our left we were passing a yellow stucco building with a
wooden sign out front showing several names. Just ahead of us
down this block was a sprawling red-brick hospital. I said, "What
office? Whose office?"

"Dulce's husband," he said.

We were past the building now. I said, "So she's married? Dulce?"

"Married," he said, and laughed. "She got six kids, man."

"And what's her husband do, that he's got an office?"

"He's a doctor. Woman doctor, you know? *He's* not a woman, he's a doctor for women."

"I follow," I said. "And what's the last name?"

"De Paula."

"Dulce de Paula."

"Dulce and Fernando de Paula. And you're Keith Emory. Except you're really Gary Brine, big movie producer."

I said, "I've been thinking about that, Arturo, and I think maybe I'm a medium movie producer. I don't work on the big things that everybody knows about, because then I'd have to talk about how I'm buddies with all these big stars and stuff, and I wouldn't like that. So I'm a producer that does the small crap."

"Whatever," he said.

We were past the main part of Marona now, headed out into Guerrera's central forest. Soon we were running along the side of a ridge, green slope upward on our left, downward to our right. From time to time I caught a glint of bright water down there past all the green.

The sign for Casa Montana Mojoca could not have been more discreet. Small plain-white block letters on a dark green background on a sign that couldn't have been larger than a foot square stood humbly beside a blacktop road on the right, giving only the name of the hotel. An even more discreet rectangular sign in the same color scheme, nailed to a tree, said PRIVADO.

Arturo took this road, and we angled down toward the Siapa. So, I thought, a riverside resort hotel: not bad.

Except it wasn't. The blacktop road, barely two lanes wide, with nothing but forest on both sides, descended the slope, and there at the bottom was the river, and on the river a ferry. In fact, two ferries; I saw one on the farther shore, just pulling out. These ferries were small and open and could carry possibly three cars. They were mostly dark green, with white highlights, the same colors as the two signs back at the main road, and they were very shiny and clean.

A wooden barrier was down across the road, just this side of the ferry slip, with a shingled guard shack next to it. A man in a dark green uniform with white piping and a tan clipboard came out and spoke with Arturo and checked something off on his list: Keith Emory, I supposed. A display of security to calm the timorous North American.

We were the only passengers on our ferry, with its polite two-man crew in dark green and white. We got out of the Impala to enjoy the ride, leaning on the gleaming white wood railing that ran down the side of the boat.

The ferry coming the other way carried only a beer truck, and as we passed each other in the middle of the sparkling river I read the brand names on its side: Corona, Heineken, Budweiser. I was willing to bet they put away a lot of Bud Light over there.

As we neared the opposite bank, Arturo and I got into the Impala again, front seat and back. The ferry bumped into position, the wooden pole barrier was lifted, and we drove past a waiting taxi with a white-haired couple in the back and up the curving blacktop road into more forest.

Somehow, this forest seemed groomed, as though it had a regular appointment at the hairdresser. The shrubbery along the road had clearly been shaped and maintained, and the trees farther back were less encumbered with vines than I was used to in Guerrera. Some distance away, at one point, I saw a group of people on horseback, riding slowly in single file. They were mostly in pastels.

The first sight of the hotel was out of a children's book. We came around a curve, and there was a medieval castle combined with a wedding cake, four stories high with setbacks, gleaming white in the middle of its own manicured lawns. To its left, extending away, I could see the beginning of the golf course.

The high porte-cochere entrance tried to suggest that this hotel had been here since its guests arrived in horse-drawn carriages, but in fact the building was surely less than ten years old. A doorman and two bellboys, all in the same dark green and white, one of the bellboys holding onto a wheeled luggage cart, came out to greet us, but then looked blank-faced as Arturo drove on by.

Gary Brine was a special case. Arturo steered the Impala off the curving blacktop onto an AUTHORIZED VEHICLES ONLY gravel drive, and we sailed around the corner of the wedding cake, seeing more of the golf course, now out ahead of us. Arturo came to a stop next to a part of the side of the building where a white door stood in a little white clapboard separate section of its own, with square double-hung windows flanking the door on both sides. A brass plate identified the door, but I was feeling a little too tense to read it.

"Okay, Mr. Brine, you're on," Arturo said.

I took a deep breath. I'm on. That's right, it's a performance, a show. I grasped my bag and, as Arturo got out at the left front, I got out at the rear right. Would Garry Brine wait for the cabby to lead and introduce him? I thought not; I opened the white door and stepped inside and said to the three women at desks in there, "Hi. Who's Dulce?"

They giggled. It was a sunny air-conditioned room, painted light yellow, with light green industrial carpeting. Five desks, each with its own computer terminal, two of them unoccupied, were spaced almost at random around the room. Large blown-up photos of other hotels were mounted on the walls.

One of the three women—they were all thirtyish and attractive, in an overblown yet muted way, like Luz dressed for the office—rose, still giggling, and said, "We all are. But you want Mrs. de Paula."

"That's right," I said, and Arturo came around me to do a quick explanation in Spanish. The woman who'd told me they were all sweet—yes, of course—replied and then looked at me with new interest. "This way, please," she said.

I followed her, and Arturo followed me, through the room to a closed door on the opposite wall. The woman knocked, a female voice spoke from within, and my guide opened the door, leaned in, and said something. Then she stepped back, smiled a bit shyly at me, and gestured for me to go inside. Movie producers, apparently, carried a bit of clout.

The office I stepped into was as large as the one outside but had only one occupant, one desk, and no computer terminals. The woman now rising from that desk, coming around it, hand out, face smiling, must have been more or less my contemporary, if she'd been Arturo's first love, but she seemed somehow older, more maternal. She was a large big-boned woman, probably five foot ten, with shortish pepper-and-salt hair in neat waves, neither fussy nor flyaway. She wore a white frilled high-neck blouse and full black slacks. Both wrists were adorned with gold bracelets that made small tinkling sounds when she moved.

"How are you?" she said, and her voice was a rich contralto.

"Much better now, Señora de Paula," I told her, and shook her firm hand. "Thanks to you and Arturo here."

"Oh, Arturo," she said, with an indulgent laugh, as though we were talking about some scamp of a boy. I saw then that maternalism was her strategy for dealing with the entire world, which of course made her perfect to run this hotel.

"I'm Gary Brine, by the way," I said. "I don't know if Arturo told you."

"Mr. Brine," she acknowledged. "But not while you're here."

"No, I understand I'm Keith Emory for a while."

"Until your problems are solved," she said.

I laughed. "Oh, Señora," I said, "if it were only that easy!"

Arturo now came around from behind me, a kind of sheepish grin on his face. "Dulce," he said, exactly like that scamp of a boy bringing an apple to teacher. Or a mango here, I suppose.

"How are you, Artie?" she said, making it clear she enjoyed him and saw no reason to take him seriously.

"Feelin' fine," he said, and took her hand, and kissed it.

Arturo's usual greeting for a woman was a bear hug, but I could see where Dulce de Paula wouldn't get much of that sort of treatment. Still with the same indulgent smile, she said, "How's Ifigenia?"

"Not yet gone to her reward," Arturo said.

She laughed, delighted with her scamp. "Artie, that's a terrible thing to say."

"*Ifigenia* is a terrible thing to say," he told her. "Why'd you ever let me go, Dulce? If I'd stuck with you, *I'd* be a doctor today and Fernando would drive my cab."

"You'd both probably like that," she commented, and turned back to me. "And I think *you'd* probably like to get settled."

"Yes, please."

"Would you like someone to show you to the room? I see you don't have much luggage."

"I've been moving fast and light," I explained. "Is it complicated to get to the room? If not, I'll just go there." Because, of course, I had no cash for a tip.

"It's very easy," she promised me. "Come look."

Arturo said, "I'll go see are there any customers out front. See you later, Mr. Brine."

"Thanks for everything, Arturo," I told him, with just the proper distance between the rich North American and the poor Hispanic cabby.

"*De nada,*" he told me. "Adios, Dulce."

"So long, Artie."

Arturo left, and I heard the women in the outer office giggle again as I bent over the hotel map Dulce de Paula opened onto her desk. This was a very snazzy four-color map, the various floors projected at angles that made the whole thing simple. Everything was color-coded, with an index of the hotel's features.

"We are here," she said, and pointed first to the map, then to a second door on the left side of her office. "When you go out there, you'll be in this hallway. You see?"

"Sure."

"You go straight down here, and turn left, and that's the elevator bank. You're on the third floor, Room Three-twenty-three."

"Okay."

She handed me a folder. "Your key and the minibar key."

Minibar key. Have there ever been more beautiful words in the English language? "Thank you," I said, and took the folder.

"You're already checked in as Keith Emory," she assured me, "so you won't have to go through any of the formalities."

"That's wonderful. I really appreciate this."

She extended her hand. "Do enjoy your stay with us, Mr. Emory," she said.

"I know I will," I told her, and now *I* kissed her hand.

She liked that. "Oh, go on," she said.

I had become her latest scamp.

3²

The bathroom! Never mind the minibar, look at this bathroom! The lights, the plumbing, the gleaming tile! The mirrors! The thick towels! You could jump off the roof of this building, and if you landed on these towels you'd be safe.

The room itself was not very large, a typical Holiday Inn sort of room, which has become the hotel industry standard. The king-size bed was not too soft, not too firm, but just right. The television set got CNN, HBO, Showtime, and pay-per-view. The minibar had one of everything and two Bud Lights. Above it the snack bar contained, among its many familiar wonders, macadamia nuts.

The view out the window was of part of the golf course. Men in madras pants and women in madras skirts made their slow way past, giving obeisance to the little white ball.

I showered for a long long time. Then I lay on the bed and watched a Steve Martin movie on HBO. I laughed whether it was funny or not.

Safe. Safe at last. Manfredo and Luis and the other Luis with the bad arm and José and Pedro and *poco* Pedro with the machete can't get me here; they can't get across that river, not on *those* ferries. The insurance investigator and Rafael Rafez can snoop around all they want; they'll never find Barry Lee alive and never find proof he isn't dead.

If only Lola could be here with me. I tried to dream up some way to make it possible for her to fly down, check in as a single. We could pretend we didn't know one another by day, sleep together by night.

And how long would it be before the insurance investigator arrived, sniffing around, checking out the guest list? There was no way, dammit, no way. Lola couldn't use a false name because she'd have to show her passport. And I couldn't dare get the terrific Señora de Paula to slip in a second person incognito because it would screw up the original story. So I just had to be patient.

When the phone rang in the room Wednesday afternoon, I assumed it was a wrong number. This was my third day here, and I'd been keeping strictly to myself, eating alone, swimming alone in the hotel pool, and (of course) sleeping alone.

But it wasn't a wrong number, it was Señora de Paula, saying, "Mr. Emory, I hope I'm not disturbing you."

"Not at all," I said, amused at her using the cover name in a phone call. "I haven't been this relaxed in years."

"Away from the cares of Hollywood," she suggested.

"Exactly," I agreed. "When the phone rang just now, I hardly knew what that noise was."

She laughed. "It is an invitation, actually. An old friend of my husband's from his college days is in the country on business, and he's coming to the hotel for dinner this evening. He says he has a very interesting story to tell about why he's here, and I thought as a film producer you might find him intriguing."

"Ah-hah," I said.

"Would you like to join us? I don't mean to intrude, if you'd prefer to—"

"No, no," I said. "That sounds fine. Thank you for asking me."

"I'll keep your secret, of course," she said. "You'll be Mr. Keith Emory."

"Thank you." She enjoyed being a conspirator, Señora de Paula, I could see that. She was a bit of a scamp herself.

"It will just be the four of us," she assured me. "In the dining room. At eight o'clock?"

"I'll be there," I said.

The insurance investigator.

Why hadn't that occurred to me? An old friend is in the country on business for a reason that has an interesting story attached to it. Why had I assumed the old friend would be South American? Señora de Paula's husband was a doctor; why wouldn't he have had his schooling in the United States?

I was here now. There was no turning back. I'd timed my arrival in the dining room for three minutes after eight, to give the others time to get here and settle themselves, and the smoothly smiling hostess said, "Of course. This way," when I said, "De Paula." I followed her, and she said, "The others are here."

"Good," I said, and looked out past her at the large corner table where Señora de Paula sat facing me, smiling, in conversation with a large robust mustachioed man to her left—the doctor husband, of course, Fernando—and, to her right, a man I recognized immediately. The last time I'd seen him had been in sunlight, in the street in front of Mamá and Papá's house in Sabanon, talking with Rafael Rafez.

He'll have seen Barry Lee's picture, won't he? Candid photos taken over the years, on vacation and here and there. Maybe my driver's license, from the wreck. I'm eight pounds lighter now, I have this thick mustache, I'm more tanned than ever before; will that be enough?

Well, sooner or later I would have had to test this theory anyway, that whoever I am now can look like Barry Lee without *being* Barry Lee, so here comes the experiment, ready or not. Smiling a greeting, happy to be here, I approached the table.

"And here he is," said Señora de Paula, and the two men turned their faces my way.

"Don't get up," I said, as they both got up.

"Mr. Keith Emory," Señora de Paula said, "please meet my husband, Fernando, and an old friend of his from Boston, Mr. Leon Kaplan."

"How do you do."

"How do you do."

"How do you do."

We all took our places, and a waiter appeared out of nowhere to help me slide my chair in. "A cocktail, sir?"

Absolutely. Leon Kaplan was looking at me quizzically, his sharp nose and sharp eyes all pointed at me. On the other hand, I'd better keep my wits about me, so I canceled my order for a vodka martini on the rocks with a twist just at the second I was about to voice it, and instead said, "Just a glass of white wine. That Kendall Jackson chardonnay, that's nice."

"Yes, sir."

Off he went, expeditiously. It's a different experience, when you're in a restaurant, to eat at the boss's table.

Leon Kaplan said, "Have we met, Mr. Emory?"

"I don't think so," I said. "I'm based in Santa Monica now, would it be from there?"

His small smile was also dry. "No, I'm strictly eastern," he said. "Boston area."

"Don't know Boston," I said. "I grew up in New Jersey."

Fernando de Paula said, "Leon and I went to college together in Boston."

"Fernando was premed," Kaplan explained, "and so was I for the first year."

Fernando, who had a robust man's robust voice, now gave a robust laugh. "Then he got smart," he said, "and switched to business."

"Ah," I said. "And are you in business now, Mr. Kaplan?"

"Leon, please," he said.

"And I'm Keith," I lied.

Fernando said, "Leon's an investigator."

I raised an interested eyebrow. "Investigator? With the police, you mean?"

"Insurance," my new friend Leon said, and my chardonnay arrived.

"Like *Double Indemnity*," I said, and lifted my glass with a hand that didn't shake even the tiniest bit. "Cheers," I said to the table.

We all toasted one another, I tasted the chardonnay, and Leon said, "Not that glamorous. Usually, it's pretty boring."

"But not this time," Fernando said.

Leon smiled his small dry smile, pleased with himself. "No, not this time."

"The truth is," Señora de Paula said, "Leon is just wonderful at catching the bad boys. And the reason he's wonderful is, he's a bad boy himself." And she shook a mock-chiding finger at Kaplan as he smirked.

Fernando said, "Oh, now, Dulce, that isn't fair. Leon was just a little wild in the old days, that's all." To me, smiling, trying to come across like a man with secrets, he said, "I confess I was a little wild myself, at one time."

"But Leon, and he knows this is true," Señora de Paula said, "had a real talent for deviltry. I'm sometimes surprised he switched sides."

Kaplan, grinning, said, "Maybe I was just never given a good enough offer on the other side."

"That's probably true," she agreed, now mock-solemn, and said to me, "That's why he's so good at catching the crooks, because he can think like them."

I couldn't help saying, "Is that true, Leon? Can you think like a crook?"

"I've had my successes," Kaplan admitted modestly.

"And he's about to have another one," Fernando said, "right here in Guerrera."

Señora de Paula said, "Tell him about it, Leon, I know he'll be interested. He's in the film business in Los Angeles."

Leon raised his eyebrows, intrigued. "Are you?"

"On the production side," I said. "Also not that glamorous. But Dulce told me you had some sort of interesting reason for being in Guerrera."

"It wasn't even supposed to be my file," Leon said. "But then I saw it was Guerrera, and I said, 'Wait a minute, I have an old friend down there; this is a chance to visit.' So I got the folder, and here I am."

"That's terrific," I said. "What is this folder?"

"It's an accidental death, a life insurance claim," he told me. "I'm with Hartford National, and we've had a number of these the last few years. You mentioned *Double Indemnity*. They really killed the husband in that one, but what *we've* been getting is the people who *fake* their deaths."

I said, "They can do that?"

"They can try," he said. "If they feel they need the money bad enough, they'll go for it. Not all of them are smart, or they wouldn't be in so much trouble in the first place."

"You're right about that," I said.

"A lot of them forget," he explained, "that they have to go on being somebody after it's all over. It isn't enough to fake a death and get a death certificate and all that. They have to find a brand new ID somewhere."

"I wouldn't have the faintest idea how to do that," I said.

"Some know," he told me. "And I think we've got one now."

"And that's why you're here."

"We've had a claim on a person—I can't mention names, of course."

"Of course."

"It looked straightforward," he said. "Accidental death, so it *is* double indemnity, and quite a lot of money."

"But it's a fake?"

"To tell you the truth, I can't be sure, not yet." Leon shook his head. "If it weren't for the letter, we wouldn't have had any question at all."

Politely curious, I said, "Letter?"

"Let me explain. These days, the majority of the life insurance fraud cases we get come from offshore. A country like this, or a country in Africa, say, or other parts of the world, the record-keeping isn't that exact. It's maybe a little easier to get a death certificate."

"Not in *my* hospital," Fernando said.

"I know, Fernando," Leon assured him, "but not everybody is as scrupulous as you people."

"You mentioned a letter," I said.

"Well, before that," he said, "we'd already done the usual check. Any time there's an offshore death and a large-figure pay-out, we look to see if there's anything that doesn't seem right, and we did it in this instance, and it seemed as though fraud wasn't even remotely a possibility. The circumstances were open and unimpeachable."

"And yet," I said, "here you are."

"One week after the claim was put in," he told me, "in fact, just at the moment the payout was being approved, a letter arrived at the national police station in San Cristóbal. Now, if Fernando will forgive me, the post office in this country isn't the greatest."

"Believe me, I know," Fernando said, and his wife said, "We beg people, Fax us the dates of your stay. Don't write."

"I've heard it said," Leon told me with his dry smile, "that the post office here is nothing to write home about."

"I've heard that about the mail here," I agreed. But I was thinking, Get on with it, man. What the hell is this letter?

"So the letter," Leon said, "had been mailed more than a *month* earlier. It got screwed up in the postal system, but then finally it did get to the police."

"And what did it say?"

"It said our client was planning to stage a fake death, in order to defraud our company. It said the letter writer's husband was involved in the plot, even though the letter writer had begged him to have nothing to do with it. It asked the police to warn our client that his plans were known, in order to force him to give up the whole idea." He spread his hands. "You see? The letter was written a month *before* our client's alleged death, but it wasn't found until *after* the death—if it really was a death—had already occurred."

I said, "Do you know who the letter writer is?"

"No. Some disgruntled wife. She doesn't matter, and her husband doesn't matter. In fact, the client doesn't matter, if he's still alive someplace."

"He doesn't?" I was distracted, because I did know who the goddamn letter writer was. The angry Ifigenia, the bitch. What had I ever done to her?

Leon was saying, "The widow—or the wife—has put in a claim. If I can establish fraud while I'm here, that lady is going to jail."

"Won't that be easy to do?"

"You'd think so," he said. "Once we're on the trail. But the circumstances are just so solid. It was an automobile accident, seen by a restaurant full of people, none of whom knew our client. It was a local mortician, who also did not know our client. There's even a videotape of the funeral, believe it or not, with grieving family members. I've been to the cemetery, and the grave is there. I've talked to the mortician who wrote the death certificate, and he described the body, and it would seem to be the right man. I've visited the stonemason, and the headstone is being carved right now."

"If it was an automobile accident," I suggested, "maybe it's one of God's little ironies. The man came down here to fake a death and was killed in a freak accident before he could do it."

"I know," Leon said, as the waiter distributed menus. "I've thought of that." After the waiter left, Leon added, "I almost believe that could be the truth, but I just have a feeling about this one."

"Leon and his feelings," Fernando said, with comradely pride. "He's almost never wrong."

"Oh, I could be wrong," Leon said. "But, Keith, you know the one thing that keeps me going on this one?"

"What?" I asked, and I was honestly interested in the answer.

"It's *too* perfect," he said. "A restaurant full of eyewitnesses. Videotape of the funeral. It's as though these people said to themselves, 'What will the insurance company look for? What flaws can we cover?' And they covered every last one. I can't prove it yet, Keith, but the reason I'm here is I believe they polished the apple just a little too much."

Fernando said, "Leon's a true bulldog when he puts his mind to something."

"I can see that," I said.

Dulce smiled at me. "Didn't I tell you it would be interesting?"

"And you were right," I told her. "You were definitely right."

33

The real bombshell came over coffee and dessert. I followed my half-eaten green salad and my picked-over sole meunière with orange sherbet and decaf espresso, tasting nothing, having trouble maintaining my part of the conversation, thinking about that damned Ifigenia. I'd never heard her name until this week, although I'd always known she existed, in some shadowy other part of Arturo's life. And now, with her letter, she'd maybe undone us all.

Why couldn't she have kept out of it? Or, alternatively, if she absolutely had to poke her oar in my eye—I know, but that's what it felt like—why couldn't the damn post office get the letter to the cops *before* we pulled the scam? Come warn us, you know what we're up to, and we'll give it up, no problem; we'll think of something else. But no.

Conversation had been general through the meal, mostly Fernando telling college anecdotes from the good old days in Boston with Leon, but then, just as I was taking my first cold mouthful of orange sherbet, Dulce said, "Leon, could I ask you a question about that case you were talking about?"

"Of course," he said.

"You said people have ways to get new identification for themselves," she said. "Do you mean forged? But isn't there a big risk in that?"

"Sure, there's a risk," he said. "And that's where we catch a lot of them. But there's other ways, better ways."

Fernando said, "Like what?"

"Well, take this fellow," Leon said. "His wife is Guerreran, from a pretty large family. Now, the odds are good, you know, that somebody in that family, some cousin, maybe even a brother, was born around the same time our man was born, and died young. So there's no records on him except his birth certificate and his death certificate."

"I *see*," Fernando said, in the tone of someone who suddenly grasps the entire scheme.

Dulce said, "Do you mean he'll pretend to be this other person?"

"More than pretend," Leon told her. "The first thing he'll do, he'll get that other person's birth certificate."

I pushed away my uneaten sherbet.

"Then," Leon went on, "he'll use that identification to get whatever else he needs. A driver's license, maybe even a passport."

I pushed away my undrunk espresso.

Dulce said, "So he can pretend to be that other person *here*. But what if he wants to go back north?"

"Why not?" Leon said. "He has ID."

Dulce shook her head. "It's hard to believe such people exist," she said.

"Oh, they exist," Leon assured her. "The statistics are amazing. In New York State alone, the fraud division of the state Department of Insurance handles twenty to thirty of these cases a year. In your state of California," he told me, "it's more like fifty a year."

"Wow," I said.

Fernando said, "So you think that's what happened this time. He's borrowing one of his wife's relatives."

"Exactly."

Dulce said, "Is there any way to check?"

"Absolutely," Leon said. "I have an appointment at the Hall of Records Friday morning. I intend to spend the day there."

"Doing what?" I tried to say, but my throat clogged. I cleared it and tried again. "Doing what?"

"Our man is thirty-five," he told me. "I'm going to check every death certificate from his wife's family from around thirty years ago. Any time I find somebody in the right age range I'll check the birth certificates to see if there's been a request for a copy recently."

"That's brilliant!" Fernando said.

"Just legwork," Leon said modestly. To me, he said, "You aren't eating, Keith."

"I may have caught a bug," I said. "I'm sorry, I wish I was better company."

No, no, they assured me, I'd been fine company. And so had they, I assured them, and I'd very much enjoyed the conversation, but I thought maybe the best thing for me right now was early to bed; thank you very much, yes, I'm sure I'll be fine in the morning; don't let me break up the party, you go on; I'll just go up to my room; good night, good night.

And phone. Mamá said, "Artie's out."

"Tell him it's Keith Emory," I said. "Can you tell him that?"

"Sure. I thought your voice—I thought you was somebody else."

"Keith Emory," I repeated. "I'm at Casa Montana Mojoca, and I want to do that tour we talked about, Arturo and me. I want him to pick me up at the hotel at nine tomorrow morning."

"That's kinda early," she said, sounding doubtful.

"In fact, it's late," I told her. "You tell him. Keith Emory. Nine in the morning."

34

"Good morning, Mr. Emory."

"Right on time."

Arturo held the door for me and I slid into the Impala's back-seat. He got behind the wheel, looked at me in his mirror, and put the car in gear. As we drove out from under the porte cochere and around the curving drive away from the grand hotel, he said, "You look like you got something on your mind."

"Ifigenia," I said.

This time the look he gave me was puzzled. "*My* Ifigenia?"

"I'd hate to think there was more than one of them."

"Why? What's up?"

"You told her about this scam we're doing. You told her a while ago."

"Sure, man," he said. "I tell Ifigenia everything."

"And she tells the cops."

His frown now crumpled his face into a mountain range. *"Ifigenia?"*

"She didn't want you involved with me, and she told you so."

"Sure," he said. We were driving now through the manicured forest, neither of us paying any attention to the scenery. Arturo said, "Ifigenia never likes nothing I'm gonna do. She bitches at me all the time."

"A month ago," I told him, "more than a month ago, she wrote a letter to the police, telling them what I was going to do and how you were gonna help, and asking the police to come tell us they know what we're up to so we won't do it."

"No!" he said.

"Yes," I said.

"Ifigenia sent that letter?"

"Anonymous, but yes. My name is the only name she mentioned."

"A month ago?"

"Or more."

"Come on, man," he said. "How come we didn't hear from the cops?"

"The letter just got there. Your goddamn post office strikes again."

"You're sure, man?" He really didn't want to believe it.

I said, "I had dinner with the insurance investigator last night."

This time, when he looked at me in the mirror, he was half smiling, as though we were telling jokes together. "No, man," he said.

"Yes, man," I said. "His name is Leon Kaplan."

"That's what he told us, yeah."

"That's what he told me too. He went to college years ago in Boston with Dulce's husband Fernando."

"Oh, man, that's crazy," he said. "That's a, whaddaya call it. *Coincidencia.*"

"Coincidence," I said.

That delighted him. "Yeah? The same word!"

"Another coincidence," I said. "Except it isn't, not exactly.

Guerrera's a small country, not that many people go to college in the North. And it wasn't Kaplan's case to begin with; he took it over because he wanted to see his old friend again."

"Huh."

I leaned forward, my forearms on the seat back behind him. "Arturo," I said, "they were gonna pay off. They were all ready to pay the money when that letter showed up. The reason that son of a bitch is here is because that letter showed up."

"Oh, I'm sorry, *hermano*," he said. "I wouldn't think she'd do a thing like that."

I sat back again. The river was just coming into view. "Well, she would," I said. "And she did. Not to hurt you, to protect you."

"She always nags and pushes at me, you know," he said. "That's why I can't be with her all the time. I love her, man, but she drives me crazy. But this. . . . She musta figured, Get the cops in ahead of time, nobody's gonna be in trouble."

"I trusted you," I said. "You trusted Ifigenia. She trusted the post office. We were all wrong."

"Oh, *hermano*, don't say that."

The ferry was there, and the man in the green-and-white uniform gestured for us to drive aboard, so Arturo couldn't say anymore until we'd boarded and stopped. Then he turned around to look at me directly and say, "I don't know what to do about her. The letter's already gone. Whaddaya want me to do?"

"Nothing about Ifigenia," I said. "We've got another problem. Let's get out of the car."

The ferry was moving. There was another taxi aboard, in front of us, with an old couple in it. Their driver got out and nodded to us, but the old couple stayed in the cab.

Arturo and I stood at the rail and looked at the river. Across the way, the other ferry was just pulling out. Arturo said, "What's our other problem?"

"Tomorrow, Leon Kaplan plans to spend all day in the Hall of Records. He's gonna look at death certificates from the Tobón family from thirty years ago and compare them with recent requests for birth certificates."

Arturo sighed. "He's gonna find Felicio, man."

"If I was still at Luz's," I said, "or still at Carlos's, I wouldn't know a thing about this, and tomorrow Lola would be on her way to jail."

"Oh, man."

"He told me so. Last night. He smells the fraud and he wants to prove it, and he said, and I'm gonna quote him, That lady's on her way to jail."

"Not Lola," he said.

"We've got today," I told him. "I don't know how we do it, but we get that death certificate out of the records."

Arturo scrinched his face up. "Get rid of Felicio's death certificate? How we gonna do that?"

"We've got a whole ferry ride to come up with an answer," I said.

The ferry approaching us also had two vehicles on it, both of them trucks bringing provisions to the hotel. One was a slat-sided truck weighed down with cartons of canned goods, and the other was that same beer truck we'd seen the first time. The driver of the beer truck waved, and I waved back. Beside me, Arturo sighed.

35

Arturo's house in San Cristóbal turned out to be more upscale than I would have guessed. It was on a nice residential street in the outskirts of town, all the houses along here being concrete block covered with stucco and painted bright colors, most with cement porches and painted tin roofs. Several, including Arturo's, had chain-link fences defining the property. There was a driveway gate, but it was open, so Arturo just turned in and stopped on the concrete pad beside the house. A number of toys and tricycles were on the weedy lawn.

Arturo had insisted on coming here first, because he said he needed to speak severely to Ifigenia and also because he had an idea involving a cousin of hers. "More cousins," I said.

"We got cousins by the dozens," he agreed, "but some cousins are better than other cousins."

So here we were, and Arturo got out of the car and went marching into the house. I was still in the backseat, the window open beside me, and the first thing I heard was a very loud female voice. Then I heard a very loud male voice. Then I heard them both, and then I just heard him, and then it became very quiet.

Too quiet, for too long. What was going on in there? I sat for ten minutes, not liking this, wondering if I should go into the house, a little afraid of what I would find there. Arturo was usually an easy-going guy, but he was also big, and if he got mad he could do some real damage. What should I do?

The front door opened, and a woman came out. She carried something in front of her in both hands, like a cake. She was buxom, in a sexy kind of way, with great billowing waves of gleaming black hair all around her face. She wore a lot of makeup and a scarlet peasant blouse and black toreador pants and a white apron. Her stiletto heels clacked on the concrete floor of the porch.

She came down the stoop and turned toward me, and I saw she was crying. Not sobbing, just with tears running down her cheeks and a tragic expression.

It took her awhile to get to the car because her heels kept sinking into the lawn. She'd take a step forward, rock back, take the next step forward, rock back; and all the while weeping. What she carried was actually a white cake of some kind, round, about seven inches wide, with something dark gold poured over the top and running down the sides here and there.

Was this Ifigenia? Was she going to throw a pie in my face? What was going on?

Behind her, Arturo came out the front door, looking solemn. The woman reached the car. She extended her arms, putting the cake through the open window, offering it like a sacrifice, lowering it so I had to take it and hold the cut-glass plate it was on from underneath on both my palms.

The woman looked at me with great dark eyes in a wet tragic face, all her makeup running. "I sorry," she said, and turned around, and step-rocked, step-rocked, back toward the house. Now that her hands were free, she wiped her eyes with the corner of her apron.

She and Arturo passed each other on the stoop, he coming

down. He started to say something to her, but she vigorously waved him off, turning her head away, holding the apron to her face. She hurried on up the stoop and into the house, as Arturo came back to the car. He gave me a weak grin and a headshake as he walked around the front, and then he got behind the wheel.

I said, "Arturo? What was that?"

"Ifigenia," he said. "I 'splained the situation to her, and she's sorry."

"She said she was sorry."

"Well, she is," he said, and started the engine, and backed the Impala into the street. "She just gets too whaddaya call it, dramatic. Dramatic."

I hefted the cake or whatever it was. I said, "But what's this?"

"That's to say she's sorry, man." We were driving down the street now, turning toward downtown San Cristóbal. "She just make that, so she give it to you, say she's sorry."

"But what am I supposed to do with it?"

He raised an eyebrow at me in the mirror. "Do with it? You're supposed to give it to *me*. That isn't gringo food."

"Wait wait wait," I said. "What is it, Arturo, what is this?"

"*Quesillo*," he said. "It's like a caramel custard, like a flan. It's a great dessert. Ifigenia makes great desserts. But not for you."

"She gave it to me, Arturo. She gave it to *me*."

"We don't have to fight over it," he told me. "You wanna know what it tastes like, I'll give you a piece."

"Arturo, she gave it to *me*. And," I said, "I am getting tired of holding it on my lap. But if I put it on the seat, it'll fall over or something."

He pulled to a stop at the curb and twisted around. "Give it to me, I'll put it on the floor in front."

I didn't trust him. "Arturo," I said, "just remember who she gave it to."

"Sure, sure," he said. "We'll talk about it later. Gimme."

So I gave it to him, and he put it on the floor in front on the passenger side, and wedged it into position with a couple of beer bottles against the edge of the plate.

"There. It's safe now," he said, and we drove on.

I said, "Arturo, excuse me, can I ask you a personal question?"

"Sure," he said. "Why not? You're my brother now, remember?"

"That house back there," I said. "Can you really afford that?"

"Who, me? No way, man."

"Then who pays for it? I'm sorry if I shouldn't ask that—"

"No, no, man, Ifigenia pays for it. She's rich, man."

"Oh, yeah? What, did she inherit money?"

"Naw. Her family's poorer than us. She's a writer, man, and an actress."

"She is?"

"In the—you know—photo novels. You know what I mean?"

"Luz had a million of them," I said. "I read some. Mostly, I looked at the pictures."

"Then you probably seen Ifigenia. She writes those things she always puts in a nice little part for herself. She makes a ton of money, man. See, that's the dramatic thing in her. Anonymous letters, call the police, all this. Her head's full of that stuff all the time."

"Well," I said, "I can see where it might be a little wearing to be around that every day."

"But every once in a while . . ." he said, and grinned like a baby.

36

There are two local television channels in Guerrera, neither of which is beamed to any satellite. Substations boost the signal so both channels can be picked up in almost every corner of the country, if anybody cares. Mostly they do tapes from other South American stations: soap operas, movies, game shows, variety hours. They both carry local news programs and the occasional local political program, but that's about it. One of them is TRG, Guerreran Revolutionary Television, and the other is RIG, Guerreran Independent Broadcasting.

Ifigenia's cousin Carlita Camal worked for RIG, as an interviewer, news reader, researcher, and general utility infielder. Arturo had decided we needed somebody who maybe knew something about the Hall of Records and how the records were maintained, and how we might possibly get at them, so when he had Ifigenia penitent he got her to phone her cousin Carlita and beg her to help us.

So where we went now was a café across the street from the art-deco headquarters of RIG—a twenties television station only looks really weird when you remember there *were* no television stations in the twenties—where Carlita Camal had promised to meet us as soon after eleven o'clock as possible. We got there at five to eleven and ordered coffee, and I tried to take this opportunity to learn patience.

It isn't that I was panicking, not quite yet, but we did have only today in which to pull this particular chestnut out of the fire. I did not want Lola to go to jail, not for a minute.

Arturo and I had worked out our story on the drive into town from Ifigenia's. We couldn't exactly tell Carlita Camal the whole truth, but we had to tell her something fairly close to the truth in order for her to be able to advise us on our next move.

To begin with, we couldn't tell her we were engaged in a life insurance scam, or in anything else illegal that might turn her against us. In addition, I couldn't tell her I was Barry Lee, because Barry Lee's spectacular death had been covered by local television, both channels. Carlita Camal had probably even been the one to report it on RIG.

So what could we say? I'm Garry Brine again, and I'm the movie producer, only based in New York, not LA. Lola Lee, the widow of Barry Lee, is my secretary, and I've just found out that, in her grief over the sudden horrible loss of her husband, she did a very dangerous and foolish thing, with her brother Arturo's help. I'm fond of Lola, and I want to keep her as my secretary, so I've come down to undo the damage, if possible.

It seems that Lola and Arturo have another brother, Martín, younger than them, and Lola wanted Martín to come live with her in the States until she got over her bereavement. Martín was willing to go, but he unfortunately had a drug-transporting conviction in his irresponsible youth—he's perfectly legitimate now, scared straight by that one fall—and he's banned from the United States.

So what Arturo did, to help Lola out, was go get a copy of the birth certificate of another of their brothers, Felicio, who'd died young. They meant to get Martín new identification as Felicio, who of course had no bad record. But now it turns out the American immigration service found out about the scheme somehow, and they've sent an investigator down, and tomorrow he's going to the Hall of Records to compare death certificates in the Tobón family with recent applications for birth certificates. If he finds the request for Felicio's birth certificate, and the death certificate, he'll have the proof he needs.

Arturo is safe, because he's here in Guerrera and doesn't plan to go anywhere, but Lola's in custody in New York. If one or another of those documents isn't removed from the files, they'll charge her with a crime and put her in prison. So—to save a poor grieving widow, who didn't mean to do anything wrong, from a life behind bars—we need to know what the physical situation is at the Hall of Records and how to get our hands on one of those papers and make it disappear.

I could hardly wait for Carlita Camal to get here, so we could try the story on her and see how it would fly. Well, I could hardly wait anyway.

But I had to wait anyway, because it was twenty after eleven before she walked in the café door. When she did, I knew immediately that's who she must be. Her hair was blond and nailed in place, her face was clear and attractive and generic, and she strode with great self-confidence. Her matching skirt and jacket were peach and very tailored, her blouse was white, her jewelry was small gold earrings, a slim gold watch, and one string of pearls. Her shoulder bag was a huge bulging leather briefcase that bounced on her hip and looked as though it must weight a hundred pounds, more filing cabinet than purse.

She paused just inside the door to look around the room, and everybody in the room looked back at her. Arturo stood at our table, so I stood too. She nodded and crossed the room to us, and everybody else went back to their food and drink and conversations.

"Artie," she said, when she arrived, and offered a smile and her

cheek for an air kiss. This was someone else Arturo was not going
to bear hug: not twice, anyway.

Arturo gestured to me and said, "This is Gary Brine from New
York."

She gave me a metallic smile and her bright-eyed look and said,
"How are you?" She had no accent at all, like Lola.

"I'm fine," I lied. "Sit down. Thank you for coming."

We all sat, and Carlita Camal said, "When Ifigenia calls, it's
always some wonderful dramatic adventure."

"There, see?" Arturo said to me. "Dramatic. I told you."

Carlita leaned her bag against her chair leg and said, "Somebody's in trouble, I take it. You, Artie?"

"No, my sister," Arturo said, and started the story, and I added
a detail or two as he went along. She nodded, remembering the
death of the American Barry Lee; she did remember there was a
beautiful widow, Lola, but hadn't realized she was Arturo's sister.

Arturo went through the rest of the story, and Carlita watched
him, almost without blinking, smiling sometimes, nodding her
head sometimes, never interrupting. Then he was finished, and she
nodded and said, "Okay. You got an application for a birth certificate in the records, and you need it out."

I said, "Or the death certificate. Either one."

"Well, forget the death certificate," she told me. "At that time,
thirty years ago, the deaths were recorded in big ledger books,
sixty-two lines, sixty-two deaths on a page. When you want a death
certificate, they go look in the book, copy down what's there, fill
out a form for you. You can't take one line out of sixty-two lines
out of one page of a great big book."

"Then the birth certificate," I said. "The application."

"That should be easier," she said. "That's just Artie's written
application, in the file." She smiled at me and said, "Now, the
story he told me doesn't hold up. I hope you know that."

I looked at her. "It doesn't?"

"No. Things don't work that way. We don't have to go through
the details, do we?"

"Not on my account," I said.

She looked at Arturo. "Artie," she said, "I know you're not a bad guy, so let's just say you need this piece of paper for whatever reason, and you'd like to know could I help."

"That's it," Arturo said. He acted humble before her, and I felt pretty much the same way myself.

She looked back at me. "So it isn't really *bad*," she said, "but it's illegal."

I cleared my throat. She raised a well-shaped eyebrow at me. Her eyes were large, hazel, with large clear whites. She had a very intense gaze. I decided not to speak.

The eyebrow lowered. She said, "I'll make you a deal. Okay?"

"Probably," I said.

"I'll see what I can do to help you," she told me, "and then, if you get caught—not because of me, I won't get in your way—but just in case, if you get caught, you don't speak to any reporter from anywhere in the media, not American, nobody, until you talk to me. First interview. Okay?"

"There's nothing to get caught about, I—"

"Is it okay?"

Arturo said, "It's okay."

I said, "Sure, it's okay, 'cause it can't happen."

"That's great," she said. "So if you *don't* get caught, once it's all over and you're safe, you'll tell me all about it. Exclusive. Deal?"

"Absolutely," I said. "No problem at all."

"And you buy me lunch today," she said.

"Sure," I said. "Here?"

"No, it's too early," she said, looking at her watch. "And not here anyway. And I've got appointments. Artie, I'll meet you two at Carla Fong's as close to twelve-thirty as I can make it."

"We'll be there," I said.

Arturo said, "Thank you, Carlita."

"Don't thank me yet," she said, gathering up her huge shoulder bag and getting to her feet. "But when it's time to thank me, I'm gonna want enthusiasm. See ya, fellas."

And she marched on out of there.

37

There are Chinese restaurants all over the world, but in each part of the world they're a little different, altered by local tastes. In Guerrera, the local taste runs heavily to jalapeño peppers, so in that country, when the Chinese menu describes a dish as "hot and spicy," it means something even more dangerous than the same dish in the States.

In Guerrera, it is generally agreed that the finest Chinese restaurant is Carla Fong's, on Avenida de Doce de Julio in San Cristóbal. Mrs. Fong is not herself Chinese; she is Guerreran, and she runs the front of the house from her seat at the cash register. Her husband, Fong Fang, is the chef, and a good one. The place is simple and clean, mostly Formica, with exotic travel posters on the walls, mainly not Chinese. There's Mount Fuji over there, next to the Taj Mahal.

Arturo and I got to Carla Fong's a few minutes early, having phoned for a reservation, and the place was quite full. I would guess most of them were lawyers and a few were shoppers. There were no tourists. Tourists don't go to South America to eat in Chinese restaurants, no matter how good they are.

Arturo had explained, when he'd made the reservation, that we would be lunching with Carlita Camal, a local celebrity, so he'd asked for a quiet corner table, and our hostess, Mrs. Fong's daughter, who looked Chinese but was named Tiffany, smilingly showed us to a table near the back that was partly shielded from the rest of the diners by a Chinese screen crawling with ferocious dragons.

Carla Fong's was the only place I knew of in Guerrera where you could drink Tsingdao, the very good Chinese beer. We ordered two from Tiffany, she went away, and I said again, as I'd been saying for the last hour, "I'm still worried."

Arturo, as he'd been doing for the last hour, tried to reassure me, saying, "You can trust Carlita. She won't turn us in."

But that wasn't what I was worried about. I had thought Arturo and I had been very clever in our cover story, yet Carlita Camal had seen through it as though it were plate glass. Were all our cover stories that stupid and obvious? Had *nobody* in Rancio believed I was a deaf mute? Had the good folk of Sabanon snickered behind their hands at the idea of my vow of silence?

To put it in a nutshell, which I was afraid to voice out loud, was I not good enough for the whole original scheme? Was insurance fraud, after all, beyond my capabilities? I was suffering from massive doubt and a deeply lowered self-esteem. When I contemplated myself, all I could see were inadequacies and failings. *He isn't up to it*, a tiny voice kept whispering at my inner ear.

I sighed. Arturo looked concerned. He said, "*Hermano*, what we got to do is not worry. What we got to do is plan."

"I know. You're right."

"Carlita's gonna come through for us," he said. "So I been thinkin', you know? And I think what we do, we go in there, in the building, late this afternoon."

"We let it go that long?"

"No, wait now," he said, and Tiffany brought our beers and three menus and went away. We drank beer from the bottle and

Arturo said, "What I think we do, we get like a map from Carlita, like what hall we go down, what door, where the file cabinets are, that kinda thing."

"Probably," I said. "She'll probably be able to do that."

"So we go in late this afternoon," he said. "With sandwiches."

I put my bottle on the table. "Sandwiches?"

"Because what we gonna do, we're gonna hide in the men's room, see?" he said. "When they shut down for the night. Then, real late, we go there, to the files, and we get the paper, and then we find someplace we can sleep awhile, and then we go back in the men's room, and come out when they open the place in the morning."

"So there's no break-in," I said.

"You got it," he told me. "No break-in, so nobody's suspicious."

"What if we oversleep?"

"We'll buy a little alarm clock," he said. "And the sandwiches."

I said, "And the *quesillo*."

He gaped at me. "What? That Ifigenia give you? How you gonna carry *that*, man?"

"We'll get a little box," I said.

"Naw, forget about it, forget the *quesillo*."

I said, "I'm not forgetting it, Arturo, and you're not getting it from me. I'll get a little box, and we'll carry it in with us, with the sandwiches and the alarm clock."

"But no beer," he said, and drank some beer. "They got water fountains there, we'll just do water."

"That sounds good," I agreed, and Tiffany came around the screen again, this time escorting Carlita Camal.

"Hi, guys," she said. She took her seat, thudded her shoulder bag onto the floor beside her chair, and looked at our beer bottles. "I love that stuff," she said, "but I can't drink it. I've got to watch my figure."

"Everybody watches your figure, Carlita," Arturo said.

"Right," Carlita said, dismissing that pleasantry. Reaching for her menu, she said, "Have you two picked yet?"

"Not yet," I said, and opened my own menu.

Arturo said, "Carlita, how'd it go?"

"Oh, fine, fine," she said, airy as an éclair. "Lunch first, I'm starved."

I said, "You know this place, do you?" Because, though I'd been there several times, I thought it best to pretend I didn't know it.

She said, "Do you want me to order for you?"

"I'd love it."

"Smart man. How about you, Artie?"

"Sure," Arturo said.

Tiffany reappeared then, with a bottle of local seltzer for Carlita, complete with glass. She put them down and took out her little pad and pen, and Carlita walked Arturo and me through the menu, helping us choose. She was clearly very knowledgeable, much more than me.

Tiffany went away, and Arturo said, "Just tell us, Carlita. Do you know how we can get it?"

"Yes," she said. "But I really can't talk all that stuff on an empty stomach. Is Ifigenia still suing that publisher in Venezuela?"

Arturo grinned. "You know I can't talk about that," he said.

"It was worth a try," she said, and looked at me. "Your first time in Guerrera?"

"Yes," I said. Unfortunately, at the same moment, Arturo said, "No, he—"

"*I'm* sorry," I said, into her grin. "I was thinking about the restaurant, first time in the restaurant. No, I've been in Guerrera several times. I was at Lola's wedding." Looking at the abashed Arturo, I said, "How long ago was that, Arturo?"

"Fourteen years," he said. "I remember you there."

"Before my time," Carlita said, and Tiffany arrived with a pot of tea and little handleless cups. Now all I need, I thought, is for Tiffany to recognize me as an old customer, though she's never recognized me before.

Nor this time. She went away and came back with food, and then she came back with more food. It was all very good, as expected, and we didn't talk again until we'd finished every last bit of it.

My fortune cookie was in Spanish. I handed it to Carlita, saying, "How'm I doing?"

She looked at the fortune, then smiled at me. "It says, 'You will be rescued by a beautiful woman.' "

"Good," I said, thinking of Luz but knowing that isn't what she meant. In fact, knowing that wasn't what the fortune had said. "I've been wanting to be rescued by a beautiful woman," I said.

Arturo said, "Carlita, *now* will you tell us? And maybe draw a map, where we go?"

"I'll tell you about it," she said, and finished her tea. "I know the clerks there, naturally," she said. "So I went in and told them a story, some research I was doing, not about *those* records but property records I know are kept nearby. I said I just wanted to look through them for a while, and they're used to me there, so they left me alone."

She bent down to her shoulder bag, found what she wanted in it immediately, and pulled out a letter-size envelope, which she tossed on the table in front of Arturo. "So I got it," she said.

I gaped at the envelope, and so did Arturo. Then he picked it up and opened it, while I said, "That's *it?* You already got it?"

"Well, I was there," she said, "and it was easy. Easier for me than for you."

Arturo had taken the form out of the envelope. He looked at it, wide-eyed, then folded it and put it back in the envelope. He folded the envelope and put it in his pants pocket. Then he looked at me and started to laugh.

So I started to laugh. Then Carlita started to laugh. Then Arturo lunged toward her, as though he were going to give her that bear hug after all, and she pulled back, still laughing, hands up defensively as she said the Spanish equivalent of *Down, boy, down.*

We gradually stopped laughing. I said, "And it was going to be so hard."

Arturo said, "We had it all plotted out."

"The whole caper," I said. "Carlita, I feel like hugging you myself, and you know us cold Northerners."

"I know all about you cold Northerners," she said, with amused skepticism.

Arturo said, "Why you didn't *tell* us?"

"I thought it would be more fun," she explained, "if we ate first, so I could have my scoop a little longer."

"I don't even mind," I said. "This is wonderful."

"Good. And thanks for lunch." She reached for the strap of her shoulder bag. "I'm off." She stood, shrugging the shoulder bag into place, and pointed at me to say, "And remember the deal. If they get you, I'm the exclusive."

"Promise," I said. "Carlita?"

"Yes?"

"What do you think? Are they gonna get me?"

"Well," she said, "they get almost everybody sooner or later."

"I'll keep beautiful women around," I suggested, "to rescue me."

"A good idea," she said. "Artie, say hello to Ifigenia, and be *good* to her for a while."

"Okay," Arturo said.

She grinned and winked at me. "See you later, Felicio," she said, and was off.

38

In a funny way, I was disappointed. I'd wanted to do the caper. Hiding in the men's room, eating Ifigenia's *quesillo* in the Hall of Records at midnight, sliding out in the morning just before Leon Kaplan would march in; then all of a sudden, it became too easy.

But that was a quibble; basically, I was delighted. We'd had a terrible danger hanging over our heads—mostly Lola's head, but mine too—and now, as far as we could see, it was swept away. So I returned to the back of the Impala, Arturo got behind the wheel, and he drove me back to Casa Montana Mojoca.

And along the way, we also resolved the question of the *quesillo*, though not quite as easily. Arturo was very hoggish about that dessert, until finally I said to him, "Arturo, what am I gonna say, the next time I see Ifigenia and she asks me how was the *quesillo?*"

"What makes you think," he wanted to know, "you're gonna see her again?"

"I'll make it my business to see her again, Arturo," I said.

He glowered at me in the mirror, but he knew when he was beaten, and there was no further discussion on the subject of *quesillos*.

Being basically a sunny guy, Arturo had gotten over it by the time we reached the ferry, because, as he himself said, "She'll make another."

"I'm sure she will," I said.

It was midafternoon by the time we reached the river, and two other taxis shared the ferry with us, containing two middle-aged couples dazed by sightseeing. They wanted to chat and smile and share their experiences, but I did not. The ferry coming the other way had one taxi on it, with two Guerreran businessmen inside— white guayabera, powder-blue guayabera—arguing furiously. My old friend with the beer truck was nowhere to be seen.

Arturo deposited me at last under the porte cochere, and I rescued the *quesillo* from among the beer bottles on the floor in front. "Let me know what's going on," I said.

"I will," he promised.

"See you later."

"So long," he told the *quesillo*.

Two days later, Saturday afternoon, Arturo phoned to say that Leon Kaplan was gone, had flown out from San Cristóbal that morning. Arturo, being a cabdriver at that moment—though not Kaplan's—had been at the airport and had seen him go.

It was over. Kaplan might still have his suspicions, but he had no proof and he wouldn't get any proof. Guerrera was the only place there could possibly be evidence, so if he was leaving Guerrera, it meant he'd given up.

After Arturo's phone call, I was too restless to stay in the room, so I went out and walked the manicured grounds for a couple of hours, alone with my thoughts. This had been much trickier, much more difficult and dangerous, than I'd guessed, with jail for Lola and murder for me, but it was over now. What a relief.

I got back to the room around five-thirty. What would I do till dinner? Nap? Shower? HBO or CNN?

There was a knock on the door. What was this, another invitation from Dulce de Paula? I called through the door, "Yes?"

"Rooh sehvice."

"Wrong room," I called. "I didn't order anything."

"Tree two tree," called the voice. "Emory."

Well, now what? I opened the door and in they came, the six of them: Manfredo and Luis and the other Luis with the bad arm and José and Pedro and *poco* Pedro. Without, at least, his machete.

39

"Listen," I said, talking fast, "let me explain something. The situation isn't what—"

One of them, walking by me, gave me a casual open-handed push on the chest that made me sit down quite suddenly on the bed. So I stayed there and went on talking, while they fanned out around the room.

"—you think it is, there isn't that much money anyway, not as much as you think, and anyway you aren't getting any—"

They were gathering my stuff. They put the green vinyl bag on the desk and started dumping my stuff into it, talking to each other in that guttural Guerreran Spanish all the while. They weren't listening to me, I knew they weren't, but I kept on anyway.

"—of it, none of it is coming down here, you don't gain anything by killing me, the scam worked, will you *listen*—"

Two of them went into the bathroom and came back out with

my toilet kit and the hotel's shampoo and body lotion, and dumped everything into the vinyl bag.

"—to me, this isn't necessary, you're only going to get yourselves in terrible trouble, the insurance company's paying off, there's nothing to worry about, there's no risk in me being alive and you aren't getting anything out of it anyway, and—will you *listen* to me, for Christ's sake, will you just *listen*?"

No. One of them came over, pulled a long length of cord out of his pants pocket, that hairy kind of cord that's put on packages, blond in color, and stood in front of me to say, "*Manos*."

He didn't speak English. "You don't speak English?" None of them spoke English. "*None* of you speaks fucking English?"

"*Manos*," he said. He was beginning to look impatient.

I didn't want to give him my hands. I didn't want to give him anything. For Christ's sake, *why* can't I speak adequate Spanish? Or why can't at least *one* of these brain-dead assholes speak English? Why do we have to have all these different languages anyway? Why can't we all speak together, all understand one another, why can't we all be brothers?

No. We've got to be fucking homicidal cousins.

"*Manos*."

Two of the others came over. One of them lifted my left forearm and the other lifted my right forearm. They didn't seem to notice I was resisting, I was even fighting back. I was still saying words, too, in that useless English, but by now even I wasn't listening to me.

The two assistant executioners moved my forearms closer to each other until my wrists touched, when my pal Manos tied them together with the hairy cord. I knew enough to clench my hand and forearm muscles, so I'd have at least a little slack when he was done, but it was still pretty tight.

Meantime, another one had gone to one knee in front of me and was tying my ankles together with a similar piece of cord. Over to my left, my clothing was being removed from the closet and dresser and jammed any which way into the vinyl bag. The one who'd pushed me onto the bed in the first place came over now and pulled something out from under his shirt.

Oh, they're going to slit my throat right here, I thought, in horror and despair, but what he brought out was a bundle of white cloth. He shook it open, and it was a giant cotton laundry bag, with CASA MONTANA MOJOCA stenciled on it, the kind of bag they would use for dirty sheets. Full, it would stand about four feet high, with a white drawstring at the top. The bag was frayed here and there, but I'm afraid it looked sturdy.

The guy holding this bag gave me a second push, which flopped me onto my back on the bed. The two who'd helped with the hands now lifted my tied-together feet, and the pusher slid the opening of the bag over my shoes.

"Hey, wait a minute," I said, and one of the others came over from my vinyl bag to stuff one of my socks into my mouth. A clean one, but still.

"*Ngngngngng,*" I said, which they understood about as well as they'd understood everything else I'd said so far and cared about as much, too.

They stood me up. They raised the bag up around me. They pushed down on my head, crumpling me so that I bent at the ankle and knee and hip and neck and would have bent at other spots too, if I could. They drew the drawstring closed over my head and I heard them knot it. And then I heard the vinyl bag zip shut.

They weren't going to kill me here. They were going to remove me, along with everything connected with me, so that I would never have existed in this room. They were going to take me and my vinyl bag away to somewhere private. I wasn't sure what they'd do with the vinyl bag once they got it there, but I was pretty sure I knew what they meant to do with *me*.

I was completely off balance, scrunched up in the laundry bag, but they didn't let me topple over. They held me, casually but firmly, and after a minute I was lifted, and two of them carried me, one with an arm wrapped around my ankles, the other holding the laundry bag knot over his shoulder, so that the back of my head

was against his shoulder blade and I would be transported head
first.

I heard the hall door open. I felt myself being lurched forward.
Behind me, I heard the hall door shut.

We moved in sporadic treks. I suppose two of them stayed out
ahead to be sure the coast was clear, and two brought up the rear to
be sure no one overtook us, while my two porters bore me on.
Then, as we stopped yet again, I heard some sort of metallic rattling sound, and a pause, and my stomach spasmed as we *dropped!*

No, not drop. An elevator. Not the regular elevator, the service
elevator.

Of course. Somebody who worked here was connected to the
cousins somehow and had recognized me, or learned about me,
and passed the word on. How the cousins had got onto the ferry I
had no idea—maybe they had a boat and came down the river—
but their inside man (or woman) had led them straight to me and
was now leading them—with me—back out again.

But how could they possibly get me across the river? Was there
reason for hope after all?

The elevator stopped with a *whump*. More metallic rattling
sounds, which I now realized was the elevator door opening, and
then the stop-start progress began again.

We were outdoors. Even within the bag, I could sense the difference in the air. We were outside, and we'd stopped again, and I
heard a metallic rattling sound once more, but slightly different.
Another elevator?

No. I was turned upright—head at the top, fortunately—and
then I was jammed into something tall and narrow, hard sides
pressing close against me, and I had a moment of panic, thinking
it was a coffin—they weren't going to take me across the river, they
meant to bury me right here on the hotel grounds, bury me alive—
and then my back hit hard things that moved, bumpy uncomfortable things that were a bit unsteady, rocking this way and that, no
more than an inch or two in any direction. I was trying to figure
out what the hell this was—where am I? what's going on here?—

when I heard the metallic rattling sound again, and the light went away from in front of me as something descended.

Something sliding downward in front of me, cutting off the light. Various square-shaped boxy things behind me, jerking around slightly. A faint familiar smell in the air.

All at once, I knew where I was, and then I understood the whole thing: who had betrayed me to the cousins, and how they would get me across the river.

I was in the beer truck.

40

The body of the beer truck was divided into walled compartments on both sides, each the width of two cases, each with its own door that could slide up out of the way or slide down to be locked. I don't know how deep those compartments were, but I was wedged into the space available when the front stack of cases is removed. One inch in any direction and I met a wall or a beer case or the door.

And I wasn't alone. Faintly I could hear voices around me, and I realized at least some of the cousins would be traveling in this manner too, except not tied up in a laundry bag. That's the way they had gotten to the hotel and the way we all would leave.

I don't know how the cousins felt about that journey, but I hated it. The beer truck rocked a lot, even on the decent access road of Casa Montana Mojoca, and the ferry, when we got to it, didn't merely rock, it also rolled. I truly did not want to throw up with a bag over my head, but it was a close thing.

We reached the other shore, and the beer truck ground its way through the gears as it went up-slope from the ferry landing. Hands up to my face, sock spit out, I was now trying to undo the knots in that nasty tight cord with my teeth, but being jounced around so much by the beer truck meant I was mostly biting myself on the wrists. Still, I kept at it, having no other course of action I could think of, except to fill my pants, which I was trying very hard not to do. Let's let everything on the inside stay on the inside and everything on the outside stay on the outside, and let's see if I have any wits at all to keep about me, because somehow or other I have got to get *away* from these people.

Sure. Tied hand and foot, knotted into a laundry bag, locked in the compartment of a beer truck driving thirty miles an hour through the jungle. Over to you, Mr. Houdini; what I'm mostly doing is biting my wrists.

The beer truck slowed. It tilted way over, bouncing me into the door. Was it going to capsize? You can't capsize on dry land. What the hell was it doing?

Coming to a stop. On the side of the road, obviously, the right side—we drive on the right in Guerrera—and I was in a compartment on the right side, so when the truck stopped, since I had neither hands nor feet to help me support myself in here, I sagged helpless against the door.

Which, a minute later, opened. *That* was painful. The door was a series of connected slats, like an overhead garage door, so it could follow its track on a curve up under the truck roof, and every one of those slats shaved my entire body on the way by. But what could I do? I was off balance; I couldn't get away from it.

And then the door was open, so naturally I fell out. Fortunately, the rocky ground stopped me, starting with my head. I rolled over, stunned, and hands pulled me up to a sort of seated position: what would be a seated position for Humpty-Dumpty immediately after the fall. There was a tiny pause, and then I was hit *hard* on the side of the head, just above and behind my right ear.

Everything before this had hurt, but that blow *hurt*. However, I was quick enough, thank God, to realize at once that the purpose of that hit, with a piece of wood or something, was not to chastise me for misspelling *quesillo* but to knock me out. Therefore, if I moved around or yelled *ow* or anything like that, they would know I was still conscious and they would hit me again. So I did the only thing I could do, which was flop over onto the ground and play dead. Or play unconscious, anyway.

They accepted the idea. They believed I was unconscious, so they didn't hit me again. I had been bound and gagged and bagged, I hurt all over, I was developing a truly terrible headache, I was on the ground amid six brutal maniacs determined to kill me, but I didn't get hit again. We take our victories where we find them.

They picked me up, a lot of them, not gently, and carried me over uneven ground awhile, not gently, and then dropped me onto a hard metal surface, not at *all* gently. The hard metal surface then dipped a couple of times. Boots made ringing noises against it near my ear.

Their pickup truck. I was lying in the bed, and my kidnappers were boarding. In the distance, I heard the beer truck drive away. And then some sort of tarp or something was thrown over me, making it much darker inside my bag, and the truck moved forward, and all of a sudden, some kind of delayed reaction took place, and I *wasn't* conscious.

The sound of rain. No, not rain. I was still in the bag, in the bed of the pickup, covered with a tarp, but the truck was not moving. And that sound I heard was six men pissing.

I worked my wrists up to my mouth again. I've *got* to get out of this. I don't want to die, I'm already dead, I want to live. I can't give up; we never say die, do we? Do we?

The truck dipped and bounced as they all climbed back aboard. The truck jolted forward, and I felt the cord with lips and teeth.

The knot is too tight, I can't pull it loose with my teeth. If I try, they'll see my head moving, and they'll clobber me again to keep me quiet.

Can I bite it? Can I gnaw it, like a rat? If I can't I'm a dead man, so the answer better be yes.

There was one little area, between my wrists, below my thumbs, where the cord did not stick into my flesh but stood out plain. By loosely cupping my hands around my eyes and sticking my nose into the space between my thumbs, I could just get to that cord with my front teeth, the sharp ones. Sharper. I kept licking the rope, licking my teeth, licking my lips, and in between I chewed on the rope, which tasted something like Shredded Wheat without the milk and sugar.

I don't know how long we traveled, but a long time. An hour? More. I was wearing my Rolex, but under the circumstances I couldn't exactly consult it. If they were taking me home to Tapitepe, that would be a trip of 200 miles. In this pickup it could take four hours. It seemed to me horribly likely they'd prefer to get rid of me sooner, but on the other hand, they did have to go home to Tapitepe anyway, and they might know the countryside better around there, have more secure places to stash me where I'd definitely never ever be found.

So, after one long time, they stopped and only one or two got out, and I couldn't figure out what was going on until I smelled gasoline. Then, being as egocentric as anybody else, my first thought was, They're going to burn the body! Before it's dead!

But then I realized, No, they were just filling the pickup's gas tank. Which they did, and we rode on.

This was boring work, gnawing through hairy cord, but I didn't have anything else to occupy my time, so I kept at it. Every once in a while, somebody would poke me with a foot to see if I were conscious and ready to be slugged again, but I always lay doggo and spared myself further punishment.

Up until the stop for gas, I had no real feeling of accomplishment with the cord. I had it nice and wet, and it was less hairy, while my teeth were more hairy, and it seemed thinner and more wirelike, but I wasn't noticing any loss of strength. Sometime after the stop for gas, however, I felt it start to give. A faint loosening around the wrists. The ability to move my thumbs just a tiny bit farther apart. Encouraged, damn near elated, I gnawed on.

This kind of cord is not one rope but a lot of thin twines braided. I suppose I must have gnawed my way through half of those twines before I felt that first slackening, but after that it all went much faster. *Sprong! Sprong!* I could feel them on my lips as they popped apart, losing their tension. And all at once, my hands were free.

Oops. I must have moved, because here came that probing foot again. I lay still, but it wasn't enough. I'm going to get hit, I thought. The side of my head is against this metal truck bed, and coming down from above is this—

Stop. Bounce. Dip. Jerk. Darkness. Conversation. Men farting.

Memory and horror returned together, hand in hand. The truck had stopped somewhere, and they were getting out. Are we *here?* My hands were free, but my ankles weren't, and I was still inside the bag, and they were still six to my one, and they were armed at least with clubs and machetes while I was . . .

Feeling doomed, is what I was.

The male voices and fartings receded. A screen door somewhere to my right opened and slammed.

What was going on? Was I alone? Very hesitantly, because I didn't want to get whomped again, I moved my left hand until I could see the Rolex, and the little numbers gleamed in the dark: 10:09. This dear little machine would tell me the time in other places, too, if I wanted to know; Madrid, say, or Adelaide. It could not, however, tell me how to get to one of those other places now, right now.

Four and a half hours on the road. We must be in Tapitepe, at one of their houses. They'd come for the shovels and things they'd be needing soon, unless I figured something out this second.

How strong was this damn bag? I poked it, and I felt new frays, new scratches in it. That would mostly be from when the beer truck door was opened, doing as much damage to the bag as to its contents. I poked at a weakened spot down below my chin, scratched at it with nails I was glad I hadn't gotten around to trimming recently, and after a few little *scritch-scritches*, my finger went through.

A hole. I widened it, first slowly and then rapidly. I widened it until my head and shoulders could fit through, so there was nothing above me any more except the tarp. I wriggled and wriggled and got the bag off the rest of me, and then spent five frustrating minutes working the knots of the cord holding my ankles before I finally managed to loosen the damn thing and free myself.

And now what? Cautiously I moved under the tarp to the right, the direction from which I'd heard that screen door slam. I found the edge of the tarp, peeked out from underneath it, and saw a million stars in an indifferent sky. It can look cold even in the tropics. A mosquito buzzed me, and I blew on it, and it tumbled away somewhere.

Beside me was the side wall of the pickup. I snaked over to it, and lifted my head, and looked out at a many-windowed shack lit by some candles and some kerosene lamps. To left and right, some distance away, were similar shacks. I saw no electric light anywhere at all.

Tapitepe. It's a very poor town, Tapitepe, and I suspected this was one of its poorest neighborhoods. These people wouldn't mind at all trading some gringo's life for their share of millions and millions of dollars.

Movement in the house. They were all in there, talking together, perhaps arguing about where to bury me. I saw a couple of them drinking beer. I saw a couple of them eating what looked like burritos. On the other hand, I also saw one of them carry a shovel over and put it down next to the screen door.

They'd driven four and a half hours, and they were tired and hungry. They'd have dinner, and deal with the inconvenient but trussed-up Barry Lee later.

I lowered myself to the truck bed. On top of the tarp now, I squirmed myself forward. I had two options. If they'd left the keys in the truck, and in these rural places people mostly leave the keys in the truck unless they're staying in for the night, then I would try to escape by stealing the truck. If they had not left the keys in the truck, even though that would be uncommon and unfair, I would try to escape by climbing over the side of the truck away from the house and scampering into the darkness.

Most of the back window of the truck was gone. I looked through the space, but it was too dark in there. I couldn't see if the key was present or not.

All right. All right. We don't have time to stall around here, they won't keep eating forever. I made it to the left side and went sliding over like a snake, riding down, clinging to the door handle and whatever other parts I could find to keep me from falling straight to the ground yet again.

Out. Knees on the ground, left hand on the driver's door. When I opened this door, I knew, the interior light would go on, alerting the six in the house. So I wouldn't have much time, whichever option I got. I took a deep breath, held it, and opened the door.

No interior light. Of course not. This was a no-frills truck. On the other hand, I still couldn't see if the goddamn key was in the goddamn ignition. I leaned into the truck, feeling around the steering column, the dashboard . . . the key. There it was, in the ignition. Dangling from it by a little chain was a key-ring decoration shaped like a sombrero. How nice.

Quickly I slid up behind the wheel. I didn't even bother to shut the door; acceleration would do that. I put in the clutch and ground the accelerator.

Pandemonium in the house. They came *barreling* out of there. The engine coughed into life, sounding as though it would prefer death. But I would not; I shoved the gearshift into first, ground gears like mad, and the truck jolted forward just as the first of them got to the right side door. He clung to the door, he got his arm inside, he was trying to climb in the open window.

Where were the goddamn lights? I was driving in the dark, no idea what was out in front of me, hand pawing all over the dashboard, turning on the windshield wipers—then *huzzah!* Light!

I was on a dirt road, flanked by scrubland featuring broad-trunked, wide-leaved trees, with shacks spaced here and there among them. Such a tree was just up ahead to the right. I steered for it, pointing at it, yelling, "You're gonna *die!*"

The guy half through the window looked out his side of the windshield, yelled, and decided not to try to live without his bottom half. He shoved himself backward and disappeared from the window; I swerved to avoid the tree. Looking in the truck's only mirror, its interior one, I saw that my recent passenger did not avoid the tree; his momentum kept him rolling along the dusty ground until he smacked straight into it. He stayed there, arms around the tree, kissing it, and moved no more.

The others were moving, though. They'd given up chasing the truck on foot, which did not mean they'd given up chasing the truck. Engines roared back there, and here came two more pickups and one motorcycle.

A wider road was up ahead. Which way was which? I had no idea. I hung a left because it was easier to make the wider turn without slowing down.

Still no electricity anywhere in this neighborhood, still just kerosene lamps and candles making small warm glows in the darkness. No other traffic either, except me and my retinue. The other two pickup trucks were as beat up as this one, but the motorcycle was faster. I could not stay ahead of him, he was catching up, he was trying to pass me, I was swerving left and right to keep him from coming around me.

I didn't know which one he was, but he had a machete, and he was using it like a polo player, trying to swing it at my tires. I veered this way, veered that way, and he was constantly there, trying to disable me by destroying my tires.

So I did the only thing I could. I veered right, and he angled left behind me. I veered left, he angled right behind me, and I *stood* on the brake.

The truck squealed to a near stop. The motorcycle didn't. It crashed into the back of the pickup and went I knew not where, while its driver flipped up over his handlebars, over my tailgate, and crashed into the bed of the pickup.

That must have hurt. True, the tarp and my ex-bag were there to cushion the fall, but they couldn't have helped much. In any case, he just lay there, spread-eagled on his back, and didn't move, which was fine by me.

Past him, in the mirror, in the headlights of the oncoming pickups, I could see the motorcycle still on its wheels, weaving drunkenly this way and that in the road. The first of the pursuing pickups tried to avoid it and therefore hit a tree instead. The second pickup juked like a basketball player around everything, motorcycle, first pickup, trees, whatever, and kept coming—but farther back.

There was more darkness around me now, fewer of those warm little lights. I was on a reasonably good blacktop road, and I appeared to have chosen the right direction. Tapitepe is a border town, abutting both Venezuela and Brazil, and clearly I'd been in the outskirts, so my choices would be either to go toward the border, which would mean I'd first have to pass through the center of town, or to go northward, back toward Marona. Since the town was petering out along here, I was northbound.

So was that pursuing pickup truck, of course, but he was still well back. And my passenger seemed to be asleep, which was nice for him.

That other pickup truck was apparently in even worse condition than the one I'd stolen, which was why this was the one they chose for cross-country voyages. Whatever the reason, every time I looked in the mirror those slightly wall-eyed headlights were a little farther behind, and at last, one time that I looked, there was nothing back there but night.

I smiled a very shaky smile, full of hairy rope. I'd got away.

41

When my passenger awoke, I almost didn't notice in time. The darkness was nearly total. True, there was moonlight and there was starlight, but my truck's headlights, while necessary, ruined my night vision to the point where I couldn't see much of anything except what the headlights showed me. So when the guy in the truck bed came to and started creeping toward me, I almost missed it.

Thank God for gold teeth. I suppose he was grimacing, not smiling, but for whatever reason his mouth was open, and a tiny ray of the not-so-good dashboard lights bounced off that gold tombstone and into my eye, and when I looked in the mirror, there he was, a darker shape against the countryside, on all fours, halfway to my broken window.

It worked once, it'll work twice. I stood on the brakes again, and over the squealing of the truck's already bald tires there came the satisfying thump of a cousin's head crashing into metal, with a reverberation I could feel all through the seat.

Instead of driving on, I kept braking, more gently, until I stopped the truck right there, on the road. It was almost eleven at night, and most people in this part of the country tended to stay home after sundown, even though there haven't been verified reports of bandits along this stretch of road for months.

I got out of the truck, leaving its engine coughing along in that dispirited camel-on-a-bad-day manner, and went first to the rear of the truck to open the tailgate, which turned out to be done not by the manufacturer's original method but by untwisting two lengths of wire. Then I climbed up into the truck, grabbed the cousin by the ankles, and dragged him backward. I eased him to the ground, somewhat more gently than they'd all done for me, though not *that* much more gently, and kicked him into the roadside ditch, so he wouldn't startle any stray motorists.

So much for him. I got my green vinyl bag out of the bed to put on the passenger seat beside me for safekeeping, left the tailgate down rather than go through that wire-twisting process again, and drove on.

But where to? My first thought had been to return to Casa Montana Mojoca, but I knew the ferry didn't run between midnight and 6 A.M., and I would never get there by midnight. Also, I'd been through a lot, and I looked it, and I just didn't see myself walking through that lobby in the morning looking like the only survivor of the Alamo.

Besides, this whole horrible experience was supposed to be nearly over. Next week, Lola would get the money and fly to Guerrera and we could start the process of getting out of here and back to our lives. So the hell with it. I would go back to Sabanon, back to Mamá and Papá's house, and I would start to be Felicio *now*, and the only reason I'm not speaking is because I'm a cranky guy, and by this point I *am* a cranky guy.

Also, Arturo could tell the surviving cousins—I certainly hoped I'd wasted some of them—that if they ever bothered me again I would announce *publicly* who I really was and that I was still alive, and there would go their share of the millions and millions of dollars.

Enough is enough. I'm driving straight home.

And then I ran out of gas.

Twelve thirty-seven in the morning it was, by my invaluable Rolex, so I was still at least an hour and a half by vehicle from Marona, plus another eighty-five miles to San Cristóbal and another hundred miles beyond that on to Sabanon.

This country could use some more direct roads.

The engine had coughed and sputtered three or four times before it gave up the ghost completely and rolled to a stop on the weedy verge. I'd been worried about how much gas might be left in the tank, but of course that gauge was one of the many things in the truck which didn't work, and in any case it wouldn't have mattered, because I hadn't passed any gas stations or anything else that was open at this hour along a road rumored to be the haunt of bandits.

Bandits? I'm 250 miles from Mamá and Papá's house, as the crow does *not* fly. I look a mess, and I don't have any money. I don't need bandits to be in trouble.

So I changed my plan. I would walk through the night. After sunup, I would try to hitch a ride as far as Casa Montana Mojoca. I would clean myself up as best I could before I got there, changing into fresh clothes from the vinyl bag, and when I reached the hotel I'd call Arturo and ask him to come get me.

It wasn't much of a plan, but it was all I had, so I started walking, vinyl bag over one shoulder, truck looking after me with a mournful expression that didn't bother me at all. *You* ran out of gas, not me.

So I trudged along, tired and sore but at least free and alive. Moonlight gave me enough illumination to make my way. All I asked was that I not run into any of those alleged bandits.

42

No. What I ran into was worse than bandits.

I became aware of light from behind me and looked over my shoulder, and here they came, a set of extremely bright headlights barreling toward me through the night.

No. Not at night. I didn't want a lift at night, didn't want to meet anyone at night. It could be the cousins again, it could be somebody worse, it could be somebody who would tangle my stories and my identities even more than they already were. In the morning I'd be happy to thumb a ride, when I can see who my driver will be, but not now.

So I immediately ran off the road to hide in the thick shrubbery along its side, hoping I'd been too far away to be seen by whoever was in that car. Just let them zoom on by, okay?

I crouched down, and the dark roadway out in front of me got lighter and lighter, swept by the washed-out white light from high-beam headlights, and then the vehicle behind it appeared, moving very slowly, more slowly, more slowly . . . stopped. In front of me.

I hunkered down. They'd seen movement, far away. It was an animal, that's all; it was a deer, or whatever they have in Guerrera instead of deer; it was nothing, drive on.

A spotlight switched on. It was mounted on a swivel at the left side of the car, by the driver. He angled it across the car body to shine along the right verge, where I was hidden.

I hunkered lower and lower. I wasn't breathing. The light moved this way, it moved that way, it moved this way. It stopped.

Pointed at me.

A voice called to me to come out, in Spanish.

I didn't move. In the first place, I was afraid to move. And in the second place, I didn't know which way to move. Toward them? Away from them into the jungle behind me? Who were these people, that they had a spotlight like that mounted on their car?

The voice called a second time. There was a brief silence while no response was forthcoming, and then the rear door on this side opened and somebody stepped out.

A light had clicked on in the inside of the door when he'd opened it, and he left it open, standing beside it, so I could see his tan lace-up shoes and the bottoms of his light-gray trouser legs. Above that he was a kind of silhouette.

He called something. This was a different voice, so the first caller must have been the driver. He waited, called something else, and then reached inside his jacket and came out with a pistol.

Oh, my God. I could see the light bounce off its gleaming blackness as he pointed it in my direction. Did bandits drive cars like that, with searchlights like that? Well, what else would they do with their loot?

For a third time, the man standing over there called to me, and for the third time I didn't respond, so he took a shot at me. I heard, or thought I heard, the bullet slice through greenery above my head.

"All right!" I yelled. "All right!"

And I jumped up and stumbled through the undergrowth out to the road, hands in the air, the straps of my vinyl bag around my upper right arm.

The man sounded surprised. "An American?"

"Yes, yes," I said. "Hi, there. American. Hi. Yes, that's me."

"Put your arms down," he said, sounding insulted, as though I were making fun of him.

So I put my arms down, and stepped up onto the blacktop in front of him, and it was Rafael Rafez.

Oh, no. I didn't need this. Fervently wishing my mustache was still a removable fake, long since removed, I said, "I didn't know who you were," to explain my hiding. But then I realized what I'd said implied I now *did* know who he was, so I quickly added, "But now I see you're all right."

"Do you," he said. He was looking me up and down, and I knew what I looked like. He put his pistol away. "I must admit," he said, "I am confused. I don't expect to see a person such as you here so late at night."

"Neither do I," I said. "I'm staying at Casa Montana Mojoca. I have a rental car, I wanted to drive to Tapitepe, see it, see the border. I took too long, and it was after dark when I started back."

He nodded, not quite unsympathetic. "And?"

"I was driving along," I said, "and there was a pickup truck beside the road."

He looked interested. "Yes?"

"There was a man, he had a withered arm," I said, implicating Cousin Luis. "he flagged me down, something was wrong with the truck."

"And you stopped," he said, deadpan.

"I thought, it's only one man, he's got that bad arm, it's safe to stop, but *then*—"

"More men," he suggested.

"From the other side of the car," I told him. "I don't know, five of them, maybe more. They had machetes. I think they were going to kill me."

"I'm surprised they did not," he said.

"I had this bag," I said, slapping it, "in case I found a place to go swimming, you know."

Briefly he closed his eyes. Even for a Northerner, my stupidity was amazing. "No," he said. "You do not find places to go swimming. But never mind. You had this bag."

"I hit the first one in the face with it," I said, "and I ran. The rest were on the other side of the car. I ran into the woods and hid, and after a while I heard my car drive away. I went back to the road and the truck was still there, but I couldn't get it to start, so I started walking. When I saw your lights, I thought you were them again."

The driver, who stood on the other side of the car with the spotlight still aimed at the spot where I'd been hiding, said something, and I thought I picked up the word *camión*. Rafez replied briefly, not looking away from me.

"Did he say something about a truck?" I said.

"We have seen the truck," he told me. "It is out of gas."

"Oh," I said. "So that's why I couldn't get it started."

"You are very lucky, Mr. . . . ?"

I was so busy making up stories, it was hard to go back and repeat an older one. At the Casa, who the hell was I at the Casa? Not Garry Brine, that's who I *really* am. Oh, shit. "Emory," I said. "Keith Emory."

"Mr. Emory," he said, not offering to shake hands. "I am Inspector Rafael Rafez of the national police."

"Oh, am I glad to see you!" I cried, and I did offer to shake hands. He seemed bewildered by the gesture but accepted it. "Am I lucky you came along!"

"You are," he agreed. "It happens I was at a conference in Tapitepe this evening on the very subject of the banditry along this road; otherwise you would have found no one out here tonight. That is, if you were lucky you would have found no one. But are you all right?"

"Now I am," I said.

He said something to the driver. I didn't realize what he meant to do until suddenly the spotlight turned to catch me in its glare. Not the full glare, just enough so Rafez could see me clearly, search my face for bruises and scratches.

And recognition. He frowned at me. "But I know you," he said.

"I don't think so," I said. "I'd remember you, I'm sure."

"And you say your name is—?"

"Keith Emory."

"Keith Emory." He tasted the name, like a dubious recipe. He squinted at me, and then faintly he smiled. Gently, he said, "Why don't you sit beside the driver, Mr. Emory, and I will return you to your hotel."

43

Except he didn't. In the dark, despite this car's intensely bright high beams, I hadn't noticed that modest Casa Montana Mojoca sign as we whipped by it, so I didn't realize we'd already passed the turnoff to the hotel until I saw a dim city glow out ahead of us, smudging the black sky with ocher, like a poor erasure. I said, "Isn't that Marona?"

"Yes, we'll be there in ten minutes," Rafez told me. He was still being pleasant.

I said, "But we missed the turnoff. For the hotel."

"Oh, I'm sorry," he said. "Didn't you understand? The hotel ferry is idle until six, and of course you wish to make a report about the theft of your automobile and the attack by the bandits. There's a police substation in Marona. We'll go there, we can be comfortable, perhaps have a cup of coffee, you'll make your statement, and then we'll drive back when the ferry begins its work again."

That's when I knew I was in trouble. Up to that point, we'd had merely an hour and a half of pleasant chat, with long periods of silence, as though there were no suspicious elements in my story or appearance at all. Rafez had asked me where I was from, and I said New York, and he told me of his hopes to visit there someday, but didn't tell me, as he'd told Lola, that he intended to be a policeman in New York eventually, because of his special knowledge of fighting criminals who speak Spanish.

He had also asked me how I liked Guerrera, and I'd told him it was just fine except for tonight's unfortunate events, and he smoothly apologized on behalf of his entire nation. He then told me some anecdotes about crime fighting in Guerrera, most of which concerned his brilliant intuitive deductions—he was apparently the Sherlock Holmes of 221B Calle Panadero—and I told him some stories about crime in the greater New York area that I remembered from newspapers and television and that had nothing to do with me.

But now this wasn't after all just a pleasant chat to kill time until I was dropped off at my hotel. It was the beginning of an interrogation.

I was sure I wasn't going to like this.

Marona at three in the morning is not a happening place. The downtown shops are sealed behind solid metal gates, there are no moving cars or pedestrians, and the only illumination is the streetlight at every intersection. The Marona police station, on a downtown corner, is a three-story adobe structure with bars on every one of its small windows—from which very little light leaked— and an overhead garage entrance on the side street, which opened upward when our driver touched the control hooked to the visor in front of him.

Inside, a black ramp curved steeply down to a basement parking area, while the garage door clanked downward behind us with a certain finality. This concrete space belowground could have held a dozen cars but contained only five, including something that looked a lot like a smallish tank; armored personnel carrier is what they call it, I believe. In case the muggers ever get nukes, I suppose.

The driver stopped us at a parking slot near a red metal fire door, and we all got out. The driver was a uniformed cop, not tall but bulked up, with a sidearm and a certain flat way of looking at things.

"The elevator is out of order, I'm afraid," Rafez said. "We'll have to walk."

"That's okay."

It was the top floor we were going to, so it was up three clanging metal flights of stairs, inadequately lit by low-wattage bulbs. At the top, we went through another red metal fire door into a hallway even less adequately lit; one overhead fluorescent in the middle of a thirty-foot-long corridor.

"This way," Rafez said, and we three walked past several closed doors until we found the one he liked. He opened it, flicked on fluorescent ceiling lights inside, and gestured smilingly for me to go in.

I didn't like Rafez's smile. I didn't like anything about him. I was glad Lola had punched him in the nose.

I stepped through the doorway, and this was clearly nothing but an interrogation room. Under the flat fluorescent lighting, a gray metal desk stood in the middle of the black linoleum floor, not facing the door but sideways to it. A padded swivel chair was to its right, behind the desk, and an unpadded wooden armchair faced the desk on the left. Four armless wooden chairs were ranged at unequal intervals along the left wall, behind the wooden armchair. There was nothing else, no filing cabinets, no wastebasket, no telephone, no calendar on the wall—in fact, nothing on the walls.

Well, at least there wasn't blood on the walls.

I hesitated, as though unsure which chair was supposed to be mine, and Rafez courteously gestured me toward the interrogatee's place, saying, "Have a seat, why don't you?"

"Thank you."

We positioned ourselves traditionally, Rafez at the desk, me facing him, the driver out of sight—but not out of mind—behind me.

Rafez opened a desk drawer to take out a long yellow pad and a ballpoint pen. Placing them on the desk, he smiled at me and said, "This automobile. From whom was it rented?"

"Pre-Columbian Rent-A-Car."

"Ah." He made a note. "And what kind was it, please?"

I didn't want to say it was a VW Beetle, because I didn't want to give Rafez any reason at all to remember that terrible accident at the Scarlet Toucan three weeks ago, so, remembering another car that was typically rented in this country, I said, "A Honda Accord. It was red."

"Red. Ah, I see," he said, as though that were significant. Making another note, looking down at the pad, he said, "Did Carlos Perez recommend Pre-Columbian?"

Who? Did I know that name? I said, "Who?"

He looked up at me. His smile was still pleasant as he said, "Carlos Perez, your friend. I just thought naturally you would have consulted with him when you wished to rent a car."

"I'm sorry," I said. I shook my head in honest bewilderment. "Perez? I don't know any Carlos Perez." I frowned, trying to think. Somebody at the hotel? "No," I said.

He watched me very intently, and now I could see doubt in his eyes. He could tell I wasn't faking, but he tried once more: "No? Carlos Perez from Rancio? You don't know him?"

Oh, for God's sake, Cousin Carlos! I'd never known his last name. Carlos and María, that's who he meant. Carlos and María Perez.

In that instant of realization, I lost control of my face. I immediately got it back, but with Rafez immediately was not soon enough. I blinked at him, while doubt disappeared from his eyes, and that small smile returned to his mouth. "You recall him now?"

He knows, he already knows, so what can I say, how do I get around this? Denying I know Carlos Perez will only make things worse.

So I had a second sudden moment of realization. "You!" I cried, startled, and pointed at him so explosively that I heard the creak of leather from the driver behind me. "You were the policeman! When I was with María!"

He sat back to think that one over. Had he caught me out, or had I somehow slipped through his net? Why had I suddenly made his job so easy for him? Temporizing, he merely repeated what I'd just said: "When you were with María."

"When I was pretending to be the chauffeur," I said.

He looked at me, completely without expression. "When you were pretending to be the chauffeur."

Was he going to use that as a tactic forever, merely repeating my own words back to me? I said, "On the road to San Cristóbal. *You* remember." I laughed lightly; I'll never know how I managed it. "That could have been very embarrassing," I said.

"Very embarrassing," he said.

There's an echo in here, I thought. I said, "Since I was pretending to be a Guerreran chauffeur, and I don't speak Guerreran Spanish."

"You don't speak Guerreran Spanish."

"My accent makes grown men weep. María told me, 'I'll tell you to let me handle it and you don't say a word.' So that's what I did. In fact, I was afraid to look at you."

"Afraid to look at me."

"Afraid to look at you," I agreed. Two could play at this game. "That's why I didn't recognize you before this. I just sat there and looked out the windshield, straight ahead."

For a wonder, he didn't repeat that. What he did instead was put down the pen so he could rub the point of his jaw with the soft flesh of his hand between thumb and forefinger. Brooding at me like that, he looked as though he were trying to unscrew his head.

A long silent moment went by. Leather creaked behind me. Rafez, more quietly than ever, said, "You were pretending to be the chauffeur."

A very early repetition, now repeated again. I'm in a time loop here. "That's right," I said.

"Why?"

I looked flustered. I looked embarrassed. I said, "Inspector, you know what it's—certainly you can—María and I—"

"You are suggesting," he said, inventing a sentence all his own, "that you were having an affair with Señora Perez."

"Inspector, María and I—"

"With the consent of her husband."

I sat ramrod stiff in the chair, startled, showing a bit of fear. "*No*, sir! If Carlos thought for a second . . ." I looked left, I looked right, I lowered my voice as I said, "Please, Inspector, promise me, none of this will leave this room."

"You had his car," he pointed out.

"It's her car too."

He thought some more, unscrewing his head. Then he took the hand away so he could shake the head, emphatically and firmly. "No," he said. "You were there for the beating of Alvarez."

I said, "The man on Sunday, after church? Was that his name?"

"You *know* his name," Rafez snapped, beginning to show his exasperation. "You know Carlos Perez's name. You know *everybody's* name. But I'm not sure I know your name."

Uh-oh. Let's change the subject, shall we? I said, "Honest, Inspector, I went to mass with María and Carlos that morning, and Carlos just said he wanted to talk with a man afterward and would I come along, and I said sure, and we walked, and Carlos and this man—Alvarez?—they talked about I don't know what, and all of a sudden Carlos started beating up on him. I had nothing to do with it, I didn't touch him, I don't know the man, I never—"

"You *know*," Rafez snarled, "he's *my* man! You know, and Carlos knows. If he was taking, it was not for himself, it was for me, and Carlos knows *that*. How did Carlos find out?"

"I have no idea what you're talking about," I said, "and that's the truth. Alvarez is your man? I don't know what you mean by that, I don't know why Carlos beat him up, I don't—"

"The *smuggling!*" Rafez was really losing his temper now, which I didn't at all want, but I didn't see how to keep it from happening. "Are you going to sit there," he growled, "and tell me you don't know about the *smuggling?*"

"Well, smuggling," I said, using his method, repeating his word while trying to think. "Of course I know it's around," I said.

"And what was I costing him?" Rafez demanded. "A pittance. He didn't have to know, and if he *did* know he didn't have to treat Alvarez as though—as though Alvarez were not under my protection. As though it didn't *matter* that Alvarez was under my protection!"

This was weird. Rafez was interrogating me, but as we went along I was the one learning things. He was still completely at sea, and I was beginning at last to understand what had happened after mass that Sunday. I said, "Believe me, Inspector, if Carlos—Perez? I never knew his last name, I only knew those people socially—if Carlos has treated you with disrespect I don't blame you for being upset, but *I* had nothing to do with it. I'm an American citizen, I'm not involved in anything in Guerrera except—"

"You're involved in *everything* in Guerrera!" he shouted, which was going too far.

So I ignored it. "Nothing except María." With dignity, I said, "And I hope you'll keep my confidence on—"

"Pah!" he said, and sat back and glared at me. "You are not having an affair with Señora Perez," he decided.

I just looked at him. He brooded at me some more, then said, "But it may be true you are not as close to Carlos Perez as I thought."

"No, sir, I'm not."

He nodded slowly, while he thought about things. Then he said, "Let me see your passport, Mr. Emory."

"It's at the hotel." I'd been waiting hours to give that answer.

"It is not," he said, and said to the driver, "*Saco.*"

Oh, no. In either language, that's my vinyl bag. It's all over, I thought, as the driver came heavily forward. He picked up the bag, carried it to the desk, and zipped it open. Unhappily, I watched him paw through my messily packed things. Out came all the wrong ID: The passport. The driver's license. Even the birth certificate.

As the driver walked back to his chair, not bothering to look at me, Rafez studied the three documents before him. At last he looked up. He was puzzled, but he was ready to be enlightened. "Felicio Tobón," he said.

44

"I can explain," I said.

"I truly doubt that," he said, which made two of us.

Still, it was up to me to try. "I'm actually connected with the DEA," I astonished myself by saying, and then I added to my gall by explaining to this policeman what that was: "The Drug Enforcement Authority."

"Administration," he corrected me.

I nodded and decided to say nothing more. That had been panic, a perfectly sensible reaction under the circumstances, but not a helpful one. I hadn't made things worse by starting a yarn about being an undercover investigator for the DEA—Administration, I *knew* that—only because in fact things couldn't get worse. Rafez held Felicio Tobón's ID in his hands. He had investigated Barry Lee's fatal accident and had worked with the insurance investigator, Leon Kaplan. It was all over. Lola and I were both going to jail.

Well, at least she'd be going to an American jail. I tried to imagine a Guerreran jail. Then I tried not to.

Rafez at last gave up waiting for me to spin another tale, and looked at the documents again. "Felicio Tobón," he said, testing the words, assaying them. "There are Tobóns in Guerrera," he decided. "It's a large family, they're all over the country."

He looked at me as though expecting me to either agree or argue, but why should I? Let him find the way on his own; he would, soon enough. It wasn't up to me to help him.

He nodded, as though my silence had been significant, and studied the documents some more. "They're very good," he said.

"They should be," I told him. "They're real."

He lifted a surprised eyebrow at me, then held the birth certificate in both hands and lifted it so he could look at it with the ceiling fluorescent behind it. Then he did the same with the driver's license. For the passport, he took a magnifying glass out of the center drawer of the desk and bent low over the first two pages. Then he put the magnifying glass back in the drawer and held up the passport to show it to me, open to the page with my picture. "But that is you," he said.

"Yes," I said.

He looked at the picture himself, then dropped the passport on the desk. "So you are Felicio Tobón," he said.

"It would seem so," I agreed.

"Yet you are an American."

I shrugged, with a sheepish little smile. These anomalies happen.

He thought it over. He drummed his fingers on the desk. Then he doodled awhile on the yellow pad. Then he did some silent whistling as he gazed over my head at the far wall. Then he nodded, apparently agreeing with himself about something, and focused on me again. "So it's actually a case of murder," he said.

I blinked. "Murder? *Whose* murder?"

"Oh, come now, Mr. Emory," he said, "or whoever you are. You are *not* Felicio Tobón, although your photo is in his passport and you possess all his identification. How do you happen to possess his identification?"

"That's my picture on the driver's license too," I pointed out.

"I saw that," he said impatiently. "I can only assume bribes were paid."

"No," I said. "You know that's not possible. Too much bureaucracy." I felt I should be saying *warm* or *cold*, but I was damned if I would.

He nodded; he knew I was right about the bureaucracy. Then he thought a little more, eyes inward. Then, as though talking mostly to himself, he said, "All we need is the body."

Oh, for Christ's sake, Felicio Tobón's body. Good luck, pal, I thought. If that was all he needed, I was home free. Except I wasn't, and I knew I wasn't.

"Carlos Perez," he said.

I watched him. Now what?

"He is the one," Rafez decided, "who would have disposed of the body. In fact," he said, sitting up more alertly, looking more intent, "he is related to the Tobóns!"

I watched him.

"There are Tobóns in Tapitepe as well," he said. "That truck will turn out to belong to one of them, and you were in it, which is where this manure stain on your traveling bag came from. Oh, yes, Mr. Emory, I am a detective."

I watched him.

"You were in Tapitepe," he said, "dressed as Emory but with Felicio Tobón's identification. You were in that truck, which ran out of gas. A falling out among thieves? What is your relationship with the Tobóns? First Carlos Perez in Rancio, then those scoundrels in Tapitepe. What is the link there?"

Behind me, the driver said something, an explanation or reminder of something. Rafez listened, alert, then nodded and said, *"Sí, sí. Gracias."* To me he said, "There was a motor vehicle accident in Tapitepe tonight, a truck and a motorcycle, involving Tobóns."

I said, "Was anyone hurt?"

"I believe everyone was hurt," he said, "but no one was killed."

"Good," I said, by which I meant, *bad*.

"So that is connected as well," he told me.

I watched him.

I saw it come over him, like sunrise. His head lifted, and he looked at me as though I were a Christmas present. "Felicio Tobón!" he cried.

I watched him. He leaned toward me over the desk, his voice lowering, as though this were a secret just between the two of us. "Is Lola Lee your sister?"

"Now," I said, "I *can* explain." And I did.

45

He was a good listener. I left out Luz, but I told him the scheme, and about Arturo's part in it, and Carlos and Manfredo and them from Tapitepe. I included dinner with Leon Kaplan, but I left out Carlita Camal, saying merely that we "got" the application letter from the Bureau of Records. "And that's all," I finished.

"Well, no," he said. "That isn't all. But it's a great deal. You are very resourceful, Mr. Lee."

"If you don't mind," I said, "I'd rather be Felicio. I'm trying to get used to it."

"Among all those other names."

"Exactly."

He studied me. He liked me now, I could see that, because I was a rascal now, and he could control rascals. "You have been very clever," he said.

"Thank you."

"And at times very lucky."

"And at times very unlucky."

That made him laugh. "Am I one of your unlucky times?"

"I think you'll tell me," I said.

"Yes," he agreed. "It was intelligent of you to tell me the truth when you did. Or part of the truth."

"I didn't tell you any lies," I said.

He said, "Are you Catholic?"

"No. But I was married in the Church. Down in Sabanon."

"For Catholics," he told me, "there are two kinds of sin."

"Mortal and venial. I know about that."

His smile was becoming edgy. "I was thinking of a different two kinds of sin."

"Oh. Sorry."

"There are sins of *commission*," he explained, "and there are sins of *omission*. You say you told me no lies, so there are no sins of *commission*. Will you say you also committed no sins of *omission*?"

"Well," I said, and shrugged, "nobody's perfect."

"Which is what makes my job possible," he assured me. "Let me congratulate you on your wife, by the way. A very attractive woman."

"Yes," I said. "She told me you were attracted."

He shrugged, palms up. "At that time," he pointed out, "you were dead."

"I still am," I said. "Leon Kaplan gave up, he went back to the States. But if he finds out I'm alive, he'll put Lola in jail. He told me so; he said it himself."

"You aren't worried about what will happen to you?"

"What have *I* done?" I asked him. "What crimes have I committed in Guerrera?"

"You faked your death," he said, surprised by my question.

"What law did that break?" I asked him. "I made no effort to profit from that little prank, I—"

"Prank?"

"What else is it? If I were to dye my hair blond, I'd be faking something. Is that a crime? If I then tried to collect an inheritance that belonged to somebody who was blond, *that's* a crime."

He didn't like this. He didn't like the idea that I'd been doing all this scamming and scheming without breaking a whole bunch of laws. "What about the funeral?" he demanded. "You buried *someone*."

"An indigent," I told him, quashing my own doubts on that score. "An unknown person provided by Señor Ortiz."

Scornfully, he said, "Impossible. It isn't that easy to—" And then he stopped, and blinked, and immediately became tough again. "Very unlikely. We'll check into it."

Ah. I can be quick too. We will *not* check into it. The body Señor Ortiz provided—and the name *Ortiz* had struck Rafez between the eyes, I'd noticed—was actually something to do with Rafez himself, and now he knows it. He will not want that grave opened, though it would probably not be a good idea to force his hand by letting him know I know it. People who traffic in mysteriously dead bodies should not be toyed with.

So I merely said, "It was a funeral, that's all. Señor Ortiz provided the body, he was paid, and he hasn't complained."

He cast around for something else, something to distract me from the body in my grave. "You destroyed an automobile."

"A terrible accident, declared so by yourself, I believe, plus all those witnesses. The car rental people are insured, and they haven't complained."

"These forged documents," he said, gesturing at my ID on his desk.

"Not forged at all," I told him. "Legitimate documents issued by your government. I have not used one of them in the commission of any crime."

He sat back to think about me. "So," he said, "as far as you're concerned, you have done nothing criminal, and there's no reason to arrest you."

"Not in this country," I said. "Not unless you decide you're angry with me and rig something up. If Leon Kaplan finds out I'm

alive, and if then I went back to the States, he might want to press
charges against me as an accessory to Lola's crime. But he'd never
be able to extradite me from here on a charge like that; everybody's got more important things to do."

"So you could stay here and be safe, you believe."

"Safe from Leon Kaplan," I said. "I don't know about being
safe from you, or the cousins in Tapitepe, or all the curious people
around who might figure out there's something wrong with me."

"Yes, of course," he said. "You're right to worry about being
safe from me, because now I know the one thing you don't want
generally known."

"That's right."

"And you're wondering what I'm going to do about it," he said.

"I'm thinking of nothing else," I assured him.

"I'm wondering that same thing myself," he admitted. "On the
one hand, it would be satisfying and a very good mark on my
record if I were to uncover this . . . what is the word? Old-fash-
ioned English word."

"Dastardly," I suggested.

"Yes, exactly! I knew you'd know it. Thank you."

"*De nada.*"

"Were I to uncover this dastardly plot," he said, and beamed at
the sound of that, "it would be a great good mark for me, which by
the way I could use. It might mean a reward for me from the insurance company."

"Or not. I think they're pretty miserly."

"Possibly," he said. "But the sad thing, of course, would be
that, even if I couldn't find a Guerreran crime to attach to you,
and possibly I could, but even if I couldn't, your lovely wife Lola
would still go to jail."

"I'd hate that," I said.

"I'm sure she would too."

"Absolutely."

"Now," he said. "What if I took a different course? What if I
went along with this rather Jesuitical idea of yours that none of

your sub-rosa activities have been actual crimes in terms of Guerreran law? What if I decided that it wasn't up to me to discover an American criminal residing in America?"

"Lola, you mean."

"Yes, exactly so. What if, further, I thought it would be of aid to the public peace and tranquillity if I were to take you under my wing until it is time for you—or Felicio Tobón, I mean, of course— to fly off to America? How long do you suppose that will be?"

"Lola should get the check by the middle of the week," I told him, "this coming week. Then she'll fly down, I'll get my visa, and we're out of here."

"A week, then," he said. "You would be under my protection for a week. Those oafs in Tapitepe would not bother you. No one in Guerrera would question you."

"Would I go back to Casa Montana Mojoca?"

"No, no," he said. "That's not the best, not after you disappeared."

"Too bad," I said.

"You would stay with your in-laws in Sabanon," he decided. "No one would wonder a thing, not if I decide to protect you."

We looked at one another. He smiled slightly. He waited for me.

I said, "The check Lola is to get is supposed to be six hundred thousand dollars."

"A fine amount of money," he said. "And which I know to be the truth, because our friend Kaplan told me the same figure. How wise it is of you to be truthful with me."

"I can see that," I said. "Tell me, do you have any thoughts? Anything that might help you decide?"

"The term that floats in my mind," he said, "is ten percent."

Sixty thousand dollars. It could have been a lot worse. "That seems very decent," I told him.

"Thank you."

"I'll tell Lola to bring it with her," I offered.

"That would be best," he agreed. "You understand, between us, it could not be a check. It would have to be cash."

"Yes, of course."

"Not *siapas*," he said.

I couldn't help laughing. "I'd love to see that much money in *siapas*," I said.

"I'd like to see it in dollars," he said.

46

We did not shake hands. It wasn't that kind of deal. We simply smiled at one another, and stood, and the driver stood, and we went back down to the car.

I would now be under the protection of Rafael Rafez, which meant, of course, I would now be under the eye of Rafael Rafez, but that was all right. We were now useful to each other, so we were on an equal footing. It is true he was shaking me down, but not very badly, and in fact I would be getting something of value for my sixty thousand dollars. After three weeks of constant bobbing and weaving, constant trouble, constant worry, my final week in Guerrera would be calm and serene. I would be back in our bed in our room in Mamá and Papá's house, waiting for Lola to join me. I could relax now, and so could Rafez, because he knew he would get his sixty thousand dollars. If he didn't, he could easily block my departure from the country. And he could do it without having to open any ambiguous graves.

Once again, in the car, I sat next to the driver, with Rafez enjoy-ing the expansive solitude of the backseat. Mostly, between Marona and San Cristóbal, we talked about Casa Montana Mojoca, a place he knew only from brief daytime visits on duty and about which he was naturally curious. I answered his questions and tried to give him a sense of the place, but I'm not sure I succeeded. The American lifestyle can be observed more readily than it can be described.

At San Cristóbal, we dropped Rafez off at police headquarters. "Enjoy the rest of your stay," he said, as he got out of the car.

"Thank you, I will," I said.

Now there was the final hundred miles to Sabanon. I stayed in the front seat, mostly because I was too weary to move, it having been a hectic night and it now being past four-thirty in the morn-ing. The driver was not a garrulous type anyway, so as the lights of San Cristóbal faded behind us I went to sleep, not waking up until he made the right turn onto our street in Sabanon, which caused me to fall over against him. He had to elbow me out of the way while steering around the turn, and it was the elbow in the ribs that woke me.

Dawn. I blinked at the familiar street. Some workers were already up and out, trudging barefoot to their jobs. The driver stopped in front of our fuchsia house, and I got out, as Madonna greeted me with a *snurf*. I would have forgotten the vinyl bag on the floor at my feet with everything I owned in it if I hadn't tripped over it.

"*Gracias,*" I told the driver, who nodded at me with that flat look of his. I shut the car door and trudged up the outside stairs and into a living room full of empty beer bottles.

I thought I might be hungry, but I didn't care. Home is Felicio, the prodigal son. Home and very very sleepy.

I went straight to bed.

47

The first question, of course, was how we were going to tell Lola to bring sixty thousand dollars in cash with her. Was her phone tapped? Was this one? I thought probably not, in both cases, but it's always dangerous to assume you have privacy. We wouldn't use e-mail for the same reason, even if we still had it. That is, Arturo was webbed up here in Guerrera, but at home on Long Island we'd lost our Internet access to insolvency months ago.

I had finally gotten out of bed sometime after noon on Sunday. The family, back from mass, was sitting around in the living room, starting the day's beer consumption and watching soccer on television. They hadn't known I was in the house, so when the spare room door opened and I staggered blearily out, a certain amount of beer was spilled.

Once that was cleaned up and the TV switched off, I could tell them all my most recent adventures. Arturo made angry noises about the behavior of Manfredo and them from Tapitepe, while

Mamá and Papá clucked and expressed horror on my behalf for all the trouble I'd gone through. Arturo, through being a cabby, knew Rafael Rafez by reputation, and the reputation was not good. "He's a bigger crook than the crooks," he told me.

"He wants that money from me," I said, "and that's all he wants, and he's going to get it, so there won't be any trouble. I know he's a crook, Arturo, that's why he's taking a bribe, but he has reason to stay bought, including whoever's in my grave out there, so I believe he will stay bought. The question is, How do we tell Lola to bring the money?"

Arturo said, "You think somebody listenin' to her phone?"

"Or this one."

He shook his head. "Not this one," he said. "Nobody around here got stuff to do that kind of thing except they get it from the CIA, and the CIA don't care about us."

"All right," I said, "the other end. So what you do, when she calls, you say it's a bad connection, it's probably her phone, she should go out to the pay phone by the gas station and call you from there, because the pay phones are always better."

"Bullshit, man," he said.

"What you tell her, Arturo," I said, "is that you remember Barry saying it one time, about the phones in the States: that the pay phones are always better."

"Oh, yeah," he said. "Yeah, you said that, I remember now."

The first time the phone rang, at six-thirty, Arturo took it, and it was Dulce de Paula. When he hung up, he told me, "Keith Emory disappeared."

"Think of that," I said.

"She reported it to the police."

"Good."

The second call came a little after seven. Arturo took it again, and talked a long time, and then hung up and nodded at me and said, "Okay."

I said, "What took so long?"

"She didn't want to do it."

"What?" I couldn't believe it. "She didn't want to *do* it?"

"She says it's cold up there."

"Of course it's cold up there. It's winter."

And the first thing she said, when the phone rang again ten minutes later and Arturo answered and then handed it to me, was, "It's *freezing* out here."

"I wish I was there to warm you," I said.

"So do I," she told me. "What's going on? I told Artie, we can't get the check until next week."

"Lola," I said, "hold on. There's something else."

"What?"

It was awfully good to hear her voice, but this wasn't exactly the love scene I'd had in mind. It was all too businesslike, and I could hear her teeth chattering. I said, "In the first place, I miss you a whole lot."

"I miss you too," she said, but I know her; I could hear her humoring me.

So I got to it. "Okay, I know you're cold there. The thing is, we got a little complication here. I can't tell you about it now, I'll tell you when you get here—"

"What is it?"

"I'll tell you when you get here. But the thing is, you'll have to bring sixty thousand dollars in cash with you."

"*What?* That's a whole lot of money!"

"It's ten percent, if you think about it," I said. "And I need it in order to leave the country."

"Something's going on," she said.

I said, "Of *course* something's going on! It got very complicated down here, wait'll I tell you about it."

"I can hardly wait," she said.

I said, "And *I* can hardly wait to see you again. To hold you again. You know what I mean."

Softer, she said, "I do. And I feel the same way."

I could sense the family's eyes on me. "I can't tell you everything I want to," I said, "you know, in the living room here." And from the family's expression, I understood they saw no reason for all this northern restraint.

"Well, I can tell *you*," she said.

"Please do."

"I want you inside me," she said.

I believe I moaned. The family looked at me with quickened interest. I said, "Oh, yes. Burrow in. Hibernate."

"Well, don't go to *sleep*," she said.

"Very active hibernation," I assured her. "Rolling and stretching. Snuggling in."

"Mmmm," she said. Then she said a few more things I couldn't properly respond to, and I could tell she wasn't feeling as cold as earlier. Her teeth had stopped chattering.

And what power words have to evoke memory. All the senses had come alive. "Come home soon," I whispered. By that point, nothing much above a whisper was possible to me.

"I will," she promised. "Wet dreams, sweetheart."

"Count on it," I said.

48

She didn't call Tuesday. She didn't call Wednesday. She hadn't called by two o'clock Thursday afternoon when Rafael Rafez came by.

I was in the living room, looking out at nothing happening in the sunshine out there, when that white Land Rover stopped out front and Rafez stuck his head out the car window. He'd seen me up here, and he gestured I should come down.

He was out of the Rover, strolling in the shade of the house, when I came down the stairs. He was snappily dressed, as usual, this time in a flowing amber gaucho shirt and ecru linen pants. "How you going, amigo?" he asked me.

"Pretty good," I said. "*Bueno*, I guess."

"What do you hear from up north?"

"Nothing," I said.

"Nothing?" He didn't like that.

"I talked to Lola on Sunday," I explained. "Told her to bring the cash but didn't say why. She'll bring it."

He nodded. "When, that's the question."

"As soon as she gets the check," I promised. "Believe me, I want this as much as you do. But you know these bureaucracies."

"Sure," he said. "Well, I'll be around."

"Great," I said, and he drove off, with a wave and a smile.

When Arturo came home at four-thirty Friday afternoon, I said, "Arturo, call her. You gotta call her, that's all. What's the problem? What's the delay? Is Kaplan making trouble again? Is he coming back down here? Is there a screwup someplace?"

"Slow down, *hermano*. I'll call her, okay?"

"Okay."

It was a fairly long call, though probably not the six hours it felt like. At last he hung up and said, "Sit down, *hermano*, stop pacing; you're gonna wear out the floor; we're gonna fall through, land on Madonna."

"What'd she say?"

"Sit down," he said.

"She didn't say sit down," I said, but I sat down. "All right, I'm sitting down. What did she say?"

"No check," he said.

"What? They're not gonna pay? How can they—"

"No no no," he said. "No check *yet*."

"Okay," I said. "I know that much. No check yet. But how come? Did she talk to our insurance man?"

"I don't think so," he said. "She told me, if nothing comes in Monday, she'll make a lot of phone calls, find out what's the holdup."

"Monday? Another damn week!"

"What she gonna do, *hermano*? The check didn't show."

"The check is in the mail," I said bitterly.

He nodded. "That's what I figure," he said.

"No," I said. "That's an American idiom. *The check is in the mail.* It's ironic, see, it means the check *isn't* in the mail, it means they're gonna stiff you."

He said, "In America, you say, 'The check is in the mail,' when you mean the check is *not* in the mail?"

"Yes."

"Americans are crazy, you know," he said. "No offense, *hermano,* not you personally, but Americans are loco."

"Everybody's loco, Arturo," I said. "But so far I'm just *poco* loco. But if that check doesn't show up goddamn soon, I'm gonna be *multo* loco."

"Mucho," he corrected me.

"Whatever," I said.

49

No news on Monday, not a sound. "Arturo," I said, when he came back from cabbing that evening, "I can't stand this. I'm going nuts here. I feel like I'm nailed to the floor."

He shook his head, sympathetic. "It is takin' awhile," he agreed.

"We have to call her," I said.

"Why?" he asked me. "If she had news, she'd call *us*. She said, Today she's askin' a lotta questions, the insurance company, all them people. They got to get back to her, right? Maybe the check is *lost* in the mail. Maybe your post office isn't so much better than ours."

"It isn't," I said. "Tomorrow, Arturo. If we don't hear from her by five o'clock tomorrow, we call her. Okay?"

"Okay," he agreed.

Four-twenty Tuesday, and Arturo came thudding up the outside stairs, yawning and scratching his belly. He came in and saw me sitting there in that low armchair, and he said, "No call, *hermano?*"

"Time to phone Lola," I said.

"Okay. Just lemme get a beer."

He did, and came back, and made the call. I watched his face, and saw him look confused. I said, "Arturo?"

Without a word, he extended the phone toward me. I took it, and listened, and heard a recorded announcement: "*We're* sorry, the number you have dialed—(five) (five) (five) (nine) (five) (nine) (five)—is no longer in service. There is no forwarding number. *We're* sorry, the number you have—"

I pushed it back at him as though it were a snake. I said, "Arturo, she turned the phone off!"

"Oh, man," he said.

"I've got—I don't have any other way to get in touch with her, to find out what the hell is going on."

"*Hermano*—"

"Let me think let me think let me think."

Had she left me? That was inconceivable, but had the inconceivable happened? We were a tribe of two, we were each other's net, it was us against the world, we were inseparable.

But we were separated. For four weeks, we'd been apart.

"Arturo," I said, "I've got to get up there. I've got to find out what's going on." I was pacing again. "Listen," I said. "Do you need a visa between Guerrera and Colombia?"

"What? No," he said, scoffing at the idea. "People go back and forth all the time, man. But Rafez won't let you cross the border. He'll know if you try to do that."

"I'll find a way," I insisted. "Carlos can smuggle me across, he'll be glad to get rid of me. Then, in Colombia, I take a plane to New York."

"And do what, *hermano*?" he asked, curiously bland.

I looked at him, and he was watching me with amiable curiosity, head cocked to one side. Hmm. I had to remember this was Lola's brother, after all. I could feel loyalties shifting like tectonic plates.

"Arturo," I said, "I don't believe Lola's left me."

"Good," he said.

"I don't believe we *can* leave each other," I said, "not really. But what explanations do I have here? The phone is turned off. You see what I mean? The phone is turned *off*."

"It's a problem," he agreed.

"Okay," I said. "Now, it's possible somebody else knew about the money, and they waited until she got the check and cashed it, and then they killed her and buried her in the basement. And turned off our phone?"

"Mmm," Arturo said.

"Or," I said, "it's possible she put the money in our checking account, and somebody's holding her prisoner, making her write checks, and they turned off the phone so she couldn't call for help. Except I don't believe that, Arturo, and neither do you. All they have to do is leave the answering machine on."

"Oh, man," he said.

"In fact," I said, "come to think of it, that's all *anybody* had to do. I mean, let's say—let's just for an argument here say that Lola found some other guy. She didn't, but we're saying."

"Sure," Arturo said.

"So they've got all this money," I said, "and they want to get away before I come looking for them, so they go to California or London or Rio or who knows where, and what do they want?"

"I dunno," he said.

"*Time*," I said. "The longest lead time possible. So do they turn off the phone? Of course not. Why don't they just leave the answering machine on? That way, I'll just dick around here another two–three days, maybe even another week, while they're gone and lost for good. *Why* turn off the phone, Arturo?"

"Save a couple *siapas*," he suggested.

"Arturo," I said, "they've got one billion two hundred million *siapas*."

"Well, that's true," he said.

I paced. I paced. I stopped. I said, "There's only one reason to turn off the phone."

He looked interested. "Oh, yeah?"

"Yeah," I said. "Lola knows I'm waiting for her to call. She knows if she doesn't call me, I'll call her. She turns off the phone. Can't you see why?"

"No," he said.

"Because she *is* in trouble," I said, "some kind of trouble, and this is the only way she can send me a message."

"She turns the phone off to send you a message?"

"I know, I know," I said, "usually it's the other way around. But not this time."

"But what's the message?"

"That she's in some kind of trouble," I said.

"So why not call? Call on the phone? Why turn it off?"

"I don't know, I don't know." I paced some more. I stopped. I said, "What if somebody's got her in a motel room?"

He looked at me.

"No," I said, "not for fucking. To hold her there until the money comes in. Let's think about this, hold on here. Somebody finds out what's going on. They know the money's coming in; they say, Give me half, or whatever. Or they'll turn her in, she'll go to jail."

"Uh-huh," he said.

"And they make her go move to a motel," I said, "or someplace where you can't make a long-distance call, so she can't warn me or get me to help her. Or someplace where there'd be a record of the call if she did, and this person would see the call and turn her in."

"Okay," he said.

"But a call to your phone company business office," I said, "isn't charged. It doesn't even show up on your bill or any records."

"Jeez, man," he said.

I said, "What do you think?"

"I don't know *what* to think," he said. "I'll tell you the truth, *hermano*. I wasn't gonna, but now I will. When I first heard them announcements on the phone, I figure that's it, she found some other guy, and I guess I'm stuck with this one here, meaning you, *hermano*, until either Rafez puts you in jail or Manfredo and them from Tapitepe kill you. No offense, man."

No offense? I didn't have time to think about that. I said, "Lola didn't leave me. Lola sent me a message. And that means there's only one thing I can do."

He looked interested. "Yeah? You got something you can do? What's that?"

"Turn myself in," I said.

50

Arturo said, "Are you crazy? Turn yourself *in?*"

"It's the only way," I said. "If Lola's in trouble somehow, it's only because of the money. If I say I'm alive, there won't *be* any money, and she won't be in trouble anymore."

"And you don't get the money."

"But I get Lola," I said. "She and me, once we're together, we'll figure something else out. There's always a scheme somewhere."

"Hold on, *hermano*," he said. "If you say you're alive, Lola goes to jail."

"No, she doesn't," I assured him. "What I say is, it was a kind of a prank, the marriage wasn't getting along, I wanted to start over, a whole new life, I did it all myself, Lola didn't know a thing about it. She put in the claim because she thought I was really dead."

He considered me. He considered the situation. He said, "All this because the phone got turned off."

"The message," I said.

He nodded. "Yeah. But what if it ain't a message?"

"Come on, Arturo," I said. "What else is it?"

"She found a guy, like we both thought," he said, "and they took off, and she turned off the phone like it was, you know, automatic. Like make it neat, like people do. What if it's that?"

"I still turn myself in," I said, "and she still doesn't get the money."

"Only this time she goes to jail," he said.

I shook my head. "Come on, Arturo, I love her, you know that, no matter what happens. I don't want Lola in jail. My story's the same, no matter what."

He seemed dubious. He said, "What are you gonna do, go tell Rafez?"

"Not on your life," I said. "He'd put me in jail just out of spite."

"So what then?" he wanted to know. "How you gonna do this thing, when you're down here?"

"Leon Kaplan," I told him. "The insurance investigator. Did he leave a card here, a business card?"

"Yeah, I think so," he said, looking vaguely this way and that way at the room. "It's around someplace."

"Could we find it, do you think?"

"I dunno. But, if you call him, and you tell him you ain't dead, it's *you* go to jail."

"No, I don't," I said. "The second they don't have to pay out the money, they lose interest. They're not gonna pursue me all the way down here. I tried something and it didn't work, and that's the end of it."

"That's a risk, man," he said.

"I've gotta take care of Lola, Arturo," I told him. "Don't you feel the same way?"

He sighed and got to his feet. All this time I'd been pacing, and he'd been sitting there watching me, like a slow-motion tennis match. Now he got up and said, "Lemme ask Mamá, maybe she knows where that card is."

"Thank you, Arturo."

He started toward the kitchen, then turned back to nod at me and say, "Okay."

"Okay?"

"Lola married the right guy," he said.

I grinned; I couldn't help it. "You bet," I said.

"That isn't always so easy to see, you know," he said, and went away to the kitchen.

I paced. I paced. I rehearsed the story I would tell Leon Kaplan. I even threw in some gestures, though I knew the effect would be lost over the telephone.

Arturo came back, holding a small white business card. "It was in Mamá's missal," he said.

"Well, because it answers our prayers," I explained, and took the card, and looked at it. Blue letters on white. Mostly it was about the insurance company, their logo and their name and their corporate address, but in the lower right was Kaplan's name and his business number.

I sat on the sofa next to the phone. I noticed, when I picked up the receiver, my hands were trembling slightly. That's okay, we just go forward, we don't worry about that little electrical storm of panic around the edges, we just do this and then it's done.

I dialed the number. I waited forever, and then a female voice came on and rattled off the company name in such a robotic way I thought at first it was a machine. But it was a receptionist, to whom I said, "Leon Kaplan, please."

"May I ask who is calling?"

"Barry Lee," I said.

Across the living room, Arturo sat down heavily in an armchair and watched me.

"One moment," she said.

It was actually three or four moments, and then she came back on the line to say, "Would you repeat that name, please?"

"Barry Lee," I said. "Would you like me to spell it?"

"No, that's all right. And where are you calling from, please?"

"Guerrera, in South America."

"One moment, please."

This time, it was one very short moment, and then Kaplan's voice was there, rasping in my ear: "*Who* is this?"

"Mr. Kaplan," I said, "I owe you an apology. I was trying to get out of that marriage, I wanted to start over, a brand new life, I did that hoax, I faked my own death, my wife knew absolutely nothing about—"

"What the hell are you saying?"

"I'm saying I'm Barry Lee and I'm not really dead," I told him. "And I just found out my wife put in a claim on my life insurance. I forgot all about that insurance, and I don't want anybody to think Lola's trying to defraud anybody, she's as—"

"Is this some kind of hoax?"

"*Yes*," I said. "I'm telling you, I'm still alive."

"Who is this?" he demanded.

"It's Barry Lee, I've told—"

"Barry Lee is *dead!*"

"He is not. I am not."

"You damn well better be," he snarled. "What do you think you're trying to pull?"

I was bewildered. "Mr. Kaplan," I said, "I thought you'd be pleased to know the company doesn't—"

And then I got it. All at once, I could hear Señora de Paula's voice: "Leon is just wonderful at catching the bad boys. And the reason he's wonderful is, he's a bad boy himself. I'm sometimes surprised he switched sides." And Kaplan himself: "Maybe I was never given a good enough offer on the other side."

It was *him*. Leon Kaplan, insurance investigator.

Had he pulled this kind of thing before? Well, he was in the middle of it this time. I could see it. He had something, he'd found something, he knew something, and he'd decided the scam was so solid he could let it ride and count himself in and profit from it. Nobody else would ever need to know Barry Lee wasn't dead. He could take—what, half?—from the "widow" or she'd go to jail.

He'd make her sign something, wouldn't he? So he'd have more control over her. Make her move into a motel or somewhere, monitor the phone calls, let her know if she calls Guerrera she goes to jail. So by the time I'd figure it out, it would be too late.

Except, she sent me a message. She counted on me to read it, and by God I read it.

"Hello?" His voice was harsh but wary.

"Mr. Kaplan," I said, "you seemed like such a decent guy when we had dinner together, but here you are preying on a poor widow."

"What?"

"Mr. Kaplan," I said, "my next phone call, if I have to make a next phone call, will be to the police, and as part of my confession, I'll admit that you were in on it from the beginning, that's why you and I had dinner together. I'll tell them—"

"We never had dinner together!"

"We did," I said. "With the de Paulas, at Casa Montana Mojoca. I was using the fake identity you'd given me, Keith Emory. And I'll tell the police—"

There was a brief strangling sound down the phone line.

I said, "Mr. Kaplan? Are you there?"

"You—you—"

"Yes, well, listen," I said. "Pay attention. You were in the scheme from the beginning, you promised us you'd arrange it so you'd handle the case, even though it wasn't assigned to you—you did that, remember? You said you'd make sure it went through the company investigation without a hitch—and you did, even after that anonymous letter came in. That's the story I'll tell in my next phone call, to the police."

"You'll go to jail!"

"I'll be calling from Guerrera," I said. "But I probably won't stay in Guerrera. That's all right, I'll give the police enough details so they won't need me around to get the goods on you."

"You son of a bitch," he growled, "you're supposed to be *dead*."

"Well, here's what I'll do," I offered. "It's quarter to five, down here. Now, if I get a phone call from Lola by quarter to seven, saying she's free and happy, she's got *every penny* of that money, she's got whatever evidence you had hanging over her, you're never going to pester either of us ever again, and she'll be on the next plane down here, then I'll be so busy getting ready for her that I won't have time to make that phone call to the police. You see what I mean?"

"I'm not sure I can—"

"I don't care, Mr. Kaplan," I said. "Quarter to seven. Otherwise, you're gonna find out if all those awful stories you've heard about prison are true." And I hung up.

Arturo put his beer down to applaud me. "*Hermano*," he said, "you got that doped out. You did it. You're pretty grade-A smart."

"Thank you, Arturo," I said modestly.

"Lemme get you a beer," he said.

"At seven o'clock," I told him. "Then, one way or the other, up or down, I'll drink every beer in the house."

51

Wednesday, the day after my conversation with Leon Kaplan: for the first time ever, Arturo trusted me to drive his precious Impala. So here I was at General Luis Pozos International Airport, among the other cabs, waiting for the afternoon flight from New York. My white shirt was buttoned at neck and wrists, my saggy pants rode low on my skinny hips, and my mustache was growing out over my upper lip. I leaned against the hood of the Impala and grinned at the other cabbies, and they grinned at me.

Yesterday, it turned out Kaplan hadn't needed the full two hours to undo his scheme. An hour and twenty minutes after I'd hung up on him the phone rang. Arturo answered, then extended the phone to me, grinning, saying, "It's our sister."

I took the phone. "Sis?"

"Oh, Felicio," said that great familiar voice. "It's so good to hear you."

"And you," I said, and it was. My knees tingled.

"Guess where I've been," she said, sounding so chirpy and happy that I knew she must be really pissed off.

"I can't imagine," I said.

"Pine Plain!" she announced, as though it must be just the greatest place in the world.

I'd never heard of it. "Pine Plain? What's that?"

"The most wonderful rehab center. They just take the best care of you."

"Rehab?" I didn't get it yet. "You mean you were in an accident?"

"Not *that* kind of rehab, silly," she said.

Then I did get it. "Oh," I said. "Detox."

"*That's* it! Our good friend Leon Kaplan just felt it would be good for me to sign myself in there for a few days."

"Ah," I said. And wasn't that perfect. It's the way to put *your-self* in jail, hold yourself captive. Stay there and nothing bad happens, leave and the shit hits the fan.

"He thought," Lola went on, "Leon thought I'd just get in terrible trouble if I didn't go for rehab, and I just had to write him a note and say I agreed with him."

"Got it," I said.

"And it's really a very nice place," she assured me. "You have your own individual room, and group therapy sessions, and really quite good food. No wine, of course."

"Of course."

"And you even have a telephone in your room, so you can make local calls."

"Sure. Local calls. You wouldn't want to disturb anybody far away."

"That's right," she agreed.

"Well," I said, "you've always been a great communicator."

"I knew I could count on you," she told me, and my heart swelled up.

I said, "So how are you now? You're out of there? One hundred percent all right?"

"Six hundred *thousand* percent all right," she said. "And I'm taking the plane tomorrow."

"Oh! When, when?"

"Three twenty-five in the afternoon we land."

"I'll see you there," I promised her, and so here I was, the next day, at the airport, and it was three-forty, and I hadn't yet seen Lola because the plane was late, but who I did see was Rafez.

Off behind the taxis he was, stepping out of the police car he'd been in when he'd stopped me while I was chauffeuring María. He was dressed the same as that time too, in the white guayabera and black sunglasses and black cowboy hat with the gold star on the front. He also wore white chinos and white cowboy boots and his black holster, and he looked like a corrupted angel as he crossed toward me, a faint smile on his lips. Behind him, his partner remained in the car, watching us.

All the other cabbies turned away, moved off, hunched their shoulders, lowered their voices, became just subtly less present. Rafez ignored all that, which must have pleased them, and stopped in front of me to say, "Going somewhere?"

"Not yet," I said. "But soon."

"You're waiting for the New York plane."

"That's right."

"And am I waiting for it too?"

I grinned at him. "I think you are, yes."

"We could wait together."

I shook my head. "I'd rather not."

That surprised him. "But don't you have something for me? Coming in on that plane?"

"It isn't for you yet," I told him. "Not till I've got my visa and my ticket north."

"We are both wary, I see," he said, as though the knowledge saddened him.

I said, "I tell you what. When the day comes for us to leave, you can give us a lift back here to the airport, and we'll give you a going-away present."

He smiled. "How generous we both are."

Together we heard the sound of the plane and looked up to see it, high and small, gleaming white in the sun, just disappearing past the terminal. It would now make a long loop out over the savanna as it descended, and land coming back.

"I might like to see your wife again," Rafez said.

"I'm pretty sure she wouldn't want to see you," I told him. "Not now."

He raised an eyebrow at me but then decided not to take offense. "Tell me," he said, "has she ever struck you?"

I grinned at him. "Bony little fist, isn't it?"

He smiled back, pitying me. "I wish you joy with her," he said, and turned away.

The cabbies thawed as Rafez walked off. They glanced sideways at me to see if my very presence meant some sort of trouble in the general world of cabdom. I grinned at them and shrugged, and Rafez and his partner drove off, and the sun began to shine again, and the taxiing airplane got louder and louder and then abruptly switched off.

It was another five minutes before the passengers began at last to straggle out, angular with luggage, and among them here she came, out of the U.S.-built terminal, all in white, my Lola, smiling like a sunrise.

All the cabbies wanted that fare, but she was mine. She came to me, carrying her suitcase, and I took it from her, put it on the ground, and folded her in my arms. The other cabbies stood there with their mouths open, forgetting to yell "Taxi!"

All good things must end, even that kiss. Her eyes were full of sparks. "If you don't take me away from here," she said, "we'll *really* surprise those fellas."

I laughed, and we got out of there. And we lived happily ever after, the most devoted of brothers and sisters, Hansel and Gretel out of the woods; or at least until the six hundred thousand dollars ran out. But that's another story.